hearts in motion

NEW YORK TIMES & USA TODAY BESTSELLING AUTHOR

KELLY ELLIOTT

Prologue

Brighton

Present day - May

The sounds of Britney Spears's "Gimme More" filled my AirPods as I ran up the driveway to my parents' bed and breakfast, savoring the vibration of my feet hitting the sidewalk. The familiar sign, Willow Tree Inn, greeted me like an old friend. A warm feeling wrapped around my body. It had nothing to do with the spring weather or the sweat I had worked up running, and everything to do with being home. This had been my safe place for the last few months.

It was a relief that my parents hadn't questioned my reasons for leaving my job in Boston as a successful divorce lawyer—or my cute little condo I adored—and running back to Boggy Creek as fast as I could. I had expected them to try and figure out that little mystery, but they hadn't. For the last three-and-a-half months or so, I had safely hidden within the walls of Willow Tree Inn.

Too bad my heart was still as broken today as it was back in January.

I made my way toward the two-story, white colonial house, taking in all the spring flowers that were starting to bloom in the gardens my mother had planted along the front of the house. The large willow and oak trees loomed over the house, as if protecting it. The scent of the different flowers—roses, daisies, forget-me-nots—and the ivory plants that greeted guests filled my senses. I bounded up the steps and onto the large front porch. Hanging baskets filled with colorful plants were strung along the porch, framing the white rocking chairs and the swing that guests could sit in to enjoy the fresh air. May in New Hampshire was a beautiful time of year, and I was honestly surprised not to see anyone out here.

I leaned over to catch my breath, only to have the front door to the house open and my mother step outside. "Brighton! Darling, I need a favor from you ASAP."

Standing up, I pulled in some air. "Christ, Mom, let me catch my breath."

"Don't use the Lord's name in vain, Brighton Willow Rogers!"

Ahh, the joys of living back at home. I was staying in the small cottage on the back of the property. When I'd made my rush back to town, I'd thought it would be fine. I mean, I wasn't moving back in with them, just near them. My folks lived on the third floor of the bed and breakfast. They had converted what used to be the attic into a little studio apartment. There was a private bathroom and a small kitchen up there, though I was positive my mother never used the latter.

"By the way, you got home late last night," she said. "Were you with anyone?"

I stared at her as I took in a few deep breaths. It was moments like this that made me realize I had made a stupid decision moving back home and thinking I would have privacy in the cottage. My mother hadn't gotten that memo. She showed up at my place whenever she wanted, tried to set me up with random guys I went to high school with who were still single, and, for some reason, had left me a list of songs to help mend a broken heart. I hadn't even told my mother my heart was broken. But apparently, she had some weird hocus-pocus magic shit that made her know these sorts of things, because my heart had indeed been broken. Not in two, but into a million damn pieces.

"Mom, I'm thirty years old as of this morning. I don't think you can keep calling me by my middle name, nor should you be asking me about who I was with last night."

Her eyes grew wide with hope.

"But for the record," I said, "I was out with the girls. We met for dinner and drinks, and then went back to Greer's house for a book club meeting."

My mother frowned. "A book club meeting? Brighton, that's all women."

"Not true, Mom. There is a one guy in the club."

She rolled her eyes. "Kyle Larson does not count."

I had to fight not to laugh. "I'm sure he'd disagree with you on that one. Now, back to you being all up in my business. Mom, you can't question where I go or who I'm with; I'm not ten. And you can't call me by my middle name. It's embarrassing."

Her brows rose and a look I remembered all too well from my days of getting caught sneaking into my bedroom window appeared on her face.

I took a step away from her. "Or, maybe you can. What did you need me to do?"

Her scowl was quickly replaced with a smile. "We just had a guest check in." She motioned for me to come closer, so she could lower her voice. "Lord, he's handsome. No ring on his finger."

I rolled my eyes. "And?"

"Well, I told him I'd make a tray thingy with some cheese, fruit, and meat on it, but Milo Mills—you know him, he's the widower whose daughter Jenny is heading to college this fall?"

I stared at my mother like she'd lost her damn mind. I was born and raised in Boggy Creek. Milo Mills used to give me ten cents to pick flowers for his wife once a week. The fact that my mother was asking if I knew who he was made me question if she'd forgotten that

I hadn't always lived in Boston. "Yes, I know who they are, Mom. I did grow up here...remember?"

She waved off my sarcasm. "He's trying to make a surprise dinner for Jenny, but he burnt it. So I'm running over a lasagna I made up earlier. Do me a favor and make Walter his tray."

I screwed up my face. "The handsome guy's name is Walter? How old is he, ninety?"

She shot me a dirty look. "No, he's not ninety. His name is Walter Cunningham."

"How old is he?" I asked as I started for the door.

"Earlier thirties, I'd guess. Did I mention there was no ring?"

Sighing, I spun around and watched while my mother walked down the steps and headed toward the drive. The Mills family only lived four houses down from us. Granted, my folks owned three acres of property, but it still wasn't a very long walk. I knew my mother though. She'd only offered to leave so it would force me to make a tray for *Walter*.

"That doesn't mean anything, Mom!"

She laughed and lifted her hand, waving it as she called over her shoulder, "He was taking a shower. I told him to meet me in the kitchen in twenty minutes or so."

"And how long has it been?" I called out.

"Fifteen."

"Shit!" I hustled inside and drew in a deep breath. The house always smelled like fall to me. It was my mother's favorite time of year, and mine as well. Mom always had some sort of cinnamon apple candles or plug-ins throughout the house, giving it that fresh apple pie smell.

My parents had run Willow Tree Inn for as long as I could remember. The old historical house had six bedrooms, four bathrooms, two living rooms, and a large dining room and kitchen. The old barn in the back had been converted into an area where we could host parties or do movie nights. I had so many fond memories growing up in this house.

A large pillow sat on the bench that was against the wall where folks could hang up their coats. It read, *"I love you a bushel and a peck."* That saying was also everywhere throughout the house. A little nod to my grandmother, who always said it to my mother and me.

I made my way to the small half bath. "I'm going to kill her," I mumbled as I quickly splashed my face with cold water, dried off, then headed to the kitchen to get to work on the charcuterie board.

My mother had a terrible time pronouncing the word charcuterie, so every time she wanted one made, she called it a tray thingy. A meat tray thingy. A fruit tray thingy with crackers and cheese. A holiday-themed tray thingy. It was fun hearing her try to pronounce charcuterie; even my father tried to get her to say it at least once a week. She was a fan of her trays, so it was easy to tease her. Last Christmas, I had even gotten her a custom wood cutting board that had all the sections laser engraved, so she would know how to build the board. She loved it so much, she displayed it in the kitchen—and had yet to actually use it.

Opening the fridge, I took out three types of cheese, two meats, fruit, jam, crackers, and honey, and then quickly got to work making the board. I had gotten to be a pro at these boards over the last few months, and I had to admit, I made a damn good display of food. I was dying to make a Halloween-themed one. Greer, one of my dearest friends and owner of Turning Pages bookstore, thought she was the queen of charcuterie boards, so I had stepped up my game some. Once Greer started drinking, her boards got a little...weird. She once made an entire charcuterie board of nothing but different types of pickles. I gagged just thinking about it and had to quickly push it from my mind.

I glanced over at the windowsill and smiled when I saw edible flowers in a glass of water. I pulled out three different ones and placed them on the board. When I glanced up at the clock, I saw that it was fifteen minutes past the time my mother said Walter would be down, so I grabbed the board and made my way to the desk area near the front door in the large foyer. He might have fallen asleep or something; I'd look up his room number and bring it to him.

As I pulled up the reservation, a strange sensation hit me. The hair on the back of my neck stood up and I took in a long, deep breath. The smell of crisp air after a rainstorm and sandalwood hit me like a brick wall.

I knew that smell.

My body instantly heated, and I slowly lifted my gaze...to see Luke Morrison standing in front of me. Dark onyx eyes met my shocked ones. The corner of his mouth lifted into a slight smile. A sexy-as-hell smile, if I was honest with myself.

"Luke," I said softly, taking a step away from the computer. I brought my hand to my stomach, which felt like it was about to drop out of my body.

"It's Mr. Walter Cunningham," he said with a wink as his smile grew bigger.

"Why are you here?" I held onto the counter to keep my knees from giving out.

His smile faded a bit, and I let my eyes take in his appearance. His dark brown hair looked like he had run his fingers through it a few times, and his dark eyes sparkled with something that might have been happiness. "Happy birthday, Bree. Did you get your cake this morning?"

I stared at him in disbelief. What the hell was he doing here in Boggy Creek? I wasn't sure if I wanted to turn and run from him or jump into his arms. He'd remembered my birthday. And why did that make my heart melt into a freaking puddle?

I had once told Luke about my parents' tradition of presenting me with a cake at exactly four-thirty in the morning on my birthday, which was the exact time I was born. And he had remembered that too.

Damn him. Damn. Him.

Luke tilted his head and let his eyes sweep over my entire body before they landed back on my face. "Bree?" he softly asked as he took a few steps closer.

I held up my hand, drew in a sharp breath, and said, "I need a few moments, Luke."

He nodded once.

Slowly, I turned around and walked back toward the kitchen, focusing on not running away from him as fast as I could. The moment I got into the kitchen, I gripped the island and drew in a few deep breaths, trying not to let all the memories flood back at once. All the times he had whispered in my ear how much he cared about me. How much he needed me. How he'd be lost without me.

How much he loved me.

I'd been trying to tell myself that his words were all lies. But a part of me knew they hadn't been. And where had he been the last few months? He hadn't even tried to contact me...but of course I was the one who told him to leave. Ugh. And here he was, on my birthday, standing in my parents' bed and breakfast with a smile on his face that melted my heart and made my knees weak.

Closing my eyes, I felt the tears I swore I would never let fall again slide down my face. I turned and slid down to the floor. A rush of emotions hit me so hard it felt like I had run into a brick wall.

Chapter One

Brighton

Seventeen months earlier - December

"**W**hat do you mean, I'm not going to that party? What other party is there, Wendy?"

My assistant gave me a half smile as she walked over, closed my office door, and then made her way back to my desk. "Did anyone ever tell you that you lack the ability to be subtle?"

"Yes, multiple people. Now, what are you talking about?"

She drew in a deep breath and let it out before she confirmed what I thought I'd heard her say. "You're not going to the company-wide Christmas party, but rather the *other* Christmas party. The one with all the senior partners and their families. They have it on a different night, of course."

My mouth fell open. "There are two different parties? Why do I not know this?"

She nodded. "Yep, and you probably do not know because you never go to any of the work parties." Smirking, she added, "You're going to hobnob with the big folks."

I dropped back down in my seat and buried my face in my hands. "What in the hell did I do? What did I sign up for?"

"I'm not sure, but I'm so curious to know why Mr. Morrison needs to bribe someone to be his son's date. Do you think he's ugly?"

Lifting my head, I stared at the one and only friend I had in Boston. Yes, my life was so pathetic that I only had one friend, and she was my legal assistant. Okay, so I was a busy woman. I didn't have time for friends. And Wendy was easy. She got my love of clothes. She wasn't into drama, and she was there for me when I needed someone to keep me from eating a gallon of ice cream the night before I had to be in court. Wendy also happened to be my eyes and ears in the office. She could find out anything.

Well, almost anything.

I had made a bargain with my boss, Mr. Morrison. He'd overheard me on the phone with Lakewood Country Club, a golf club not far from Boggy Creek, begging them to let my best friend Willa's now-husband, Aiden, and his buddies hang out and golf on the day of their rehearsal dinner. The club was not budging unless one of the guys became a member. And that was not going to happen. The dinner was easy to book, but getting them to let the guys all golf at the country club the day of was not on the table. Not even with my best flirty voice.

That was when Mr. Morrison took my cell phone from my hand—yes, he took it—and told the guy on the other end who he was. He made all the arrangements for Aiden, Hunter, Bishop, Kyle, and Adam to have full access to the country club.

The crazy thing was, I thought he did it because he was a cool boss.

No, he did it because he saw a sucker. Once he hung up, he said I had to do him a favor in return. I was ready to kick him in the balls if he said I had to sleep with him, but thankfully he came back with, "I need a date for my son for the firm's Christmas party."

After staring at the man for a good two minutes, I nodded like a fool and said, "Okay." I didn't even ask a single thing about his son.

Nothing. Was he a serial killer? Why couldn't he get his own date? Was he even cute?

"Ugh, Willa is going to owe me big time for this!" I said as I sat back in my chair.

Wendy tried not to laugh. "I've heard whispers from time to time about Mr. Morrison's son. He lives in California and works in entertainment or something like that. One rumor says he's an actor, but I highly doubt that."

"I don't care what people think he does for a living. What does he *look* like, Wendy?"

"I don't know. Do you know how hard it is to ask questions discreetly? People have started to ask me why I'm asking. I can't tell them you're going on a blind date with him. Mr. Morrison is super private about his two kids, especially his son. Some think they had a falling out. He never talks about him. Like *ever*."

I shook my head. "Great. And no, don't tell anyone why you're snooping. I'll look desperate."

She folded her arms over her chest and frowned.

"What?" I asked.

"Aren't you?"

My mouth fell open. "I beg your pardon. I am not desperate. I have plenty of sex. Lots of sex. Hot sex."

"With who?"

I stood. "Well, for starters, I had a fun little affair with my best friend's brother."

She rolled her eyes. "Okay, before that?"

"It doesn't matter," I stated.

"Bob in the mailroom thinks you're a snob who hates men."

"What?" I cried out. "Why would he think that?"

She tapped her finger on her chin. "Let's see. You walk in, get on the elevator, don't say hi to anyone, and walk straight back to your office. You don't talk to anyone except to give them a polite hello. You never go to the Friday night happy hour, and you've turned down every guy here who's asked you out. Hence, Bob thinks you're a man-hating bitch."

I started to talk but then snapped my mouth shut. Fine, I could be classified as a workaholic. But in my defense, I was still fairly new to the firm and I wanted to make a good impression. My only job was to show up at work, lawyer the shit out of things, go home, and work more. In between takeout dinners and my daily trip to the gym, I dated. Kind of. When I had time or a guy caught my eye. There was the time I picked up yoga at the studio in my building because of the hot-as-hell guy I'd seen going in. Turned out, he was the husband of the instructor. I didn't last long in yoga.

I wasn't about to argue with Wendy. I probably did come off as a coldhearted bitch.

"So, you said Duke was a lawyer?" I asked Wendy, running my hands down my pencil skirt and sitting back down.

She laughed. "Luke, Brighton, his name is Luke. All I found out from the gossip mill is that he was once a lawyer, though not for Morrison, Becker, and Gline. Some other law firm in Boston. But he's no longer a lawyer."

I raised a brow and looked at her. "Really? Why not?"

She shrugged. "No clue."

"Do we know what type of law he practiced?"

"Corporate law, I think," she said, sitting in the chair across from my desk.

"Corporate, huh?"

She nodded. "M and A, I heard once. Don't know how true that is. No one really seems to talk about him because Mr. Morrison so rarely talks about him. The only reason we know anything about his daughter is because she makes an appearance once a quarter and struts through the office holding her little dog. I think it's a chihuahua or a yorkie."

I raised a brow. "And people say I'm a bitch? By the way, how can you mix up those dog breeds? They look nothing alike other than both being small."

"Potato, patato. And not people," Wendy said, "just Bob. But he does talk to a lot of other people, and everyone knows him. Mailroom and all."

"You're not making things better, Wendy."

She shrugged. "Just keeping it real."

"You know I could replace you with a snap of my fingers?"

With a grin that almost dared me to try, she leaned back in her chair.

I tapped my finger on my chin. "Mergers and acquisitions. That doesn't surprise me, considering his father is good at it."

Wendy chuckled. "He was also apparently a wiz at securities law."

I faked a yawn. "Boring. No wonder he's not a lawyer anymore and needs a date."

Wendy laughed again. "It's hard getting intel for you since I'm still the new kid on the block—not far behind you in that regard."

Nodding, I let out a sigh. "Well, I guess I'll find out tonight."

"Did you pick up your dress?"

Smiling, I replied, "I did. And it's fabulous."

She clapped. "Take a selfie when you get all fixed up. I'm dying to see it. Will you come to the regular office Christmas party tomorrow night?"

I shook my head. "God, no. One office party is enough, thank you very much."

There was a knock on my door and Wendy jumped up. "Coldhearted, man-hating bitch," she said softly as she made her way to the door. When she opened it, she nearly jumped back. "Mr. Morrison, how are you this morning?"

I stood and smiled while my boss and senior partner in the firm breezed past my assistant. "Good, Melody. I'm good."

It took everything I had not to laugh when Wendy shot him a dirty look. "May I get you anything?" she asked.

Mr. Morrison raised his hand. "No, thank you. Shut the door, Melinda."

I had to cover my mouth and look down so I couldn't see what Wendy did in response, but I imagined it had something to do with her middle finger.

Once the door clicked shut, I dropped my hand. "Good morning, Mr. Morrison."

"Good morning, Brighton. I take it you got the invite for the party this evening?"

"Yes, I did."

"I'll have a car pick you up at seven, promptly. Please be outside and waiting on them. Be sure to bring a coat, it's going to be cold this evening."

I had to bite my tongue to keep myself from reminding him that I was twenty-eight years old and didn't need to be told how to dress. After all, it was December in Boston and there was snow on the ground.

"Yes, sir, I'll be ready."

"Now, I need to let you know, Brighton, my son and I have a... rocky past. He has chosen a lifestyle and career that I'm not happy with at all. He only agreed to come back to Boston for Christmas because his mother asked him to. No, she begged him. She also asked him to come to the Christmas party, and instead of him bringing some...some...*person* he works with, I told him he had to come alone."

I was positive I was going to blink my eyeballs right out of my head. Holy crap, was Mr. Morrison's son gay? Great, even if there'd only been a shred of hope he was cute, there went any chance of a one-night stand. And holy crap, did Mr. Morrison have an issue with his son being gay? What in the hell?

"Is he okay with me being his date?" I asked.

"Oh, he doesn't know yet. I'll let him know on the way to the party."

I felt my mouth drop open. "Wh-what? You're going to...to... blindside him?"

He waved off my stunned stutter. "Don't worry, he'll be happy with my choice of date."

Whoa. Okay, what?

"Happy with your...choice?"

He blinked a few times, then said, "Oh, I don't mean it like that, Brighton. I meant to say you're a very beautiful woman who's smart and hardworking. I like your work ethic. You don't get caught up in the office drama or the nonsense of dating anyone at work. I'm hoping you'll be a good influence on Luke."

I quickly looked around for the hidden cameras that must have been in my office. Then I focused back on Mr. Morrison.

"Now," he said, rubbing his hands together, "I'll see you at the party. And if you need anything, you'll let Jill know?" Jill Locker was Mr. Morrison's personal assistant.

Standing, I replied, "Yes, of course."

"See you tonight, Brighton!" Mr. Morrison called out, quickly making his way out of my office.

Wendy slipped inside, shut the door, and turned to me. "Well? What did he say?"

I sank back down in the seat and let out a long groan. "I think Mr. Morrison is hoping I'll make his son like women and not men."

Wendy gasped. "He's gay?"

"I don't know for sure, but I think so. And the worst part is, he doesn't even know I'm going to be there!"

Wendy screwed up her face. "Yikes." Then she drew in a breath, leaned in closer to me, and said in a hushed voice, "This is going to sound so stereotypical, but maybe he'll like fashion and you guys will have something in common."

"What?" I asked, surprisingly amused.

She stood again and pointed to me, her face morphing into a wide grin. "Oh, and he likes dick, too, so you'll have that to talk about as well."

I glared at her with what I imagined was the same look my mother gave me when I was in trouble as a teen.

Wendy took a few steps back. "I'm going to go pick up lunch now."

"It's nine in the morning," I replied.

"Coffee, then."

"I gave up coffee."

She shrugged. "Then I'm going to go visit Bob in the mailroom."

I quickly stood and walked around my desk. "Don't you dare say a word about Luke Morrison, Wendy."

Glancing over her shoulder, she winked. "My lips are sealed."

Chapter Two
Brighton

When the Jaguar pulled up and a well-dressed gentleman who looked to be a few years older than me got out, I smiled. He was cute with his dark brown hair in a buzz cut. I couldn't tell because it was dark out, but I was pretty sure his eyes were a light color.

"Brighton Rogers?" he asked.

"That would be me."

He smiled and held out his arm to help me into the backseat. "My name is Hank, and I'm Mr. Morrison's personal driver."

"Oh, how nice to meet you, Hank."

With a nod, he said, "You look beautiful tonight, Ms. Rogers."

Heat washed over my face. "Thank you, Hank."

I did feel beautiful in the satin dress that hugged my body perfectly, yet still felt airy. The soft neckline flowed into a graceful wrap that twisted around my body. I left my neck bare and went with a silver diamond bracelet. A side slit that nearly went to the top of my thigh gave it that extra sexy touch. The sales lady at Saks had tried to talk me into a dusty blue dress, but as soon as I saw this cinnamon beauty, I knew I had to have it. It cost me a cool $520, but it looked beautiful with my gold strappy Jimmy Choos.

I held my red coat in my arms. I mean, if I was going to spend five-hundred bucks on a dress, I was damn well going to show it the hell off.

Hank shut the door and made his way around to the driver's seat.

"How are you this evening?" he asked, glancing in the rearview mirror.

"I'm doing well, how about you?"

He smiled. "Adjusting to Boston traffic."

"Did you recently move here?" I asked.

Laughing, he said, "No, I came with Mr. Morrison from LA."

I frowned. "I'm sorry?"

"I work for Mr. Morrison. He flew in from California this morning, and I arrived with him."

It took me a moment to realize which Mr. Morrison he was referring to. "You work for Luke? I was under the impression he wasn't aware I was going to be his date this evening."

Hank laughed again. "Mrs. Morrison sent me to pick you up after she canceled the car her husband ordered."

That made my brows shoot up to my hairline. "Oh, I see. So, Luke still doesn't know he has a date for tonight?"

"I believe he does now, ma'am. Mrs. Morrison informed him."

"Ah." I looked out the window, then back at the man driving. "And you work for Luke?"

"Yes," he said with a nod.

Christ, I had already asked him that.

"Does he always bring you with him when he travels?"

Oh my gosh, am I really grilling his driver?

Hank laughed again. "I'm his personal assistant."

"And part-time Uber driver, it seems."

Another laugh from Hank. "I have a variety of roles."

"I bet you do," I mumbled, remembering the toned body I'd glimpsed under the suit Hank was wearing.

"I'm sorry?"

"Nothing."

He looked at me once more in the mirror before saying, "I do believe Mr. Morrison—the *younger* one—will enjoy your company, Ms. Rogers."

"I do have a shining personality," I said with a smile. If the younger Mr. Morrison was really batting for the other team, that would be about the only thing he'd like about me. "I hope he isn't agitated that his father set him up on a blind date—and with a girl on top of that."

Hank's eyes flicked up and met mine in the mirror. He looked confused. "I'm sorry?"

I waved off my comment with my hand. "Nothing, just...just ignore me." I sighed heavily and suddenly wished I'd taken that shot of whiskey I'd been considering earlier. My nerves were frayed, and I hadn't even reached the party yet.

Hank and I drove the rest of the way in silence as I tried to think of what I was going to say to Luke.

It's nice to meet you. I'm sorry your father is a jackass, but he is still my boss. Or maybe I could tell him I had a headache and let him escort me home, so we could both get out of the party. If he was being forced to attend, he might be game for bugging out. Perhaps I could talk him into taking me somewhere I could show off my dress.

"We're here, Ms. Rogers."

Hank's voice pulled me out of my thoughts, and I looked toward the entrance of the Mandarin Oriental. It was a beautiful hotel, and I wasn't the least bit surprised that Morrison, Becker, and Gline had chosen to hold their private Christmas party here. I was going to have to ask Wendy where the peasants were having their Christmas party. I knew it wouldn't be here.

Hank helped me out of the car and handed the keys to valet before he turned back to me and held out his hand.

"Why, are you escorting me to the party, Hank?" I asked in a flirty voice.

He smiled, and it was then I noticed how handsome he truly was. He was older than me, in his mid-thirties, maybe six feet, with brown hair that was sprinkled with blond highlights. His eyes looked to be a light blue or gray.

"I am, if you don't mind."

I let out a nervous laugh. "I don't mind at all. The last thing I want to do is walk into that party alone."

He winked. "I wouldn't let that happen."

I squeezed his arm, and we made our way into the hotel. I had to admit I loved the looks I got from people as we walked through the lobby. Hank wasn't in a tux, but he was dressed in a very nicely tailored suit. As we entered the Oriental Ballroom, I tried to keep my breathing steady. I had no idea why I was so damn nervous.

When we stepped into the ballroom, I sucked in a breath. It was a magnificent room and decorated beautifully for Christmas.

"How beautiful," I whispered, looking around. Stunning, modern glass chandeliers hung from the ceilings and seemed to catch every light in the room. A large Christmas tree sat in the corner, decorated with blue and silver ornaments, twinkling white lights, and a silver star at the top. Part of me wanted to walk over to it. I hadn't put up a Christmas tree in my condo for the last three or four years. I'd always thought it was a waste of time since I always spent Christmas back home in Boggy Creek. My folks would set up two trees. One in the main living room of the bed and breakfast for guests, and one in their private living area. But looking at this one, I longed to have one of my own. Blue was my favorite color.

"Brighton! You made it!"

A female voice pulled my gaze off the Christmas tree, and I looked over to see an older woman walking toward me.

Mrs. Lucy Morrison. She was a beautiful woman. Her blonde hair was pulled up and piled on top of her head in a tight bun. She wore a light blue dress that showcased her body, which she clearly took care of. I wasn't sure what the woman did for exercise, but I prayed I looked half as good as that when I was her age.

"Hank, you delivered her to us safely," she said when she reached us.

Hank gave a slight bow and turned to face me. He took my hand and kissed the back of it, then looked at me and winked. "Enjoy your evening with Luke, Ms. Rogers."

I felt my cheeks get hot...because there was something in his eyes that said he knew something I wasn't privy to.

"I will. Thank you so much, Hank."

I watched as he made his way back out the door we'd just walked through. A part of me was sad he wasn't staying.

"Mitch has told me so much about you, Brighton. He says you're a promising young lawyer and not one to be messed with in the courtroom."

My cheeks warmed again. "Your husband is too kind, Mrs. Morrison."

She shook her head. "Tonight you'll call me Lucy."

Smiling, I said, "Lucy, it is."

With a raised brow, she asked, "Would you like a drink?"

"Yes, I'd love a drink."

Lucy laughed, then wrapped her arm around mine and led us over to one of three bars that were set up in the ballroom. About fifteen round tables sat along the perimeter of the dance floor, all decorated with beautiful silver tablecloths and stunning floral centerpieces of red, green, and gold.

"Goodness, whoever decorated the ballroom is very talented."

Lucy beamed. "Thank you, that would be me. My profession is interior decorating, so I live for events like this where I can play with different colors and patterns. I used to own my own business until I had Luke. I gave it up to be a stay-at-home mom."

"Well, you certainly knocked it out of the park. It's breathtaking."

We stopped at the bar and Lucy turned and asked for two glasses of champagne. "I hope champagne is okay for you?"

A part of me wanted to tell her I needed something a hell of a lot stronger if I was going to make it through this night. Instead, I flashed her a smile and took the flute. "Thank you, it's perfect."

"Let's find Luke. I'm sure he's itching to meet his date."

"I bet he is," I whispered before I took a drink.

I caught a glimpse of Mr. and Mrs. Morrison's daughter, Jenn, across the ballroom. I hadn't spoken to her too many times, maybe once when she came to the office, and I was on the top floor where the senior lawyers and partners had offices. She'd been wearing a tennis outfit that day and hadn't stayed long enough for me to even finish introducing myself.

"Oh, there's Mitch and Luke," Lucy said. "Come along, Brighton. I can't wait to introduce you. He's going to fall over when he sees you—and might possibly fall in love at first sight!"

Letting out a nervous laugh, all I could do was smile.

I allowed my boss's wife to pull me along like a puppy on a lead as I tried to keep my heart from pounding right out of my chest. Why in the hell was I so nervous? Maybe it was the idea of letting Mr. Morrison down, or even Lucy. With the way her eyes were twinkling, I had a feeling she was hoping her son might get lucky tonight. And he might. Maybe Hank was his lover. Or maybe he was bi and there was still hope?

Oh God, what if he wanted a threesome with Hank?

My stomach dropped, and I shook that thought away. I mean, I was always up for an adventure, but two guys at once was not something I had on my bucket list.

I pushed that visual away as we approached a group of six men, all dressed in tuxedos. Mr. Morrison was one of them; Jon Gline, one of the three partners, was another. The other three men were senior lawyers in the firm, whom I'd maybe said hello to once or twice in the elevator.

The last man had his back to me, but was broad across the shoulders and had thick, wavy, short dark brown hair that I instantly wanted to run my fingers through. That had to be the mysterious

Luke Morrison. He certainly made an impression from behind. Christ Almighty, he had a nice ass.

What in the hell, Bree? Run your fingers through his hair? And why are you checking out his ass? Get it together, woman! He's not even going to look twice at you.

"Darling, look who I found," Lucy said as she tapped on her husband's shoulder. When Mr. Morrison saw me, he grinned.

"*There* you are, Brighton," Mr. Morrison said. He looked back at the other men. "Jon, you of course know Brighton Rogers, one of our up-and-coming litigation lawyers. If you ever get a divorce, you want this woman as your lawyer."

They all laughed, and I smiled. It was, of course, true. I was damn good at my job. I was honest and fair, yet didn't take bullshit from anyone. That, and I lived, ate, and slept this freaking job.

The three men, along with Mr. Jon Gline, nodded and said hello. I turned my attention to the man who had originally had his back to me—and almost swallowed my damn tongue.

Holy. Mary. Mother. Of. Jesus. Why in the name of all that is holy does he have to be so good-looking?

Standing before me wasn't a man. He was a Roman god. Well-proportioned with his skin tanned to just the right color to give it a glow. Skin, I might add, that looked flawless and had me making a mental note to ask him what type of skin-care routine he used. The black tux and dark color of his hair made his brown eyes look almost black. To say he was handsome would not be doing this man justice. He was drop-dead, make-a-virgin's-cherry-pop-from-his-smile-alone gorgeous. He looked like a young Gene Kelly.

Why are you being so cruel to me, Lord? What did I do?

When I was able to drag my eyes from his face, I took in his body before meeting his gaze again. I had to work on my breathing to keep it even and steady. I also needed to remember this guy was the son of my boss. And I was currently eye-fucking and undressing him in my imagination.

Lucky, lucky Hank.

"Brighton Rogers, this is my son and your date for the evening, Luke Morrison."

I was going to deserve a fucking Oscar for how calm and cool I acted, while on the inside I was melting into a freaking puddle. My heart hammered in my chest.

Luke held out his hand for mine. "It's a pleasure to meet you, Brighton."

Oh God, even his voice is sexy.

"The pleasure is all mine," I replied with a smile. *Impressive, Bree. You spoke words that made sense.* With a tilt of my head, I added, "Has anyone ever told you that you look like a young Gene Kelly?"

He smiled brilliantly. "As a matter of fact, yes."

"Can you dance like him?" I asked, then immediately wished I could take it back.

He laughed, and holy fucking shit, it sounded sexy. Damn. Why were all the good-looking ones batting for the other team?

"Luke, take this beautiful woman out for a spin on the dance floor, won't you?" Lucy said as she pushed me—yes, *pushed me*—toward her son.

I wondered if Lucy knew my mother. She seemed to have all the same moves as her.

Luke smiled and held his arm out for me to take.

The moment I touched him, I felt a strange sensation race through my body. I swore he felt it as well, because those eyes of his almost seemed to flare before they turned darker.

Right. Stop being wishful, Brighton.

"I'm sorry?" Luke asked as we headed to the dance floor.

Shit. Shit. Shit. Did I say that out loud?

"Um...ahh...um..." *Words, Bree. Find your words. You have a law degree. You know how to use words.* "Nothing. I didn't say anything. Not a word. No words came from this mouth."

His gaze dropped to my mouth, and he smiled again. Except this time a freaking dimple appeared on his right cheek.

It's official. The entire world hates me.

The band was playing a Christmas tune. Luke drew me closer, and we started to waltz across the dance floor.

He glanced down, and his eyes flashed with amusement. "Tell me, Brighton, how did my father talk you into this whole blind-date thing?" He gave me a smile that made my lower stomach pull with a wave of desire I wasn't sure I had ever felt before. Weird.

Forbidden fruit. That's what this is. Damn it.

I looked at him and grinned. "He bribed me."

Luke's brows shot up, and he sputtered, "Wh-what?"

Laughing, I said, "He used some of his pull at Lakewood Country Club for me. My best friend got married not too long ago, and Mr. Morrison arranged for her husband and his friends to spend a day at the club."

"Guy stuff?" he asked with a chuckle.

I nodded. "Yeah, stuff guys do, but you probably aren't into that kind of thing."

Okay, could I sound any more stereotypical right now?

He looked confused but shook it off. "So, he arranged it, but only if you agreed to be my date for tonight?"

"That's right."

Luke shook his head. "I didn't ask for a date, just so you know. My mother has been bugging me to come home for a few years now, and my relationship with my father is rather...strained."

"He told me."

That surprised him. "He did?"

I nodded. "Why do you have a strained relationship? Is it because of your sexuality?" I asked before I could stop myself. "I'm sorry. That's none of my business."

Now he *really* looked confused...and stunned. I didn't blame him. *Christ, Brighton, scream out that the boss's son is gay, why don't you?*

"I don't mind answering, but I'm a bit confused about what my sexuality has to do with it."

I chewed on my bottom lip and looked around. Then I stretched up some and whispered, "You know, because you're gay?"

His eyes nearly popped out of his head.

"It's okay," I said, "I honestly could not care less. I don't think your mom knows, though. Your dad said he wasn't happy with your lifestyle and career. I'm sorry he isn't more supportive of you."

Luke stared down at me and blinked a few times before he let out a laugh.

I frowned. "I get it, believe me. My folks have been hounding me for years to settle down and stop working so much. I'm just glad they don't live closer to Boston, or I'm positive my mother would have a different guy lined up each weekend for me to go out with. If I have to hear about my eggs growing old one more time, I swear I'm going to scream."

Luke nodded, and I really couldn't read the expression on his face. He still seemed confused.

I sighed and looked up at him. "Anyway, since you're giving me permission to snoop—and when I'm nervous I tend to talk on and on—tell me why your dad doesn't like your career choice? Are you in the entertainment industry or something?"

A look of amusement crossed his face. "Something like that. My father stopped talking to me when I quit my job as a lawyer and moved to California. I was pretty into the whole drama club thing in high school and college, and acting was sort of my passion."

I raised my brows. "Acting, huh? I could see why that would make him blow a gasket." Laughing, I added, "Then add in Hank."

"Hank?" Luke asked.

"Yeah," I said with a smile. "Your *assistant*."

He slowed us down and stared at me. "He *is* my assistant."

I winked. "Sure, he is."

"No, he really is."

I stopped dancing. "So Hank isn't gay too? Damn, I pegged that one all wrong."

Luke pressed his lips together in a tight line as if trying to keep from laughing. "He's probably fucking someone in the backseat of the Jag right now. By someone, I mean a woman. He has no problem picking them up."

I crinkled my nose. "Eeeeww. I think I'll take an Uber home."

Luke tossed his head back and laughed so hard, I started to laugh with him. Then he looked at me and slowly shook his head. "Goddamn, you are refreshing, Brighton Rogers."

I grinned. "I try. Do you like fashion at all?"

"Um, not really."

Frowning, I said, "Well, damn."

Luke cleared his throat. "How about we go get a drink and step out onto the balcony for some fresh air? They have some heaters out there."

I nodded. "Sounds good."

He placed his hand on my lower back, and my stomach did a little flip. *Down, girl, he isn't into you.*

When we stopped in front of the bar, Luke turned to me. "What would you like?"

"A French 75, please."

"And for you, sir?" the bartender asked.

"Double whiskey, neat."

The bartender quickly got to work on our drinks.

I looked at Luke and gave him a good once-over before I spoke. "Double, huh?"

"Trust me, I need it. And don't look now, but my mother is currently watching us and most likely planning our wedding."

"What?" I asked with a slight chuckle as I turned back in the direction of Luke's parents. I nearly started laughing when his mother waved, smiled, and gave me a thumbs up.

"Told you."

Facing Luke, I asked, "Why don't you just tell your mom?"

The bartender placed our drinks on the bar and Luke slid him a tip.

Reaching for mine, I said, "Thank you."

Luke nodded and picked up his drink. "Tell my mother what?"

"You know," I whispered.

He ignored me and took a drink of his whiskey. "If it was up to my mother, I'd be living in the suburbs of Boston, married to a beautiful wife who lives for charity work, and we'd have two-and-a-half kids already."

"Two and a half?" I asked.

"Two kids and a dog."

Laughing again, I raised my glass to his. "Your mother and my mother sound very much alike."

"Pressuring you to marry, huh?"

I shrugged. "Among other things. She thinks I work too much and hates that I'm not dating anyone. And if I left it up to her, I'd be living in Boggy Creek and working as a kindergarten teacher or some bullshit like that."

Luke chuckled. "Is that where you're from, Boggy Creek?"

Nodding, I took a sip of my drink. "Born and raised."

"Cute town. I remember driving through plenty of times on the way to Lakewood. It's beautiful in the fall up that way."

"I like it there too. And, yes, it is. I'm sure I'll get tired of the city life eventually and move back to open my own law firm or help my folks run their bed and breakfast."

He stared at me for a moment. "Is that what you want to do?"

Looking down into my drink, I ignored that small little voice in the back of my head that said I wanted what all of my friends back home were getting.

Marriage and kids.

I was tired of working long hours and hearing about marriages breaking up. I wanted what my folks had. I glanced back up at him and plastered on a smile. "Yes. At least part of it."

His eyes searched my face, and I swore it was like he could read my mind. "My dad was bragging how you're an amazing lawyer, Brighton."

"Well, he had to say it with me standing there," I replied in a teasing manner.

"People."

I laughed and shook my head. "Well, I don't know about amazing, but I do work my ass off."

He let his eyes drift down my body, and I was positive I saw them darken with heat. Okay, so maybe he was into guys *and* girls. I could be down for that. He was beyond handsome and looked just like Gene.

He lifted his drink to his mouth and finished the whiskey in one gulp. "Let's dance again."

Before I could even say a word, we were back on the dance floor. An oldie started, and I gasped. "Gene Kelly! I love him so much, and I especially love this song. Oh, that scene in *Singing in the Rain* when Gene sings 'You Were Meant for Me.' I think that's when I fell in love with him."

Luke grinned. "A Gene Kelly fan, huh? Since you said I looked like him, does that mean I have a shot at getting more than a dance out of you?"

I felt my cheeks heat as I looked up at him. "Why, Mr. Morrison, are you flirting with me?"

He nodded. "I'm certainly trying. Is it working?"

"I am questioning a few things. Can you dance like him though?"

Leaning his head down, he placed his mouth next to my ear. "I can. Would you like to see?"

And before I knew it, Luke Morrison was spinning me around and showing me dance moves that made me want things I knew I couldn't have.

When the song ended, he pulled me close, and I swore for a hot second he was going to kiss me.

"I need to clear something up with you, Brighton, before things go any further."

My eyes widened. "Any further?" I asked in a breathy voice.

"Yes, because I *really* want things to go further, or as far as you want them to go."

My entire body heated as desire pooled in my stomach. I quickly glanced around and saw couples dancing and small groups lost in conversation—not one person was paying any attention to us. Focusing back on Luke, I softly said, "Okay."

He leaned down, his mouth only inches from mine. I felt my body lift closer to him. I wanted to bridge the distance between us more than I had ever wanted anything in my entire life.

"What...what is it? That you want to tell me? To go further?"

He smiled. He was so close I could feel the heat of his breath on my face. Smell the whiskey from his drink. "I'm not gay—and I really want to kiss you."

I felt my eyes go wide. "You're not?"

He shook his head. "No, sweetheart, far from it."

"Thank fuck," I whispered.

He laughed and drew back, leaving me slightly dizzy.

"But your dad..." I whispered.

"Doesn't like me living in California, hates that I'm into acting, and thinks I only date shallow women."

"Do you?" I asked.

"Date shallow women?"

I shook my head. "No. I mean, yes, do you date shallow women... and do you want to kiss me?"

Lord, I sound like a teenage girl right now. Get your shit together, Bree!

He slowly shook his head.

"Wait, are you shaking your head because you don't want to kiss me, or because you don't date shallow women? Oh my God, I think I drank too much."

Luke chuckled. "I don't date shallow women, and I would very much like to kiss you."

Before I could say anything else, Lucy was standing there, a wide grin on her face. Luke took a step away from me, and the heated connection between us broke.

Shit on a brick. I had never wanted to push away another woman as much as I did in that moment. What was it with moms and their terrible timing?

"All those years of dance lessons paid off, did they not, Brighton?" Lucy asked.

My feet felt like lead, and I had to force myself to get my shit together. I cleared my throat and put my game face on. "They certainly did; your son is a wonderful dancer."

Luke winked at me and then turned to his mother. "Mom, would you care to dance?"

Lucy turned to me. "Do you mind?"

"No, not at all." He was only just about to kiss me. And I had a feeling his kisses would render me stupid. "I, um, I need to run to the ladies' room."

As I started to leave the dance floor, Luke took hold of my arm and leaned closer. "I didn't scare you off with my confession, did I?" he asked.

I let out a bubble of nervous laughter. "Scare me? No, not at all. If you think you can handle it. Me. I mean, if you think you can handle me...kissing me."

His brows rose, and I took a step back, wishing the floor would open and swallow me.

"I think I can," he said, "but there's only one way to find out. Don't be gone too long."

I bit down on my lower lip and then smiled. "Excuse me for a moment."

He nodded and turned back to his mother, and they started to glide across the dance floor. If she had heard any of that, she was clearly pretending she hadn't.

Smiling to everyone I passed on the way to the ladies' room, I went over everything in my head.

He was handsome. He looked like a young Gene Kelly. He danced like a 1940's movie star. He wasn't gay. And he wanted to kiss me.

"Oh my God, dreams really do come true," I mumbled, making my way to the restroom.

I placed my hand over my stomach to settle the sudden nerves that spiked up at the thought of that man kissing me. After checking all the stalls, I hit Wendy's number.

"So?" she said without even saying hello. "What's he like?"

"I'm in deep shit."

"Why?"

I drew in a deep breath. "For starters, he's not gay. Thank fuck, he's not gay."

"Why thank fuck?"

"Because he's hot, Wendy. I'm not talking Brad Pitt kind of hot. I'm talking Gene Kelly in *Singing in the Rain* kind of hot."

Yes, I forced my assistant to watch *Singing in the Rain* with me, multiple times.

"Shut up! That's totally your type."

"I know!" I cried. "And the best part? He dances! Oh, and apparently, he's trying to make it as an actor or something in California and *that's* what Mr. Morrison meant by his lifestyle choices. I had it all wrong. I mean, he certainly has the looks...and did I mention he can dance? I'm pretty sure he just performed the scene in *Singing in the Rain* where Gene sings to Debbie on the studio stage."

Wendy paused for a moment. "I know I should probably know that scene, but I've got to be honest with you, Bree, it's drawing a blank. I've learned to fall asleep with my eyes open when we have your Gene Kelly marathons."

My mouth fell open. "That's it, block out Sunday night. We're watching it again, and you *will* stay awake."

I heard a groan from the other end of the phone. "No! No, I am not giving up my Sunday night for Gene, Brighton. I don't care if you're my boss. I've got plans, with a guy. One I actually like."

"Who?" I asked.

Before Wendy could answer, the door to the bathroom opened and Lucy Morrison walked in. I panicked, hit End, and forced myself to smile as I dropped my phone back into my clutch.

Lucy returned the gesture, but there was something strange about her grin. As she made her way over to me, I found myself taking a few steps back until I hit the opposite side of the bathroom.

"So, Brighton, what do you think of my son?"

Oh. Shit. This is where I could lose my job.

"Um, he's handsome and very polite. Nice. Dances well and carries on an interesting conversation."

Holy shit. Did that all come from my mouth?

She clapped like a teenage girl. "Wonderful! Now, do you see yourself having sex with him?"

And I'm dead. Stick a knife in me right now because my boss's wife, the mother of the man I indeed want to have sex with, just asked me if I wanted to have sex. With her son. In the bathroom. At the company Christmas party.

She raised a brow while she waited for my answer. With one quick look around, I realized I was trapped.

I should pack up my desk Monday morning...because when I opened my mouth to speak, I was positive neither of us was expecting my reply.

Chapter Three

Luke

"What do you think of Brighton, Luke?"

I turned to face my father. "I like her. She's funny."

He raised a single brow. "Brighton's funny? Mmm, I wouldn't have thought that. She seems so serious all the time."

Lifting my whiskey to my mouth, I attempted to hide my smile. Clearly Brighton Rogers had two sides, and I was certainly enjoying this one.

"Where is she?" he asked, glancing around the dance floor.

"Being cornered by your wife in the woman's bathroom."

My father let out a groan. We at least could agree on one thing. My father might have hated my decision to move to LA, hated that I was an actor, hated that I took dance lessons and had no interest in playing football, but he thought my mother should stay out of my love life as much as I did. It was the only thing we had in common.

"Good Lord. When your mother asked me to find you a date for the party, I picked Brighton because I figured your mother wouldn't see you with a lawyer or a woman like her."

"A woman like her?" I asked, glancing at him.

"Yes. Quiet, dedicated to her job. Settled."

I drew in a slow breath. "You think I'm not attracted to a woman like that, Dad?"

He sighed. "Truth be told, I don't know what type of woman you're interested in, Luke. An actress, most likely. Isn't that whom you last dated? At least that was what I read in the paper. Brighton Rogers doesn't seem like the type of woman who'd be interested in your lifestyle, son."

I tossed my head back as I let out a roar of laughter. No wonder she thought I was gay. My father stared at me like I had lost my mind.

"I think you're wrong," I said. "From the little bit I've seen this evening, she's exactly the type of woman I'd be interested in. I like her. She makes me laugh, and I want to know more about her. I also like the fact that she has no earthly idea who I am."

He turned and faced me. "And why do you think that is, son? She'd never be interested in the life you could offer her."

A strange pain hit me right in the middle of my chest. "I told her I was an actor."

My father stared at me for the longest moment and then smirked. "I'm going to go mingle. Enjoy your evening, Luke."

As he walked away, I had the urge to yell out at him. To tell him he was wrong, that Brighton wouldn't care, that me being an actor wouldn't change anything. But a part of me knew it wasn't true.

Of course, she might not know who I was because she was a workaholic, like most lawyers were. My father included.

When I glanced back toward the ladies' room, I saw her coming out with my mother right behind her. Her eyes swept over the room, and when she found me, a wide smile appeared on her face...and for the first time in my adult life, I had the feeling my father was right and I was wrong.

My mother turned and headed toward my father while Brighton practically sprinted over to me. That coppery brown dress she had on fit her like a glove. My hands itched to feel her body under it. Her cinnamon-colored hair was piled up in large curls on top of her head, and those brown eyes of hers...fuck, they were beautiful. Large and luminous and so warm in color. Most guys I knew wanted the blonde and blue-eyed women, but Brighton's eyes stole my breath. They were a light shade of brown with a dark ring that made them appear deeper in color. Rich, yet soft. Like chocolate—and I fucking loved chocolate.

"I need to leave," Brighton said when she approached, though she continued to smile.

I shook my head in confusion. "Why?"

She let out a nervous laugh as she looked over her shoulder at my mother, then back at me. "Well, it's a little hard to explain."

I placed my hand on her back and led her to one of the corners of the room for a bit more privacy. My mother had obviously said something to Brighton, and I wanted to know what it was that had her so freaked out.

"Try me," I said.

She chewed on her lip. "I may never be able to look at your mother or your father, ever again. That's going to be really hard since he's my boss and all. Oh my God...I might have to quit."

I pulled my brows in. "And why is that?"

When she looked at me, I felt my knees go weak. She was the most beautiful woman I had ever laid eyes on, and I'd worked with some very beautiful women.

"Well, she asked me if I...um...if I, um..."

My heart started to beat harder. "If you what?" I asked, clenching my fists at my side to keep from shaking the words out of her.

"She asked if I saw myself having sex with you."

I nearly stumbled back. "She *what*?" I shouted, then quickly looked around before lowering my voice. "She asked if you saw yourself having sex with me?"

Brighton nodded. "That's not the worst of it, Luke." She closed her eyes and shook her head before glancing back toward my parents. She leaned in closer and said in a low voice, "I answered her...truthfully. I have no idea why. I think it's your fault."

"Mine?"

She nodded. "You danced with me all Gene Kelly like, then whispered you wanted to kiss me, and my mind went to all sorts of dirty *ways* you could kiss me.

Smiling, I replied, "Is that so?"

"This is not funny! It's serious. What came out of my mouth wasn't something I should have said to my boss's wife."

I couldn't help it. I chuckled and took a step closer, bent slightly so I could look into her face, and lowered my voice. "What did you say?"

She blinked rapidly before she looked down at the floor.

I placed my finger on her chin. "Don't get shy on me now, Brighton."

"I said..." She closed her eyes and drew in a deep breath. "I said I wanted to have more than sex with you. I wanted to fuck you six ways from Sunday."

"What?" I said with a disbelieving laugh. "You said that? To my *mother*?"

She buried her face in her hands. "Yes! Yes, I said that. I was thinking it, and it sort of just...came out! Then I confessed to thinking you were gay and that you were off limits, but I still had this weird attraction to you. And then you said you wanted to kiss me and I got all turned on by it and my mind started to race... She finally held up her hand and *begged* me to stop talking! I, of course, told her it was your fault. Then I blamed *her* for even bringing up sex when all I'd been thinking about was kissing before she walked in."

Brighton took a deep breath in and then blew it out.

I laughed. "Well, she was the one who started it."

Her eyes went wide. "That's what I said! Apparently, she expected me to say I liked you and would like to get to know you better."

I rubbed at the back of my neck. "Why in the hell would she think she'd get that response when she asked if you wanted to sleep with me?"

Brighton shrugged. "Your mom is...well, not to be rude, but she is so much worse than my mother. I'm pretty sure my mom wouldn't

36

ask you if you wanted to sleep with me." She looked up for a moment, frowned, then added, "On second thought, she might if she got a look at you."

I couldn't help but laugh again. "Christ, I like you, Brighton. I don't want this night to end."

She dug her teeth into her lower lip as her cheeks turned the most beautiful shade of pink. "Are you saying you still want to kiss me?"

I put my hands on her hips and pulled her closer. "I'm saying I want to do more than kiss you."

"Are you asking me to sleep with you, Luke Morrison?"

"What I want to do with you will not involve sleeping, Ms. Rogers."

Her eyes went wide, and I could tell she was trying to hold back a smile. "Every sensible part of me is warning me to stay away from you," she said as she studied me. "That it's not worth risking my job."

We both looked over to where my parents were sitting. My mother waved her fingers at us and my father lifted his glass. I laughed.

Brighton turned back to me. "Do you think your dad thinks I'm easy? That maybe I'd sleep with you, and that's why he asked me to be your date?"

I shook my head. "No, I don't think that at all."

She nodded. "I don't think it would be wise for me to stay with you tonight."

Smiling, I replied, "Would you like me to call Hank? I can escort you home, at least."

Her mouth dropped open slightly. "Wait. That's it?"

I lifted my brows. "Excuse me?"

Brighton sighed. "Ugh. I'm not this type of woman...the needy kind. I never wanted a man to beg me for anything...but why would you give up so easily?"

"You said no. I'm respecting that."

She blinked a few times, then whispered, "Oh. Well, I said I didn't think it would be wise. However, I didn't say I didn't want to."

Trying not to smile again, I asked, "Do you want to spend the night with me?"

With a quick nibble on that delicious-looking lip of hers, she answered, "Yes. I want to spend the night with you, Luke. But I need you to know I don't make a habit of this—one-night stands, that is."

I traced along her jawline with my finger before I lifted her chin and leaned down. "Good. Neither do I."

The moment my mouth covered hers, I knew everything was going to change. My life was about to get very complicated, and I was going to turn Brighton Rogers's world upside down. The problem was, I wanted her too much to care about anything but being with her. Knowing what our bodies would feel like when I pushed inside of her. God, I could come just thinking about it.

We broke the kiss. I leaned my forehead against hers, trying to catch my damn breath.

"Maybe we should dance," she whispered.

"I think so, or I'll be tempted to make it an early night."

She laughed and took my arm while I led her out to the dance floor. For another hour, we danced and mingled with my father and his guests before I finally decided we should call it a night.

"Mom, Dad, I'm going to escort Brighton home."

My mother beamed with happiness. "That's wonderful, sweetheart! I hope you two exchanged phone numbers."

Brighton's cheeks went red. "We did, yes."

Dad nodded and took a sip of his whiskey. "Thank you for coming, Brighton. I hope you weren't too bored."

She blinked in surprise. "I wasn't the least bit bored. Luke was an amazing date, thank you for having me."

He nodded once more, said his goodnights, then turned and started to speak to someone else, politely dismissing Brighton.

"I guess that's our cue to leave," I said, placing my hand on Brighton's back.

My mother reached for my arm. "Call me tomorrow! I want to make sure you know where to meet us for dinner."

I leaned in and kissed her on the check, said my goodbyes, and then led Brighton out of the ballroom.

Even though I'd told my folks I was taking Brighton home, we never made it out of the hotel. One quick stop at the front desk and I had a suite booked for the night. As we headed to the elevators, Brighton kept looking around.

"Who are you looking for?" I asked.

"Your parents, other lawyers from the firm."

"So what if you see them?"

She stopped and looked at me. "They'll all know we're sleeping together."

I placed my hand on the side of her face. "Does that bother you?"

Brighton thought for a moment before a brilliant smile appeared on her face. "No, it doesn't. I mean, I pretty much already admitted to your mother that I wanted to screw you, so..."

I tossed my head back as I laughed. "Exactly."

When the elevators opened, I moved to one back corner while Brighton went to the other. An older couple was standing in the middle of the elevator talking about the play they'd been to, completely unaware of the sexual tension building around them.

I glanced over at Brighton and smiled. She was looking at me like she wanted to rip my clothes off, to hell with the older couple.

The elevator doors opened and the couple stepped out, leaving us alone. Once the doors shut, I slipped my hands into my pants pockets and Brighton fiddled with her clutch.

"You had to get a room on the top floor?" she asked.

"I got a suite; I thought you'd be more comfortable."

She tilted her head—and what came out of that pretty little mouth of hers nearly had me falling to the ground. "I don't need a suite, Luke. All I need is a comfortable bed we can fuck in."

I swept my tongue over my suddenly dry lips before I whispered, "I think I just fell in love with you."

The little minx winked at me and then opened her purse and took out her phone. She hit a few buttons and put the phone to her ear. The doors opened and we both walked out into the hall.

"You're making a call?" I asked. "Now?"

She nodded. "I am."

"Who are you calling?"

Before she could answer, she smiled. "Hey, Mom! Yeah, I'm exhausted and heading home. The party was nice. Oh, he was okay, nothing to really look at."

I stopped walking and faced her. She looked at me with mock surprise.

"Okay? Nothing to look at?" I whispered.

Brighton pushed her finger to my lips and shook her head. "Sorry, Mom. This one isn't going to work out. He's gay. Totally not into me at all."

I pulled her hand away from my mouth and placed it right over my hard cock.

Her eyes dropped to where her hand was, then she looked back up to me. "I've got to go, Mom. Talk to you tomorrow."

She hit End with her thumb and looked down again. Her hand started to move along my length, and I could hear her breathing pick up a bit.

Brighton slowly lifted her gaze to mine and said, as cool as a cucumber, "Well, if the whole acting gig doesn't work out, I'm pretty sure you could do porn from the size of this baby."

All I could do was laugh and pull her to me. Our mouths pressed together in a heated kiss as I walked her back until she hit the wall by the elevator. I moved my hands over her body, feeling the soft satin of her dress. It was a fucking tease. I needed to see her naked. Feel her against me.

Brighton drew her head back and looked up at me. "I don't know about you, but I really don't want our first time to be in a hallway."

"Why did you lie to your mom?" I asked.

She shrugged. "She'll hound me for days if I tell her the truth."

40

I nodded and kissed the tip of her nose before I took her hand in mine and led her down the hall to the very last room. I unlocked it and opened the door, motioning for her to walk in first.

Letting out a whistle, Brighton slowly shook her head and set her purse on the side buffet table. "Holy crap. Look at the view! I can see the whole city."

I shut the door and watched as she made her way through the suite. There was a small kitchenette to the right along with a four-chair table a little farther into the room. A large sofa sat near the windows with a few accent chairs placed opposite. The door to the bedroom was toward the small kitchen area.

"This suite is bigger than my condo," she said with a giggle.

I really liked that sound and made a mental note to make her laugh as much as I could.

Brighton walked up to the window and gasped. "There's a balcony, Luke!"

She opened the door and stepped out into the cold night while I placed her coat and mine over the chairs. I started to make my way to her, undoing my tie. "You're going to freeze out there, Brighton."

"Call me Bree," she said over her shoulder. The moonlight cast a beautiful glow on her skin and seemed to make her dress sparkle. She had a huge smile on her face as she drew in a deep breath and took in the city view.

God, she was breathtaking.

"Okay, you really *are* going to freeze," I said. "Come in here."

She turned and came back in before I slid the door shut.

"I wasn't worried," she said. "I'm sure we'll be hot here in a little bit."

Laughing, I tossed my tux jacket on the sofa while she slipped her shoes off and set them to the side.

"Do you always say what you're thinking?" I asked, pulling my shirt from my pants and rolling up the sleeves.

She nodded, making her way into the bedroom. She crawled onto the bed and knelt on it, looking out the large windows. "I would kill for a view like this."

"Where do you live now?"

"Off of Burbank Street. It's a cute little place, and I'm in a good neighborhood. It's just small. I'm close to Symphony Park, and there's a Whole Foods right down the block from me. What more could a girl want?"

I nodded, giving her a soft smile.

"What about you? Do you like living in California?" She turned and sat on the bed, her legs stretched out and her cleavage on full display for me to gawk at.

"It's okay."

"Do you have a nice place?"

"It has two bedrooms and two baths."

She tilted her head. "Do you at least have a view?"

I wasn't about to tell her I lived on five acres of land with a view of the Pacific Ocean. At least, I wasn't going to tell her *yet*.

"I do," I said as I crawled onto the bed. "Are you stalling, Bree?"

She nodded and let out the sexiest little giggle I'd ever heard. "I'm nervous for some reason."

I paused. "Do I make you nervous?"

With a shake of her head, she replied, "No. But I don't normally make it a habit to sleep with men I've just met. Or my boss's son."

I laughed. "Good, I don't make it a habit to sleep with women I've just met either."

She put her hand on my chest. "You're single, right? Please tell me there isn't anyone back in LA waiting for you."

"I'm single."

Bree let out a breath.

"You look beautiful in this dress, by the way," I said.

"Thank you." She looked down at the dress. "It's getting rather uncomfortable, though."

I grinned as my cock grew harder. "I think I can help you out of it."

"Will you?" she asked. I took her hands and guided her off the bed.

We sat there, staring at each other, both of us clearly hesitant to make the first move. Finally, Bree turned and looked over her shoulder at me. "Will you unzip me?"

I reached up...and saw my hands were shaking. *What in the fuck is up with that?*

When I unzipped the gown and got a look at her creamy white skin, I nearly let out a moan. Clearing my throat, I said, "There you go."

She slowly turned back around and moved each strap off her shoulders. Then she dropped her hands and the dress pooled at her feet.

I stepped back and drew in a deep breath as I took her in. She was completely naked.

Mother of God—my cock strained against my pants.

"Fucking hell," I said, "you were naked under that thing this entire time?"

"I didn't want any panty lines to show."

I brought my hand to my dick to adjust it while I let my gaze move slowly over her. "You're so beautiful. Perfect in every way."

Her cheeks turned bright pink. I loved how easily I could make her blush, because I had a feeling Brighton Rogers wasn't the type of woman who blushed easily for anyone else.

"Take your hair down now," I said, not even recognizing the roughness of my own voice.

When Bree lifted her hands, her pert, rounded breasts lifted as well. My mouth watered at the thought of sucking on her nipples.

I forced myself to look up from her tits and saw her taking down her hair. Watching as her light brown curls fell free around her shoulders was one of the sexiest things I'd ever seen. I itched to run my fingers through her hair. It looked so soft and shiny, like the satin of the dress she'd removed for me.

When she was finally finished, she shook her head, letting the curls fall where they may, and I let out a low groan.

"I believe it's your turn now, Mr. Morrison."

"Don't call me that. It's my father's name."

She curled her lip and shivered as if the thought had just occurred to her.

Never in my life had I taken off my clothes so damn fast. Once I was down to my boxer briefs, I pushed them off and kicked them to the side to join my discarded dress shirt and pants. Bree's eyes took in every inch of my body, and I had to admit I liked how she looked at me. Like a hungry predator waiting to devour her prey.

Her eyes jerked up to meet mine. "You are...like no other man I've ever seen. Everything about you is...well, it's beautiful."

I was totally giving my personal trainer a raise. No woman ever looked at my body like Bree did, and it made me even harder, if that was possible, seeing the desire in her eyes.

Smiling, I cupped her face in my hands and brushed my lips over hers. "Bree, I really hope you have condoms, because this is the last thing I thought would happen when I got ready for tonight."

She giggled again. "My assistant Wendy made sure I had some, just in case."

I moved my mouth and kissed along her jaw, then down to her neck. I inhaled, and the smell of jasmine and vanilla filled my senses. "You should give her a raise."

Bree's head dropped back, and she let out a soft moan when I moved my hand up her side and cupped one of her breasts. I loved how it fit perfectly in my hand. I ran my thumb over her hardened nipple, and she gasped.

"I'll...for sure...give her... Oh God," she moaned when my mouth covered her nipple and my hand moved between her legs. "Yes. Oh, Luke...yes."

"Do you like that, love?"

Her head jerked in a nod. "Yes. Don't stop. Please don't stop!"

She gripped my shoulders and moaned out my name as I slid my fingers into her wet pussy. Christ, she was ready. I could practically feel her vibrating with the need to come.

I was going to send my mother to fucking Paris for talking me into coming home for Christmas.

Brighton Rogers was, by far, the best Christmas present I had ever unwrapped.

Chapter Four
Brighton

Oh.
My.
Gawd.

Luke had only just started to touch me and I could already feel my orgasm building. What in the hell? The man had magical fingers and a mouth that would drive any woman insane. His kisses alone nearly made me come undone.

"Lie down on the bed, Bree. I want to taste you."

I tried to be calm and nonchalant, as if men asked to taste me all the time, when really on the inside I wanted to jump up and down with joy.

I turned too fast and tripped, and my body fell to the floor, my face barely missing the side table.

"Shit, are you okay?" Luke asked.

Nodding, I covered my mouth and laughed at my eagerness. He smiled as he scooped me up into his arms like I weighed nothing. The man clearly worked out—though that was already evident from his insanely fit body. His chiseled-perfection-without-an-ounce-of-fat-anywhere body. And his abs...Christ on a cracker, I wanted to lick them with my tongue. Hell, I wanted to lick his whole body. And that dick. I was going to feel him for days. He was big. Very big.

How in the hell did he not have a girlfriend?

Luke gently placed me on the bed, then crawled over me. I could feel his cock rub against my leg, and I had to force myself not to beg him to push inside of me.

Shit. Shit. Shit. I forgot to grab the condoms. Should I stop him and go get them? Ask him to grab my purse or—

"Holy shit! Oh my God, Luke!"

HIs mouth was between my legs doing very naughty things, and all coherent thoughts left me. He licked me like I was his favorite flavor of ice cream. My line of past lovers wasn't very long, and only one other guy back in college had given me oral sex—and it was *nothing* like this. I was pretty sure it had been his first time doing it as well.

With Luke, my body had never been so...hot. It was the only way I could describe how he made me feel. I was burning up for him, and I needed more. God, I needed so much more.

Luke's hands went to my thighs, and he spread my legs farther apart before he slid his fingers inside me. I gasped and then let out a long moan.

"God, what are you doing?" I cried out when he started to massage a place so deep inside of me that it left me feeling like I was going to pass out from the utter bliss of it all. The man knew how to pleasure a woman, and I wasn't sure if that was a good thing or not.

Then his mouth was on my clit again, and I threaded my fingers in his dark brown hair. I pulled him closer to me, even while I fought against the urge to push him away.

"Yes," I hissed. "That feels so...oh, Luke!"

He licked and sucked and did things that had my toes curling. My body trembled. and I pressed my hand over my mouth to keep from screaming out when my orgasm hit me.

Luke reached up and pulled my hand from my mouth and our eyes met.

Then he sucked harder—and I fell.

"Luke. I'm coming!"

I felt my body spasm around his fingers as he pumped them in and out and never once took his mouth off of me. He groaned in pleasure, and I swore another round hit me from the rumble of his voice, making me scream out. "I can't! I can't take it anymore!"

When I pushed his head away, Luke shot me a smirk that said he was more than happy with his performance, and I had to agree. He deserved a standing ovation. It felt like it took forever to come down from the high I'd experienced.

He kissed all the way up my body before his mouth captured mine. I could taste myself on his tongue and it caused me to moan softly.

Luke drew back and said with a wicked smile, "I want you to come in my mouth again, but this time with you sitting on my face."

My insides jumped and twisted at his words. "Sit on your face?"

He nodded.

With one raised brow, I replied, "You dirty little boy."

Luke laughed. "I may be dirty, but I'm certainly not little."

"Touché."

I moved my fingers over his chest to his abs. "I want to lick every inch of your body, but especially here."

He looked down. "My abs?"

Nodding, I replied, "Yes. I've never seen a set of abs so beautiful."

"You have my permission to lick anywhere you please, Bree."

Our eyes met, and we stared at each other for a moment before Luke reached down, grabbed his dick, and started to stroke it.

I wagged my finger back and forth. "Tsk, tsk, you don't get to have all the fun. Get on your back."

He grinned. "Yes, ma'am."

I straddled him, running my finger down his chest and over his abs. I licked my lips when I saw the precum on the tip of his cock. Swiping my finger through it, I put it in my mouth, closed my eyes, and moaned in delight.

"Fucking hell, Bree."

I moved my body so I could position my mouth over him, then slowly licked from the bottom to the top of his cock, swirling my tongue over the tip and causing Luke to jerk his hips.

"Christ above," he gasped when I ran my tongue back down his shaft.

"I have to confess, I haven't given very many blowjobs. Never was a fan. But something about your pretty dick makes me want to suck you, hard."

Luke's head popped up from the bed. "Pretty? Did you just call him pretty?"

With an innocent look, I replied, "I did. He's very—" I placed a kiss on the tip—"very—" another kiss—"*very* pretty."

Luke closed his eyes and fisted the sheets. "Bree, are you trying to kill me?"

I took him deep into my mouth, and Luke nearly shot off the bed.

"Fuck!" he called out. "That feels so fucking good. Yeah, baby... don't stop."

I wrapped my hand around the bottom of his cock and moved it in time with my mouth. I wasn't a pro at blowjobs, but by the sounds he was making, I'd say I was doing a fairly good job.

"Bree!" Luke gasped. "Bree, baby, I need...fuck, oh God. If you don't...stop...I'm going to..."

The feeling of power I had in that moment spurred me on, and I sucked him harder.

Luke reached for me and pulled me up, covering his mouth with mine as I straddled him. The kiss was needy, yet something pulled in my chest that I couldn't put my finger on. I'd kissed other men while having sex, but something about Luke... The way he made me feel, the way he kissed me back. It was like he was giving me his soul. And I greedily took it while I gave my own to him as well.

I broke the kiss and drew back to look at him with a fake pout on my face. "That's not fair. You didn't let me finish."

"I want to be inside of you, Bree. Now."

"Condom," I panted out as I crawled off of him, nearly falling again in my rush to grab my purse.

When I came back into the room, I dumped it out and found three condoms. I held them up and Luke smiled.

"Your assistant was planning on you getting very lucky tonight."

I giggled and placed two of them on the table. "I guess so." Crawling back onto the bed, I flashed him a wicked smile and rolled one of the condoms onto his shaft.

Goodness, he is big.

When I looked at Luke, I could tell he was holding his breath. "Do you want me on top?" I asked, hoping he'd say yes.

"Do you *want* to be on top?"

"Yes, very much so."

Luke put his arms behind his head and winked. "I'm yours to do with as you please, love."

I wrapped my hand around his dick and gave him a smirk. "How did you know I liked being in control?"

He laughed. "I'm good at reading people; it's what made me a good lawyer."

Ever so slowly, I sank down on him. Christ, he was hard and thick, and I couldn't wait to feel him completely inside of me.

Luke took hold of my hips and watched as I ground myself down on him, adjusting to how much he stretched me. I wished I could feel him skin to skin, but that would really be pushing things. Once I felt comfortable with his length, I moved faster.

"That's it, Bree. Fuck me. Make yourself come on my cock."

Shit, I never knew how much dirty talk could turn me on, and Luke telling me to fuck him nearly had me coming on the spot. I dropped my head back and said, "You're a dirty talker."

He moved his hands and found my clit. With one little rotation of his fingers, I felt my orgasm coming. I brought my hand up to my mouth, but Luke pulled it away again.

"No, let me hear your pleasure. I want my name on those lips when you come."

Then it hit, and I screamed out his name while my orgasm seemed to take over my entire body. I was almost positive I *left* my body and went to heaven for a few moments. I had never come so hard in my life. It felt glorious.

Before I came back down from my euphoria, Luke flipped us over and started to move slowly, in and out.

"Faster. Luke, I need all of you! Please."

"I want to last, Bree. Fuck, I don't want to come yet."

I met his gaze and silently told him we had all damn night to do this. He clearly read it in my eyes, because he picked up his speed.

"Yes. Yes. Luke! Yes! Oh my God, I'm going to come again!" I cried, grabbing a pillow and putting it over my face. Luke pulled it away and it went flying across the room.

"That's it, baby, come with me. I'm coming, Bree...fuck, I'm coming so hard."

We fell together. My body squeezed Luke's dick. Hearing him call out in pleasure had my own orgasm rippling, over and over. I closed my eyes, stars bursting behind my lids.

When I felt the last of our orgasms fading, Luke leaned over me, careful not to give me too much of his weight. Then he kissed me. I brought my fingers to his hair—it was the sweetest, most sensual kiss I had ever experienced.

And just like that, Luke Morrison ruined all future sex for me, because I was positive no man could ever make me feel that good again. Or make me come three times. I was exhausted. Spent. Thoroughly fucked and satisfied like never before.

We drew apart when we both needed more air. Luke rested his forehead against mine and we worked to steady our breathing.

"That was...beyond words," he whispered as I ran my fingers lightly up and down his back.

"It was amazing," I agreed.

Placing soft kisses all around my face, Luke slowly pulled out of me. "Shower?"

I nodded. "That sounds nice."

He pulled off the condom, tied it up, and tossed it into the trashcan before reaching for my hand and pulling me gently off the bed.

To say I was in a sex-induced euphoria would be putting it lightly. Even though I'd had three of the most intense orgasms of my life—not even my best vibrator could give me one like what I'd just experienced—I was still feeling a pull in my lower stomach. I wanted more. More of him inside me. More of his mouth all over my body. More of those naughty words whispered in my ear.

I giggled as Luke pulled me into his arms. "My God. I have never felt so satisfied in my life."

"That's what I like to hear," he said as we walked into the bathroom.

"Wow, that's a shower," I said. "You could fit ten people in there."

Luke reached in and turned on the water, then looked back at me. "I'd rather we keep it to the two of us."

"You're no fun."

He laughed and motioned for me to get under the rain showerhead. "Wet your hair and I'll wash it for you."

I stared at him. "Are you for real right now? How did you know that was one of my most favorite things ever?"

Luke shrugged and poured shampoo into his hands. I wasn't even ashamed of the little moans of pleasure I let out as he massaged my scalp.

"Do you give massages as well?" I asked.

He leaned down and kissed my shoulder before he moved his soapy hands around my body and cupped my breasts. "I do."

"God, Luke, you're going to make me either fall asleep or come again."

Chuckling, he moved his mouth to my ear. "I better stop, then, because I have so much more I want to do to you, and I need you awake for all of it."

Turning in his embrace, I wrapped my arms around his neck. "Then I'm going to need food. Lots and lots of food."

But before he fed me, he turned me around, pressed my back to his chest, and made me come once more.

Chapter Five

Luke

I watched Bree eat another piece of pizza. The girl certainly had an appetite, and I freaking loved it. She wasn't rail thin like most of the actresses I worked with. She had one of the most amazing bodies I'd ever seen, with curves and an ass that made my mouth water.

"I can say one thing," she said, "you don't disappoint with orgasms *or* your choice of food."

Laughing, I folded my pizza and took a bite.

Bree closed her eyes and moaned, and it went straight to my dick. She was dressed in my white button-down shirt, sitting on the bed with her legs crossed. I could tell she was a runner. Her legs were toned and muscular, and all I wanted to do was run my hands over them.

"What do you like to do when you're not giving your life to the law firm?" I asked, wiping my mouth with a napkin.

Letting out a breath, Bree replied, "Let's see. I've recently gotten into reading, which I don't really do unless I'm back in Boggy Creek or my case load is light. I love to run. I run at least three to five miles every other day."

Damn, I'm good. "I enjoy running as well."

"How did you get Regina Pizzeria to deliver in the middle of the night?"

I smirked. "I'm good friends with one of the owner's sons. He owed me a favor, and I called it in."

"Well, if this is your idea of a first date, you're going to have to go pretty crazy with the second date to top this."

My heart did a weird little jump in my chest at the idea of seeing Bree again. I truly wanted to get to know her better, and I could see us spending countless nights like this. At least, whenever I was able to get back to Boston.

"Are you okay with dating someone who lives across the country?"

Bree stopped chewing and looked horrified. "I...I don't know why I said that, Luke. I don't have any expectations of anything..." Her voice faded away.

"Hey, I want to see you again, Bree."

She smiled and whispered, "Okay. I want to see you as well."

"And me being clear across the country won't bother you?" I asked.

She took her time thinking about her answer, and I liked that. She wasn't one to jump the gun or go with her emotions in the moment. That said a lot about her.

"Do you want me to answer you honestly?"

That was another thing I liked about Bree. She wasn't into bullshit games and spoke her mind. "Of course, I do."

She shrugged. "I'm not sure. I've never done any sort of long-distance thing before, so the only thing I can say is...I'd have to see. I wasn't looking for a relationship, and you've sorta swept into my life and knocked me over with your talented tongue and dick."

I nearly choked on my pizza. "Christ, are you trying to kill me?"

She winked. "You said you wanted honesty. That's what I'm giving you."

And I needed to be honest with her. "Bree, it might be complicated, dating me. With my career and all."

Her eyes traveled over my bare chest, and she did a quick sweep of her lips with her tongue. "I think you're worth the risk."

I returned her perusal with one of my own. "I'm glad to hear it, and so are you, even if you are a workaholic."

"What?" she asked with mock surprise.

"I saw you checking your work email and replying to something earlier. You do know it's nearly four in the morning, and no one is going to read that email until Monday morning?"

"Ha, that's where you're wrong. I already got a reply from the other lawyer."

I rolled my eyes. "Jesus, lawyers."

She giggled and fell back on the bed. "I'm so full."

Gathering up the pizza box and our paper plates, I tossed them into the trash, then crawled back onto the bed. "You clearly don't make a habit of eating pizza in the middle of the night," I said, pulling her body next to mine where we sat up against the headboard.

She shook her head. "I eat what I want, I just run my ass off every day and hit the gym."

"I love food. All kinds of food."

Bree faced me. "I know this amazing place for breakfast, if you want to go tomorrow."

I crinkled up my face. "How in the hell can you even think about food? I'm so stuffed I can hardly move."

Giggling, she sighed and leaned against me. "Want to watch a movie? I can't go to sleep right after eating."

I reached for the remote and turned on the TV. "What do you want to watch?"

"Can you go to Amazon Prime? I'll give you my login."

"Um, sure." After logging into Amazon Prime, I asked, "What do you want?"

"Type in *Singing in the Rain*; I bought it."

Letting out a chuckle, I pulled up the movie and hit play. As it played in the background, we talked about anything and everything. Bree told me about Boggy Creek and her folks' bed and breakfast and what it was like growing up in a small town. She also talked about her best friend Willa and her new husband, Aiden. When she mentioned she'd someday like to move back to Boggy Creek, I let my imagination go wild. What would it be like to live a normal life with no paparazzi following my every damn move? To have friends who wanted to hang out with me simply to hang out and not because they wanted to be introduced to a director I worked with?

"Do you not like Boston?" I asked as Bree yawned and leaned closer to me.

"I love Boston. Love the sounds of the city, the hustle and bustle of it all. Especially during the holidays. There's a guy back in Boggy Creek, Bishop Harris, who owns a Christmas tree farm. He supplies trees to a lot of the government offices in Boston." She smiled as if lost in a memory. "I used to love to go and pick out our tree each year. My father would bring a handsaw, and we'd cut down our own tree. They had Christmas songs playing, and you could get a cup of hot chocolate. Since Bishop bought it, he's made some changes. Fun changes. They have all kinds of events throughout the season. Even a firepit where you can make s'mores."

"Sounds nice. Do you always go home and spend Christmas with your family?"

She nodded. "Yes, always. My mother would drive to Boston and drag me home by my ear if I ever said I wasn't coming home for the holidays."

I laughed.

"What about you? Do you come back to Boston for the holidays?"

"No. My folks and sister usually go somewhere. Paris, Italy, Spain. They're never home for the holidays. I honestly don't remember the last time we even spent Christmas together as a family. I think this is the first year I've been home for the holidays since moving to LA."

She looked at me with sadness in her eyes, then whispered, "I'm sorry."

I laced my fingers with hers. "Don't be. You can't miss something you've never had."

Bree blinked a few times. "What about this Christmas? You're not leaving, are you?"

Those big brown eyes studied me, and I could hear the hopefulness in her voice. God, she looked so breathtaking.

"No, I'm staying in Boston through the New Year," I said. "I take it you'll be heading to Boggy Creek for Christmas?"

She pouted, and it was fucking adorable. "No. My parents don't go away often, but they decided to treat themselves and go out of town for the first time ever over Christmas. Maybe we could spend it together?"

That made my eyes widen. "Yeah?"

"Yeah," she replied with a slight laugh as she bumped my shoulder with hers. "I mean, if you wanted to."

I pulled her onto my lap, and she quickly straddled me. I cupped her face with my hand and my heart did a little flip when she leaned into it. "I like you, Brighton Rogers. I like you a lot."

Her breath caught, then a slow smile played across her face. She ran her thumb over my bottom lip and said softly, "I like you a lot, too, Luke."

When I rolled her over, she instantly spread her thighs for me. I moved my hand down her side and between her legs. She was wet and ready.

"I want to make love to you, Bree..."

"Okay," she whispered.

"But we don't have any more condoms."

"I'm on birth control."

I swallowed hard. I'd never had sex without a condom. Okay, that was a lie. I did when I was eighteen at a college party once, drunk out of my mind. The idea of being inside of Bree with nothing between us made my heart feel as if it would beat out of my chest.

"Are you...are you sure? I haven't been with anyone in about eight months, and I've always used a condom. Except once in college when I was too drunk to remember."

She swallowed hard. "I've never slept with anyone without protection, but something about you makes me do crazy things. I'm sure. I want to feel you."

I reached between us once more and lined up my throbbing cock with her entrance and slowly pushed in. We both sighed with pleasure, and I had to stop moving for a few moments.

"What's wrong?" she asked.

"If I move, I'm going to come."

Bree laughed and wrapped her legs around my waist.

When I finally got myself under control, I moved in and out of her slowly, relishing the feel of her tight body wrapped around me.

Everything about this moment was perfect. A part of me wanted to pretend we could do this and nothing would change...but the moment I told Bree who I really was, things would be different.

And that scared the hell out of me.

The light from the morning sun shone in through the windows, and I groaned as I pulled my pillow over my face.

The sound of a door clicking had me tossing the pillow to the side and sitting up quickly. Bree smiled as she crawled onto the bed beside me. "I'm starving."

"What time is it?" I asked, scrubbing my hands down my face.

"Ten. We have to be out of the hotel by noon, and I need to get a change of clothes."

I reached over, picked up the phone on the side table, and hit the button for the front desk. "Yes, I was wondering if I can possibly book this room for tonight as well?"

Bree's eyes widened as she whispered, "What are you doing?"

I held up my finger. "Great, thank you. No, that's it for now."

When I hung up, Bree crawled on top of me and pushed her hands onto my chest, forcing my back against the headboard. "Luke Morrison, we cannot stay in this hotel forever."

I flipped her over. Now that the whole condom problem was a thing of the past, I *could* keep Bree in this hotel and naked in this bed for another twenty-four hours, if not more. A part of me never wanted to leave this room. I wanted the simplicity of being here with Bree. In here, I could leave the real world behind.

"I think the idea of staying naked and in this bed for another twenty-four hours sounds amazing," I said.

She giggled. "Well, when you put it that way. But honestly, I'm starving."

"I'll make you a deal. Let's order room service for breakfast, and then I'll make it up to you by taking you to dinner at one of my favorite Italian restaurants."

Raising a single brow, she asked, "Italian? I love Italian food."

I jerked my hips. "So what do you say? A little bit of fun in bed and then dinner, just the two of us?"

She laughed. "Who else would it be?"

I felt my throat work to swallow. It was now or never. I couldn't keep ignoring the fact that once Bree found out exactly what I did for a living, it could change everything.

Clearing my throat, I said, "The press."

A confused expression appeared on her face. "What do you mean, the press?"

Drawing in a deep breath, I said, "I use a stage name when I act, Bree."

"Okay," she replied, laughing but still confused.

"My stage name is Luke Walters."

She tilted her head and stared at me. "Am I supposed to know that name?"

God, I loved that she had absolutely no fucking clue who I was. It was so damn refreshing. Most women wanted to be seen on my arm for a chance to be photographed with me or to further their own careers. Bree wasn't looking for anything from me...but me.

Reaching for my cell, I Googled my name and then handed her the phone.

With a smile, she asked, "What is this?"

"Read it," I said softly as she took the phone from me.

I waited and watched her smile fade while she read. Her eyes darted across my phone screen, and when she finally dropped her hand, she met my gaze but didn't utter a word.

"Say something, Bree."

Crawling off of me, she grabbed my shirt and pulled it over her head, then headed out of the bedroom and to the living room. I followed her, wrapping a towel around my waist. She stood at the windows, overlooking Boston.

"Bree?"

"I need a second to process this, Luke. You kissed Scarlett Johansson, for fuck's sake."

I tried not to laugh, instead smiling and pressing my lips tightly together. "That movie gave me my first Oscar win."

She spun around and gaped at me. "How many have you won? It seems I didn't read that far down."

"Two."

"Two? Two. You've won two Oscars. And I had no freaking clue who you were."

All I could do was shrug and attempt to make light of it. "Workaholic, remember?"

She rolled her eyes, then turned back to the window. She folded her arms over her body as if to hug herself.

"Bree, please don't let this change anything."

When she didn't reply, I walked over and stood behind her. She leaned back against me, and I took that as a good sign.

"How does this work, Luke?" she asked in a barely there voice.

"I wish I had the answer to that question, love."

She let a bitter laugh slip free and shook her head. "That's not encouraging."

"I do know that the moment the press finds out who you are, they won't leave you alone until they find out everything about you."

My words caused her to push away, turning to face me with a look of utter fear on her face.

"We can make sure they don't find out," I said. "Other people do it. I mean, other actors."

"Like Taylor Swift?" she asked with the sweetest expression of hope on her face. "Wait, do you know Taylor Swift?"

I shook my head. "I don't, sorry."

Her eyes lit up for the briefest moment with excitement. "Britney Spears? I love running to her music."

Christ, this woman made my insides feel something I'd never experienced before. I'd told her I won two Oscars, and she was more excited about the prospect of meeting Britney Spears. "No, I don't know her either. But I could get my manager to contact her manager."

Bree sighed. "I don't care about that. I mean, it would be cool meeting her. I really like you, Luke."

I placed my hand on the side of her face. "I really like you too. Do you still want to spend Christmas with me? I'll take you somewhere I know we won't have to worry about anything other than getting to know each other better."

When I waggled my brows, she laughed. "Is that code for staying in bed?"

"If you want it to be. If you'll give me a chance, I know we can make this work. I need you to trust me."

The tension in her body seemed to slip away. She wrapped her arms around my neck and looked up at me with a smile that said she would do that. Trust me. And that made a crazy sensation go off in my chest.

"Okay."

I raised a brow. "Okay, you'll trust me, or okay, you'll go away with me for the holiday."

She reached up onto her toes and kissed me softly on the lips. "Both.

Chapter Six

Bree

Luke and I spent nearly the entire day in the hotel room. We talked, laughed, and made love in between watching a few movies. It was one of the most amazing days of my life. When it came time for me to go home, Luke left the hotel first and had Hank drive me home.

After a quick shower, I got ready for dinner with Luke. My phone buzzed, and I smiled when I saw his text come through.

Luke: Car will be outside your place at 7

I replied that I'd be ready. A small part of me was a bit anxious about dinner. Once I got home, I'd looked up Luke's name...well, the name he used for acting. I was stunned to learn this whole other side of the man I had spent the last day with. A small part of my brain told me I needed to put a stop to this, that I was so far out of my league it was unreal. But the other part told me I was being silly. Luke was like any other guy. So he was an actor. So he'd kissed some of Hollywood's top leading ladies. I wouldn't let that bother me. The feelings I felt for Luke were more than a fling. I had never experienced the feelings I had with Luke with any other man.

My phone rang, and without even looking at who was caller, I swiped it and put it on speaker. "Hello?"

"Brighton, sweetheart. Am I interrupting your work?"

Smiling, I applied my mascara and answered, "Hey, Mom. No, you aren't interrupting. I'm not working today."

"Are you feeling okay?"

I paused. "Yes. Why?"

"You always work on Saturdays."

"Not this weekend. I decided to take some time off and pamper myself."

I almost laughed at my choice of words. I was indeed pampering myself, with one very handsome man who knew how to make a woman feel good.

"That's nice, darling. I'm glad you're taking some me-time."

"Me too, Mom. Me too. What's up? I'm getting ready to have dinner with a friend."

She didn't even bother asking who. She most likely thought I was going to dinner with Wendy, since I never mentioned dating anyone. Wendy was the only person I ever really talked about from Boston.

"I won't keep you, but did I read your text right that you're not coming back for Christmas at all?"

I could hear the worry in her voice. "Did you need me to help at the bed and breakfast for you guys?"

My mother laughed softly. "No, I've got that covered. I was surprised when you texted and said you'd be staying in Boston over the holidays, that's all. I figured you would be spending it with your friends."

"I'm really far behind on some work. I'm prepping for a deposition next week, and it's a pretty delicate divorce. I want to be sure I'm prepared."

That wasn't entirely a lie. I did have a deposition I needed to prep for.

Mom sighed. "I'm sure you'll do fine. I'm glad you're taking this weekend off, at least. I wish you were coming here, though; I'm sure Willa will miss seeing you."

It was my turn to laugh. "Willa is newly married. I'm sure she and Aiden have plenty of things to do to keep them occupied. And they also have Ben to think about."

Ben was Willa's son from her first marriage to a loser whom I helped her get divorced from as well as full custody of Ben. "I promise I'll come visit after the new year."

One glance at my clock told me I had ten minutes until Luke was here. "Mom, I need to get going. I'll call you in the morning before you and Dad take off for your trip. I love you both."

"Love you, too, sweetheart. Talk soon."

After I hung up, I put on a bit of lipstick, pulled the sides of my brown hair up and pinned them back, and gave myself a quick glance. I had on a black knit, long-sleeve shirt with a bow at the top right side. It was a nice statement piece without being over the top. I'd paired it with a double-layered skirt of caramel satin with a tulle overlay covered in black posies. A pair of black high-heeled boots finished off the look.

"Okay, why are you so nervous, Brighton Rogers?"

I placed my hand over my stomach to calm the butterflies. I wasn't sure what it was about Luke that had me in knots. Probably a small part of it in the back of my mind was because he was a famous actor, but I had gotten to know Luke Morrison, not Luke Walters. And boy, did I really like Luke Morrison.

Grabbing my coat, I slipped it on and reached for my purse before I headed down to the lobby.

"Hey, Jessie," I said as I walked up to the doorman.

"Good evening, Ms. Rogers. You look nice this evening."

I smiled. "Are you flirting with me?"

Jessie, who was probably old enough to be my grandfather, winked. "It's a terrible thing, I know. But when I see a pretty girl, I can't help myself."

I laughed. I loved listening to Jessie speak in his native Irish brogue. He'd moved to the US to work for one of his cousins when he was twenty-nine. He'd met the love of his life, Lily, at a dinner party and they'd never looked back. Four kids and five dogs later, and Jessie was just as happy. He didn't have to work, but said he needed to do something to keep from being bored after he'd retired. So he worked part time here in my building as the doorman. I was pretty positive Jessie had enough money to *buy* the building. Rumor had it he was actually the owner. I would believe it too.

"I'm telling you, it's the Irish accent that does it for me, Jessie. If only you weren't married."

He laughed and waved me off. "Are you waiting for Wendy?"

Before I had a chance to answer, a Mercedes pulled up and Hank got out.

"That would be my ride." I pointed while Jessie held the door open for me. "You don't have to come out here, Jessie, Hank's got it."

He gave me a wink. "Be careful, lass, and have a good time."

"I will!" I called back as I walked up to Hank. "Where's the Jag?" I asked with a teasing smile.

"Mr. Morrison—the older one, I mean—required it tonight."

I glanced at the back door and frowned. Why was Luke not getting out? "Is Luke back there?"

Hank shook his head. "He'll meet you at the restaurant."

I pulled my head back in surprise. "He'll meet me there?"

Hank nodded and held open the door to the Mercedes for me, as if it was the most normal thing in the world for my date's assistant to come and pick me up. I slipped into the backseat and took a long, deep breath before letting it out.

Once Hank was in the driver's seat, I asked, "Does he do this often?"

"I'm sorry?" Hank asked as he met my gaze in the rearview mirror.

"Have you pick up his dates and bring them to him?"

Hank laughed. "If I'm being honest, Luke doesn't date much at all."

I wasn't sure if that made me feel better or not, because Hank didn't really answer the question.

Twenty minutes later, we pulled up to Sorellina and Hank jumped of the car. He held out his hand, and I took it. "Enjoy your dinner, Ms. Rogers."

"I call you Hank, so you can call me Brighton."

He gave me a quick nod. "Brighton, it is."

Hank walked me into the restaurant and leaned close to the hostess. "This is Ms. Rogers."

Her eyes immediately went to me and a wide smile appeared on her face. "Good evening, Ms. Rogers, please follow me to your table."

I quickly glanced at Hank, and he smiled. "Have fun."

"Thank you, um, I will."

I followed the hostess and realized we were going into a private room. "Mr. Morrison requested a private dinner this evening," she said, looking back at me with another smile.

My stomach jumped. I'd never been to a restaurant where I got to sit in a private room before. We walked into the small room, and I couldn't help but smile as I saw Luke stand. He was dressed in a suit and had shaved since I'd last seen him. He walked up to me, and when I stopped in front of him, he placed his hand on my waist and leaned down to kiss me.

"Would you like the wine now, Mr. Morrison?" the hostess asked.

Luke couldn't seem to pull his eyes off of me while he answered. "Yes, thank you."

"Ms. Rogers, would you like me to take your coat and hang it up?"

It appeared I was just as transfixed on Luke, because I couldn't seem to find the words to speak. Luke walked around me and took off my coat, then handed it to the young woman.

I finally found my voice. "Thank you so much."

"Of course. If you need anything, please let Robert, your waiter, know."

Luke nodded, then pulled a chair out for me to sit. I placed my purse on the table and sat down. He leaned down and placed his mouth next to my ear. The heat made me shiver.

"You look beautiful, Bree."

Grinning, I looked up at him. "And you look rather dashing this evening as well."

He sat across from me and flashed that panty-melting smile of his. My heart felt like it did a tumble in my chest.

"Thank you. I hope you don't mind, I ordered an appetizer. Their burrata is amazing."

"I don't mind at all," I said, picking up the menu. "What do you recommend, since you said this was your favorite Italian restaurant?"

He looked at the menu and grinned like a damn school boy. "I've had pretty much everything on the menu. The ravioli has got to be one of my favorites, but I love the maccheroncelli as well. The veal is good too."

I screwed up my face and shook my head. "I'm not eating babies; no, thank you."

Luke chuckled. "The filet mignon is pretty amazing."

"I think the ravioli sounds good—I'll go with that."

Our waiter showed up and had Luke taste the wine, then poured us both a glass after he nodded.

"Why didn't you come and pick me up yourself?" I asked.

Luke smiled. "To the point, I like it."

"You won't get anything less from me."

Leaning back in his chair, Luke studied me for a moment. "I thought it would be best, since I knew there was some press outside my place."

"You're not staying with your parents?" I asked, lifting my wine glass.

Luke shook his head. "No, I don't want to bother them with the craziness of me being home. I've done a pretty good job at keeping my personal life private. I've never even told anyone in Hollywood my real last name."

"So how do we leave?"

He winked. "Out the back door."

Laughing, I said, "How do you explain that to the staff?"

Luke glanced around the empty room that held only the two of us. I followed his lead, then looked back at him. "They know who you are."

He nodded.

"But you gave them your real name."

"My father is good friends with the manager. My family has been coming here for a number of years. They know me more as a personal friend of the owner, rather than as Luke Walters, the actor."

"I see," I said, then took a sip of wine.

We sat in silence for a few moments before Luke spoke again. "I booked a house in Maine, if you're still serious about spending Christmas with me."

A rush of warmth filled my entire body. "I am. I told my parents I wasn't coming to Boggy Creek this year."

"They didn't mind?"

With a quick shake of my head, I answered, "No, not at all. They won't be there anyway. My mother was just happy I was going out tonight."

"You told her about me?"

I felt my face instantly heat. "Um, no. She probably thinks I'm with Wendy."

Luke nodded.

"It's complicated with my parents. If I tell her about you, she's going to want to know every single detail, and I don't want her adding pressure to the situation. Then add in the fact that you're a...a famous actor and..." My voice trailed off.

"I get it. Just to let you know, I did tell my parents that we were going out tonight."

That made me pause for a moment. "You did?"

Luke reached across the table and took my hand in his. "I did. I really do like you, Bree, and I'm serious...I want to see where things go with us. I know it'll be hard, with me living across the country and all the sneaking around."

"All the sneaking around? Will we have to do this every time we go out?"

He looked away for a quick moment before he focused on me again. "If we can, yes. It's just, once the press finds out that I'm dating someone, they'll be relentless. They'll follow you, take pictures of you, print shit about you in the rags. I don't want that to taint what we're trying to do here. The longer we can keep this—" he motioned between us—"a secret, the better."

Smiling, I squeezed his hand. "It could be kind of fun, playing cloak and dagger."

An uneasy look crossed his face, but it was gone as quickly as it appeared.

I cleared my throat. "I know I already said I'd go to Maine with you, but I have to see if I can take the time off. I don't think it will be a problem, though."

"It won't," Luke stated.

"I'm glad you're so confident."

He winked. "I already talked to my dad, told him we were going up there for the holiday."

I wasn't so sure how I felt about Luke sharing my personal information, especially with my boss. "You told your father we were going to Maine together? Do you think that was something you should have shared with him?"

He looked perplexed. "We *are* going to Maine, so why is it a problem?"

"It's a problem, Luke, because now your father—who happens to be my boss—and your mother know we're together."

His brows pulled down in confusion. "I'm not sure where the issue is with that, Bree. Just because you chose not to tell your parents, doesn't mean I want to keep it from mine."

I opened my mouth to argue, but I had nothing to say to that. So all that came out was, "Well..."

One of his brows rose, and I could see the bastard hiding a smile. "Well?"

"It's easier for you, Luke. I'm the one who has to work for your father, and I'm a little uncomfortable with him knowing I'm fucking his son."

The words were out before I could stop them.

"Is that all we're doing, Bree? Fucking? Because I kind of thought it was more...or at least I hoped it was."

I closed my eyes and drew in a breath. "It is. I'm just saying, I wish you hadn't told him about us. You could have said we were dating, but telling them we're going off together...that doesn't sit right with me."

He nodded as he thought it over. "That's fair. I'm sorry if I overstepped; I honestly don't think he'd let you go if it wasn't with me."

I chewed on my lower lip, because I knew he was right. Mr. Morrison would have given me that look he always did when I asked for time off at this time of year. Then he'd guilt me into questioning myself for even taking time off in the first place.

"I'll probably need to bring my laptop," I said. "I do have a deposition coming up, and I need to work on another file."

"You can work all you want during the day, as long as I get your evenings."

"Just my evenings, huh? After earlier today, I'd think you were a fan of afternoon delights."

He grinned, and it made my stomach flip. "Oh, I am a very big fan of them."

The way he looked at me made my body heat. His nearly black eyes turned darker with desire. Like he could devour me right then and there.

"I'll be sure not to work too much, so you don't get bored."

Luke laughed. "I love how you're looking out for me, Bree."

Lifting my glass of wine to my mouth, I replied in a sultry voice, "I'm just that kind of girl."

71

Chapter Seven

Luke

The breeze coming off the Atlantic Ocean tossed Bree's hair about as she stepped out of the car and looked up at the massive house. "Luke, this is stunning."

The white clapboard house was surrounded by beautiful landscaping and a crushed granite trail that led from the front of the house around to the back. It looked like a small cottage on the outside, but the inside of the house was massive.

Smiling, I glanced back at Hank who was currently taking luggage out of the SUV we'd rented. Bree had teased me about Hank coming with us, but he was more than the guy who drove me around: he was my assistant, my friend, and the guy who kept me fucking sane and on top things. He was also my business partner in a few ventures.

"There are ocean views from every single room in the house," I said as I stepped up next to Bree. A light covering of fresh snow blanketed the ground and added to the quaint feel of the area.

"How did you find this place?"

"My friend Kai owns it. He's a fellow actor and had the house built a few years back. I've stayed here a few times when I've needed to get away. No one in this town gives two shits who I am or who I'm with. There's no press walking around snapping pictures. It's just normal."

Bree nodded. "I get wanting normal."

She thought she got it, but she had no idea.

"Shall we go inside and see the house?" I asked, placing my hand on the small of her back and guiding her up the steps.

The moment we stepped inside, Bree let out a gasp. Windows covered nearly every wall, allowing the ocean to feel like it was part of the house. The kitchen and living room were all one big open space, giving it a light and airy vibe.

"This is beautiful. I think if I owned this, I'd never leave."

I walked up to where she stood by the windows, staring down at the Atlantic Ocean. "The beach is private, so no one will be on it."

She looked over her shoulder and gave me a wicked smile. "Are you suggesting sex on the beach?"

"I wasn't, but now that you mention it... Although, it might be a bit cold."

Bree laughed.

Hank walked into the room. "I put the bags in the main bedroom, Luke. Anything else?"

I shook my head. "No, man, go enjoy some much-earned time off."

Hank gave me a quick nod, then looked at Bree. "Enjoy your time at the beach, Ms....um...Brighton."

She chuckled. "I will. You enjoy your time off as well."

After Hank closed the front door, Bree looked at me. "Where is he staying?"

"There's a guesthouse right next door."

"Do you bring him everywhere you go?"

I nodded. "Mostly, but not always."

Bree turned back to the windows and let out a contented sigh. "This place is going to be healing for my soul, I can feel it."

Wrapping my arms around her, I kissed the top of her head and gazed out over the deep blue waters. "I think you're right, love."

For the next few days, we explored the little private island we were on. There were two other houses on the island, but both appeared to be vacant, so it felt like we were completely and utterly alone. It was so nice to walk along the beach and talk to Bree without worrying if anyone had a telescopic lens and was taking our pictures. I had booked a flight to Belize and mentioned to a reporter that I'd be staying there over the holidays. No one in their right mind would think I was in Maine.

When Bree wanted to go to Harpswell, we spent the entire day exploring the area. She had a thing for lighthouses, so we visited Halfway Rock Lighthouse. We spent a lot of time hiking and enjoying the beautiful nature that surrounded us. We even headed into the next town over and shopped along the historic downtown area, where Bree bought a few things for her friends and family.

I loved how genuine her heart was and how easy it was for her to talk to people. And her sense of humor never ceased to amaze me. She was quick-witted and kept me on my toes.

It wasn't hard to see why I was quickly falling for her. I wouldn't put the word love with it quite yet. But I could see myself loving her. Being with her...having a family with her.

What I couldn't see, though, was her thriving in my world. It would slowly pull the light from those beautiful brown eyes of hers. We didn't talk at all about my career, and for that I was thankful. I had managed to bring us to a place where we could get to know each other without the outside world sticking their noses in.

I was stopped once by a younger couple who asked me to take a photo with them. Bree offered to take the picture and didn't seem the least bit put off by it. That was also refreshing. For the most part, though, no one knew who I was, and being able to walk openly without worrying about anyone following us was freeing.

I loved my fans, don't get me wrong. People asking me for a photo never bothered me. It was the media who went to extra lengths to snap pictures of me, especially if I was on a date, that I hated. It was why I never truly got serious with anyone. Well, one of the reasons. I honestly couldn't see myself settling down with an actress, especially when I wasn't even sure I wanted to keep acting. I had loved it the first few years. Now it felt more like a job. Like a job I no longer had as much passion for.

I sighed and glanced at Bree as we strolled down the empty beach. The press would eventually get wind of us. I just hoped they wouldn't be able to find out who she was. I needed to keep my guard up, especially in Boston, when I was around her. She'd be easier to track if they knew she lived there. But in somewhere like Harpswell, Maine, they'd probably assume she was from here or from LA, as well, and we were visiting. We'd been lucky so far though. At least, I hoped we had been.

"Penny for your thoughts," Bree said as she bumped my shoulder with hers.

"Just thinking about how nice the last few days have been with you."

A brightness filled her eyes. "It's been amazing. I don't think I've felt this relaxed in a very long time. Thank you for that."

I pulled her to me and kissed her forehead. I hated that our jackets kept me from feeling her body. "Thank you for coming with me."

She ran her fingers through my hair before she rubbed her cold nose against mine. "I'm freezing and hungry. Should we head back to the island?"

I waggled my brows. "I know a way to warm you up."

Her eyes twinkled. "Where do you get so much stamina?"

Draping my arm around her shoulders, I pulled her closer. "I work out a lot, sweetheart."

Bree laughed, and it made my chest feel warm and tight. Yes, I could see myself falling for her. And falling hard.

Four months later — April

"The plane is ready and waiting, Luke," Hank said as he stepped up next to me.

Glancing to my right, I gave him a quick nod.

"Jetting off somewhere again, I see," Janice Rothwell said, batting her fake eyelashes at me. Janice was the leading lady playing opposite me in the movie we were finishing up. The director had called some of us back to reshoot several scenes he wasn't happy with. The movie was set to be released on Christmas Day, so he'd insisted that we spend a week in San Francisco to finish it up. Most of the film had already been shot there.

I flashed Janice a smile. "I am."

"Where to this time?" she asked.

"I'm heading to Florida." It was a lie, of course; I was heading to Boston. So far Bree and I had been able to stay out of the press, and as far as everyone knew, I was still very much a bachelor and enjoying my life just as it was.

Janice walked over and ran her finger down my cheek, leaned up and whispered against my ear, "I could join you, Luke."

Taking a step back, I quickly glanced around. The paparazzi were always hanging around somewhere. Last month, they'd taken a photo of me sitting outside a café with my friend Rich's future wife. The couple had flown in from Boston to spend a few weeks with me, and Rich had asked Mary to marry him while they were in Napa Valley. We'd gone out to eat that night, and I'd been holding her hand, looking at the ring. Someone took a photo, and before I knew it, I was engaged to a secret woman. Never mind the fact that Rich had been sitting next to her, with his arm around her shoulders.

Luckily, I had snapped my own pictures of the happy couple, and my manager had released one of them with a statement saying I was having dinner with two old friends and had been admiring Mary's engagement ring. I had called Bree the moment I found out it was on some news outlets. She, of course, hadn't even seen it. Another thing I loved about her. She didn't keep up with the gossip mill.

Love. Another thing I *loved* about her...

I couldn't help but smile. I was in love with Bree and had every intention of telling her tonight at dinner. It had been easy to fall in love with her. I was pretty sure I fell the first time I turned and saw her looking up at me with those big doe eyes of hers.

"Goodness," Janice said, "what are you thinking about that's making you smile like that? Me joining you?"

Right, I hadn't answered her. "I'm going to Florida for business." Turning to look at Hank, I asked, "Did you get that meeting set up for tonight?" Knowing he would know I was talking about Brighton.

He gave me a quick nod. "I did."

"Great," I said, clapping him on the arm and then looking at Janice. "Janice, it was a pleasure working with you, as always. I'll see you at the premiere."

Her smile never broke. She was indeed a very good actress, and me giving her the brush-off didn't appear to faze her in the least.

"A pleasure, Luke. Enjoy your...business trip."

"I will," I said as I leaned down and kissed her softly on the cheek. "Tell Phil I said hi."

That caused her smile to falter for the briefest moment. Phil being her husband and all.

By the time I got to the airplane, I was about ready to bounce out of my own skin. I couldn't wait to see Bree. It had only been three weeks since I'd last seen her, but I usually tried to make it back to Boston every weekend if I could. My mother would kill me if she knew how often I had been home and hadn't told her. Every so often, Bree and I would join my parents and sometimes my sister for dinner, but most of the time we were holed up in her place or mine the entire time. My favorite thing to do was order food and sit on Bree's sofa and watch movies. She had a strong love for Gene Kelly, so we always played at least one of his movies while we were together.

I stared out the window of the private plane before I turned to Hank. "What time are we landing?"

He rolled his eyes, most likely because I'd asked him the same question at least five times already. "Six forty-two."

I nodded. "And you told Brighton dinner was at eight, right?"

Now he sighed. "Yes. I told her eight, and you texted her about it earlier. She'll be there, Luke."

I pulled out my phone, looked at the last text from Bree, and smiled. I had never met a woman like Brighton Rogers before. She had no problem saying what was on her mind, and didn't take shit from anyone. I hated that we couldn't have a normal relationship, but it didn't appear to bother her. At least not yet.

> Bree: I'm thinking of hiring a rent-a-date, so I don't look like a loser walking into all these places by myself.

> Me: We can eat at my place or yours if you don't want to go out.

> Bree: Are you kidding? And miss the opportunity to eat at Ralph's? Um, I'll meet you there.

> Me: LOL. Are you more excited about having steak tonight or seeing me?

> Bree: Trust me, I can handle a lot of meat in one night.

> Me: I just laughed out loud. You're something else. I can't wait to see you, Bree.

> Bree: I can't wait either. Have a safe flight, Luke.

"Do you think I'm being overly cautious by having Brighton meet me at the restaurant?" I asked Hank.

He looked up at me and frowned. I could see the concern in his eyes. "I don't blame you for wanting to protect her and the relationship the two of you are building. You know more than anyone the type of pressure and strain that comes from dating a celebrity. I'm not so sure Brighton is ready for everything that goes along with that."

I slowly nodded. "There've been a few times where I've told myself I need to let her go...but I can't. I think about her nearly every moment of the damn day when I'm not with her."

"Because you're falling in love with her?"

Leave it to Hank to get right to the point. He never failed me on that.

I didn't even have to think about it. "I do love her. I think I fell in love with her the moment she looked at me with those big brown eyes of hers and said I looked like Gene Kelly."

Hank laughed, and so did I.

"And what happens when she wants more of a normal relationship, or gets tired of the sneaking around?" he asked. "Or living on two different coasts?"

I rubbed at the back of my neck. "I haven't let myself think that far ahead."

He tilted his head and gave me a look that said he was disappointed in me. "You can't ignore it forever, Luke."

Dropping back in my seat, I let out a heavy breath. "Fuck if I know anything. No, that's not true, I do know I don't want to lose her. If the media gets wind of our relationship, they'll invade her privacy. She hasn't even told her parents about me because she's worried they'll say something. Brighton is content with how things are, for now. I don't honestly know how long she'll stay that way."

"What about how long *you* can keep this up. You know you can't keep flying back to Boston every weekend."

I exhaled. "This is why I'm glad you're my friend, Hank. I would lose my goddamn mind if I didn't have you."

He laughed. "I highly doubt that. You would, however, never show up anywhere on time."

I smiled.

"Have you talked to Brighton about how things will be once you two go public with your relationship?" Hank asked.

"No. Right now we're in this fucking bubble, and she's having as much fun as I am. To be honest with you, I'm afraid to take the relationship public. Brighton isn't the type of woman who wants that kind of attention. Don't get me wrong, she's tough, and I know she can handle gossip. But at the same time, she didn't really sign up for it, and I don't want the press to taint it."

"She knows you're an actor."

I scrubbed my hand down my face. "She knows what I've shown her. She didn't go to the Oscars with me, or any public event. I haven't had to leave the country for weeks at a time yet, since I haven't shot a full movie while we've been dating. I feel like I'm playing a goddamn role and I'm the only one aware of it. Brighton seems to be blissfully happy the days I'm in Boston. When we were in Maine, it was like we were two normal people. That's what she saw as the beginning of our relationship. She's perfectly content hanging out at her place or mine. At least, she seems to be. I don't want to risk what we have to be able to walk into the front door of a goddamn restaurant."

Hank stared at me for a moment, then said, "Maybe you need to give her a taste of what your life is really like."

I drew my brows in. "I'm not sure either one of us is ready for that."

"Let her see what it's like when people know it's you and how they react. Give her a preview of what her life could eventually be like. I mean, if you love her—and I'm pretty sure she loves you—it's going to have to happen at some point."

I was hit by a sudden urge to throw up so fast I had to swallow a few times to keep the bile from moving up into my throat. I knew what it would be like once the press found out about me and Brighton. They would tear us apart. Not at first, but eventually.

I couldn't lose her.

I shook my head. "No, no. Not yet."

Hank sighed. "You're gonna have to do it eventually, dude."

"Not yet, Hank. Everything is too new."

"Too perfect, I think you mean, and you've been dating for over four months. When does the new wear off?"

I shot him a dirty look.

Hank gave me a small smile. "Just be honest with her, Luke."

"About what? I'm not even sure where my own future is going to be in a year or two."

He sat up straighter. "You still thinking of leaving LA?"

I rolled my neck in an attempt to ease the tension there. "I don't know. I wouldn't mind living away from it all."

"Luke, if this thing you have with Brighton is meant to be, it'll all work out. You have to trust in it."

I lifted my eyes and met his. "I trust the *us* part of it, I just don't trust the *them*. The moment the vultures dive in, everything will change. You and I both know it, Hank."

He gave me a solemn expression. "It will, but plenty of people make it work. Don't give up the fight before you even throw the first punch."

I didn't say anything else, just gave him a nod and then stared out the window of the plane.

Chapter Eight
Brighton

"**B**righton, what are you doing here?"

The female voice caught me off guard as I looked up from the table I was seated at in Ralph's Steakhouse. It was a popular restaurant in Boston and one I had been dying to go to. It had taken a bit of convincing for Luke to eat here, but he'd finally given in. I knew how much he wanted to keep our relationship out of the press, and truth be told, I did as well. I wasn't really sure how much things would change once people found out I was dating an actor. A famous one. Plus, the moment my mother found out, she'd start hounding me. A part of me liked keeping Luke all to myself.

I stood and made my way over to my old college friend. "Carol, it's so good to see you."

We hugged, and she stepped back and gave me a quick once-over. "I see you're still the fashion diva you've always been."

Glancing down at my dress, I smiled slightly. The black knit dress was simple yet sexy at the same time. It hugged my body in all the right places but was so comfortable it had quickly become one of my favorite dresses to wear. Ralph's wasn't a casual restaurant, and if I was being completely honest, I also wanted to eat here so I could show off the dress I'd bought earlier this week. It was on sale at this darling little boutique down the street from my place. The moment I saw it, I knew I had to have it.

"You know me, always looking for a reason to dress up," I said.

Carol gave my outfit another glance and then turned to the guy on her arm. He was also giving me a slow perusal—or more like a good eye-fuck. Carole frowned when she caught him staring.

When his eyes met mine, I raised a brow and tilted my head slightly. He at least had the decency to look away.

"Bradly, this is Brighton Rogers. We knew one another in the last few years of law school."

"Aw, you're a lawyer?" Bradly asked, his gaze locked on my breasts, not my eyes.

I bent down and waved my hand, catching his attention. "I am. Are you okay? Your gaze seems to be everywhere but where it should be, which is here," I said as I pointed to my face. Then I pointed at my breasts. "Not here."

Bradly's cheeks turned pink while Carol let out a laugh. "Still the same Brighton. You haven't changed a bit."

Smiling, I said, "And most likely never will."

She looked toward my table and then back at me, giving me a pout. "Are you alone, darling? You're more than welcome to join us for dinner. We're meeting another couple, as long as you won't feel like the fifth wheel."

I forced a smile. "I'm waiting for my boyfriend."

Carol held her hand to her chest and faked a surprised look. "You have a boyfriend?"

"She does, and he's very sorry for being so late."

I turned to see Luke standing behind me. My heart nearly leapt from my chest when he looked at me and smiled. That damn dimple in his cheek made my knees weak every single time.

Before I could say anything, Luke leaned in and kissed me. "I'm sorry I'm late, love."

The simple kiss nearly left me breathless. "I'm just glad you're here safe and sound."

"Has anyone ever told you that you look like that actor from the movie *The Time Before Us*?" Carol asked while staring at Luke.

"Yes, and I've also been told I look like Gene Kelly. I like that comparison over the bloke in that other movie."

Carol laughed...a flirty laugh.

"Well, don't let me hold up your evening with Bradly here," I said, flashing her a dead-ass fake smile.

"The offer is still on the table if you'd both like to join us," Carol said as she continued to stare at Luke. It was clear Bradly was not happy. Jackass didn't like it when the roles were reversed.

Luke wrapped his arm around my waist. "Thank you, but we'll pass."

Bradly tugged Carol away, mumbling, "Nice meeting you both."

Carol waved goodbye and went to say something as Bradly picked up his pace and pulled her away.

"Friends of yours?" Luke asked, pulling my chair out for me.

I laughed. "No. I knew Carol our last two years of law school or so. I do feel sorry for her, though."

"Is that because old Bradly wouldn't stop staring at your breasts? Which, by the way, look fucking amazing in that dress."

Grinning, I replied, "Thank you. And yes, the dickhead didn't even try to hide it."

The waitress came up to the table and asked Luke for his drink order. To my surprise, he ordered water.

"Not drinking this evening?" I asked.

He shook his head. "No, I have a little surprise for you after dinner."

I raised a brow. "A surprise where you can't have a drink?"

All he did was nod. He gave a quick glance around the restaurant before he looked at the menu.

"I did ask for a more private table, but this was all they had," I said.

"It's fine," he responded, his voice sounding a bit distracted.

"Was the flight okay?"

"Yep."

I sat back in my seat and stared at the menu he was holding up in front of his face. He was clearly trying to keep people from seeing him. I reached for my wine and took a drink.

He moved the menu down and looked at me. "Do you already know what you want?"

Nodding, I said, "Yes, I've been staring at the menu for twenty minutes."

My words made him put the menu down. "I'm sorry. I had Hank stop by my place so I could pick something up. I honestly thought I'd make it here on time."

I waved it off. "No, I'm sorry. You're acting strange."

"I don't mean to." He reached across the table and took my hand. "It's been a long week, and I really wanted to see you." He looked around once more, and I could tell he was uncomfortable.

"I have an idea, if you're up for it," I said. "There's this new pizza stand that I've been dying to try. We could take an Uber there if Hank dropped you off."

"I drove here myself."

"What?" I asked, surprised. "You drove here? By yourself?"

Luke laughed. "I do have a driver's license."

It was my turn to laugh.

"I thought you wanted to try the New York strip," he said.

Squeezing his hand, I leaned across the table. "All I really want is to be with you, not have everyone staring at us, trying to place who in the hell you are because they feel like they've seen you somewhere before."

A brilliant smile appeared on his face, and it warmed my heart. "Are you sure?"

With a wink, I replied, "As long as you give me one hell of an orgasm later, I'm sure."

He laughed, then pulled his wallet out and tossed some money on the table.

I grabbed my coat and we quickly walked out of the restaurant. It was a beautiful evening for April and a bit on the warm side, so I didn't have to put on the light coat I'd brought with me.

I waited for Luke to ask the valet to bring his car up and noticed a sports bike parked out front. With a low whistle, I said, "Wow, look at that motorcycle." The bike was black with a bit of lime green. Lord, it was nice.

"It's a Kawasaki KLR650," Luke said. "Do you like motorcycles?"

I smiled and shrugged. "I've never been on one, but I think they're kind of hot."

He raised a brow. "Is that right? And would you have a problem riding one in that nice dress of yours?"

I glanced down at my outfit and then back up at him. "If that was your bike, I'd hike this bitch up to my boobs so I could climb on the back of it."

Luke laughed.

One of the valets walked up to Luke, and he handed him some money. "Thanks for looking out for her."

"Her?" I asked as Luke took my hand and led me to the bike. When he stopped and handed me a helmet, I gaped at him.

He smiled. "Tell me you're not going back on your word, Bree. I was looking forward to it."

"Wait," I said, shaking my head. "This is your bike? *Your* bike?"

He nodded, then slipped on the other helmet.

"And you want me to climb onto it in this dress?!"

Luke took the helmet back off. "You said you would not even a minute ago. Put your jacket on too."

I glanced around, looked at the bike, then back to Luke. I slid my coat on. "Oh, I'm going to need to have sex on that bike for this."

One of the valets started to choke as Luke let out another laugh and helped me put the helmet on.

"You're lucky I'm wearing panties under this dress," I said.

A full-on grin appeared on his handsome face before he leaned in and said, "You won't be for long."

Oh my Lord. Yes, please, sign me up for that.

Luke climbed onto the bike first, then held his hand out for me. I damn near *did* almost have to hike the dress up to my boobs, but I managed to get on without giving the two young valets a sideshow.

"Ready?"

I jumped, then squeezed my arms around Luke and laughed. "Oh my God, there are speakers in the helmets?"

"And mics," he said with a chuckle.

"Men," I whispered as Luke started the bike and pulled out. I closed my eyes and tried to keep my breathing steady, but as he sped up, my nervousness turned to pure excitement. I let out a little scream and held on tighter. It took me another five minutes to work up the nerve to open my eyes.

I was in awe while Luke drove us through the streets of Boston. He appeared to be going in the opposite direction of both my place and his...and the pizza place.

"Where are we going?" I asked.

"Somewhere a little less crowded."

I held onto him while attempting to also hold onto my coat. My purse was securely over my shoulder, but I was positive we looked like raging idiots on this bike.

"Next time will you give me a warning, so I can bring a change of clothes?"

Luke laughed and turned into a parking lot, parking the bike outside of a...bar. The only thing lit up outside on the building was a sign that said *Fletchers*.

"You're bringing me to a bar, Luke Morrison? Really?"

He took off the helmet and ran his fingers though his hair. I was pretty sure I moaned, and not internally.

"I'm getting you some food, and no, we're not eating in the bar."

With a quick glance around, I tried to find the restaurant we were going to, but the only thing near the parking lot was the bar.

Luke laced his fingers with mine, and we walked in. There were maybe a handful of customers. It was a hell of a lot nicer on the inside than it was on the outside. The moment the bartender saw Luke, he called out his name, jumped over the bar, and pulled him in for a massive bro hug.

"Jesus Christ, Luke, what are you doing here?" He shook his head and smiled as he gave Luke a once-over. It was odd, but he looked a bit like him. Same hair color, same build. His eyes weren't as dark and he wasn't as handsome as Luke, but he was still good-looking.

"I needed a place to bring my girl for some dinner."

The bartender turned and looked at me. He gave me a slow perusal, then focused back on Luke. "Is this Brighton, then?"

I jerked my head back a bit in surprise. I hadn't realized that anyone other than Hank and Luke's family knew about me.

Luke wrapped his arm around me and drew me to his side. "This is her. Brighton, this is Jack Fletcher, my brother."

I extended my hand and smiled, then looked at Luke. "Your brother? You have a *brother*? I thought you only had a sister?"

Luke winked while Jack let out a roar of laughter. "I'm the family's dirty little secret. The bastard child our old man had when he cheated on his wife."

My mouth dropped open. "You've never told me about Jack."

Luke shrugged. "I wanted to introduce you to him first."

"And you didn't think a heads up was warranted?"

"Jack is a...touchy conversation around my mother. I needed to make sure you wouldn't slip up in front of her."

I folded my arms over my chest and glared at him. "Slip up? You do realize I'm not an idiot."

He pulled me back to him and kissed me quickly. "Yes, I know. I'm sorry I didn't tell you about him sooner."

If there was one thing I couldn't do, it was stay mad at Luke. Not when he looked at me that way, or kissed me. Or touched me. He was like a damn drug that both thrilled me and made me slightly wary.

And truth be told, I wasn't mad. I had been taken by surprise, and I hated surprises.

"Are there more Jacks I should know about?" I asked.

Jack and Luke both laughed. "Most likely," Jack said. "Come on, let's get you two fed. Lou is here today, and she happened to make your favorite."

Luke let out a groan. "Oh man, this is my lucky night."

Jack led the way for us as we walked through the bar, down a hallway, and into a small kitchen. A woman a few years older than me turned and nearly screamed when she saw Luke.

"Luke! Oh my gosh!"

Luke let go of my hand as the woman rushed around the small workstation and nearly threw herself into his arms. He took a few steps back and laughed while giving her a hug.

"Hey, Lou. How're you doing?"

She drew back and held him at arm's length. "Lord, do you get more handsome every time I see you?"

A strange sensation zipped through me, but I kept my smile in place. Holy shit, was that...jealousy I was experiencing?

I brushed it away. Until Lou hugged Luke again.

When I shot a quick look over at Jack, he winked at me, an amused smirk tugging at the corner of his mouth.

Lou finally stepped back, and Luke turned toward me. He smiled and reached for my hand, which I readily gave him. "Lou, this is Brighton."

Lou spun and faced me. She let out another scream, and before I knew what was happening, she had her arms around *me*, swaying us back and forth. "So you're the woman who's stolen Luke's heart!"

My eyes met Luke's, and like his brother, he winked. "Brighton, this is Lou Fletcher, Jack's wife."

Lou dropped hold of me and took a step back, a smile still on her face. "It's so nice to finally meet you, Brighton. Luke is like a little brother to me. If you break his heart, I *will* track you down and break you into a million pieces."

I opened my mouth but quickly shut it again as I studied the woman in front of me. I finally said, "Oddly enough, I think I already like you."

Lou clapped. "Perfect, we're starting off on the same page."

"Lou, should you be slamming yourself into other people's bodies?" Luke asked.

With a wave of her hand, Lou rounded the table again and started to pull out plates. "I'm only three months pregnant, it's fine."

"Oh wow, congratulations to you both," I said, looking at Jack and then Lou.

"Thank you!" they said in unison.

"You're in luck, I made your favorite," Lou said to Luke. "I hope you like chicken and dumplins, Brighton."

It was then I noticed her southern accent. "I love them," I said. "I haven't had them in a while, but my grandmother used to make them all the time."

Lou began piling up chicken and dumplings on four plates before looking up at Jack. "Is anyone covering the bar?"

He nodded and handed me a plate. "Yeah, Rach is out there. She can handle it. It's slow tonight."

"Perfect, shall we eat upstairs, then?" Lou asked.

Luke and Jack both nodded, then looked at me. "Sure, of course," I said.

"I'll grab a bottle of wine and some glasses, y'all go ahead and head on up," Lou stated as she handed Jack her plate of food.

I followed both men up some stairs and out onto the roof, where I gasped at the sight before me. A long table that probably sat at least twelve people stood in the middle of the roof, surrounded by a plethora of plants and trees. White Edison lights were strung up across the roof, weaving back and forth in the wind. It was a beautiful space.

"Where's Lou from?" I asked as I set my dish down and Luke held out my chair for me. "Thank you, Luke."

"She was born and raised in Atlanta," Jack said. "Moved to Boston almost ten years ago. We met when she came in and applied for a waitress job. Instead of hiring her, I asked her out, and we were married three months later."

At that moment, Lou joined us and set the wine bottle and three glasses down. "It was love at first sight for both of us."

I couldn't help but peek over at Luke. My stomach flipped when I saw he was looking at me. When he smiled, I felt myself fall even more in love with him. Neither one of us had said it yet, but there were so many times I wanted to. And I was positive Luke felt the same way.

Jack poured us each a glass of wine, with the exception of his wife. Luke lifted his in a toast while Lou held up a bottle of water. "To love at first sight," he said.

The rest of us clinked our glasses, and I tried like hell to keep my heart from pounding even harder.

We spent the evening laughing while Jack and Luke told stories about the two of them growing up. They had only ever gotten to see each other during the summers, when their father would bring Luke and his sister Jenn to Maine to see Jack. That was where his mother lived. When Jack's mother passed away from cancer, he moved to the Boston area. It warmed my heart to see the two of them together like this. To see Luke so relaxed and carefree.

"How are you handling Luke's stardom?" Lou asked as I helped her wash up the dishes. Luke and Jack were still on the roof catching up.

I shrugged. "To be honest, I haven't really seen much of it. When he comes to Boston, we're either at my place or his, and if we do go out, we meet there and never arrive together. Luke usually arranges for us to be seated somewhere we won't gain a lot of attention."

Lou nodded, and I could tell she wanted to say something but remained silent.

"It's been a whirlwind the last four months, but I've enjoyed it."

She smiled. "You're in love with him."

I paused in the middle of drying off a dish and met her gaze. Before I had a chance to even respond, the man in question appeared.

"Are you ready to go dancing?" Luke asked with a smirk on his face.

"Oh Lord. You two didn't set that up, did you?" Lou asked.

Looking between the two of them, I asked, "Set what up? Dancing where?"

Lou slipped the plate out of my hand and motioned for me to go back up to the roof with Luke.

He winked as he took my hand in his and led us up the steps. I wasn't going to lie to myself—I felt like a kid being led to her gifts under the Christmas tree.

Chapter Nine

Luke

"**W**e're dancing on the roof, huh?" Bree asked as we walked back out into the cooler night air.

"Are you too cold?" I asked.

She turned and looked at me with the sweetest smile on her face before she tried to look sad. "I was hoping for sex on the bike," she sighed.

I laughed. "Trust me, I still plan on delivering that. You told me once how much you love to dance, and since we haven't had a chance to go dancing since Christmas, I asked Jack to help me."

Reaching for a remote on the table, I hit play and Gene Kelly started to filter through the speakers.

Bree giggled, shook her head, and walked into my arms. "How did you know this was one of my favorite songs?"

"I heard through the grapevine you have a thing for Gene Kelly."

She gazed up at me. "I do. He makes me all hot and bothered."

I raised my brows. "Does he now?"

Nodding, she laid her cheek on my chest as we slowly danced to "You Wonderful You."

As we glided across the roof, I pulled out some of my Gene Kelly moves, and Bree laughed as I spun and twirled her before I drew her back to me.

"You're a wonderful dancer, Luke," she said.

I leaned my forehead on hers. "Only because I'm dancing with you, love."

Her eyes filled with tears. Cupping her face in my hands, I leaned in, but before I kissed her, I whispered, "I love you, Brighton."

A single tear slipped free and made a path down her cheek. "I love you too." She smiled.

She reached up ever so slightly and bridged the gap between us, and I wrapped my arms around her and deepened the kiss. This wasn't the place where I thought I'd tell her those three words, but it was the perfect moment.

When we finally broke the kiss, she drew in a shaky breath. With her eyes still closed, she said, "Did you only have one song planned?"

Laughing, I picked her up and spun her around while she laughed. I loved seeing her so happy and at ease. "I did. I want to get you back to my place."

Bree nodded. "I like the sound of that."

Lou and Bree exchanged numbers, we said our goodbyes, and soon we were back on the bike. Instead of turning onto the main road, I chose a side road that led to Jack and Lou's house. They wouldn't be home for another few hours and it was the perfect place to afford us some privacy.

"Where are we going now?" Bree asked with touch of excitement in her voice.

"I plan on taking advantage of that dress and the fact that you said the bike makes you hot and bothered."

She held onto me tighter as I pulled down the drive and parked to the side of Jack and Lou's place. I thanked my lucky stars they lived on four acres of land and no one would be around.

"How are we going to do this?" Bree asked while I parked and put out the kickstand.

"Wing it."

Bree laughed. "Wing it?

I shrugged and placed my helmet gently on the ground. Bree did the same.

"I've never thought about having sex on my bike, so yeah. We're gonna have to wing it."

Her teeth dug into her lower lip, and she crawled around the bike to face me. Her hands went to work getting my dress pants unbuttoned. She smiled when she saw I had forgone boxers.

"If I had known this, I would have been copping some feels all night," she said.

I couldn't help but laugh, but it turned to a hiss when she wrapped her hand around my cock and stroked it.

"Fuck, I want you, Bree. Now."

She moaned as I slipped my fingers inside her, finding her more than ready. I withdrew my fingers and put them in my mouth, sucking on them before I pulled her closer.

"Luke," she gasped when I guided her down onto my dick. "Oh God!"

"That's it, love. Yes...God, that feels good."

Her head dropped back while our rhythm increased. I needed more. The angle didn't allow me to get deep inside of her, and I needed to be nestled in all the way.

I pulled out and slipped off the bike, turning her and easing her down so that her back was lying against the seat. Then I pushed back inside, causing us both to moan.

"Yes, that's it. Luke, that's it!"

Brushing my thumb over her clit, I felt her tighten around me. She was close...and this had to be the hottest fucking moment of my life.

"Bree, I need you to come. Fuck, I need you to come!"

"I'm...so...close."

I tilted my hips and felt her body quiver. She screamed out my name and started to spasm on my cock, pulling my own orgasm out.

"Holy shit," I gasped as I moved faster, harder. "Bree, I'm coming with you. Fuck!"

I saw stars, my orgasm hit me so damn hard. My knees nearly buckled, and it seemed to last forever.

When we both finally stopped and all I could hear was our breathing, I pulled out and reached for her. She wrapped her legs around me and I held her, taking a step away from the bike. It was the first time we'd had sex while both of us were fully clothed.

"When did you take off your panties?" I asked in between peppering kisses on her face, jaw, and neck.

She lifted her head, a look of complete happiness on her face. "I never had any on."

My mouth fell open. "You lied?"

She nodded.

"You little vixen."

With a giggle, she pressed her mouth to mine for a quick kiss. "Take me home, Luke."

"With pleasure."

The ride back to Boston felt like it took forever. Bree had left her coat at Jack and Lou's bar, and we stopped at a gas station and bought her a sweatshirt that said *I Love Boston,* so she wouldn't completely freeze her ass off.

The night had been absolutely perfect. Bree loved me, too, and that had me flying high. I couldn't wait to get her back to my place, so I could undress her and make love to her all night.

I drove down Atlantic Avenue and turned onto Commercial Street, then into the gated parking garage of my condo. It overlooked Lewis Wharf Marina and had spectacular views of the harbor from the floor-to-ceiling windows and the outdoor balcony. It was one of the few condos that offered both a private outdoor space and a waterfront view.

After parking the bike, I took Bree's hand in mine and we got into the elevator. I hit the button for the top floor. I owned one of the penthouses that had an open kitchen, a decent-size living room, a large bedroom, and a bathroom that could give any spa a run for its money. The previous owner—a football player for the New England Patriots—had custom cabinets put in, and there was even a common rooftop area that I swore no one ever went to.

I unlocked the door to my place, and we walked in. The first time I'd brought Bree here, she'd fallen in love with the view. She'd walked right past the kitchen with its high-end appliances and dark walnut cabinets without giving them a second glance. To the left of the kitchen sat a small dining area with a round table and four chairs my mother insisted I buy. If it had been left up to me, there wouldn't even be a table, since I ate nearly every meal either on the sofa or out on the balcony.

My bedroom offered views of North End and Zakim Bridge. I liked that I was centrally located on Waterfront and North End, with all of its restaurants, cafés, and bakeries. And Bree had fallen in love with all the shops that were nearby.

Bree kicked off her heels and made a beeline straight for the balcony. It was always her first stop. She would step outside, draw in a deep breath of the ocean breeze, and close her eyes. I loved to watch her in moments like that. Totally lost in the elements around her and never looking more beautiful.

I grabbed a bottle of wine and two glasses. "Do you want to sit out here for a bit?"

She turned and leaned against the rail. The moonlight danced off her light brown hair and when she smiled, I swore I fell even more in love with her.

"Do you mind if I get out of this dress?"

"Do you plan on sitting out here naked?"

She chuckled. "No, I was going to put something warmer on. That drive home on the bike nearly froze my tits off."

It was my turn to laugh. "I'll change with you."

Setting the wine and glasses down on the balcony table, I followed her back inside and to my bedroom. Bree kept a few outfits here, mostly sweatpants and oversized T-shirts, which I'd quickly discovered was her go-to comfy wear. She looked stunning in whatever she put on.

I slipped into a pair of sweats and a long-sleeve shirt while Bree put on yoga pants and a sweater. We spent the next hour or so on the balcony, lost in comfortable conversation. Talking to Bree was so easy. I never had to pretend with her, and she seemed to be able to read my mood like no other person ever had.

"How long can you stay in Boston this time?" she asked, finishing off the last of her wine. When I held up the bottle, she shook her head. "I've had enough, thanks."

"For a while. I don't have any reason to go back to LA right away."

Her eyes lit up.

"I thought maybe we could head out to the beach," I said. "My father has a house on the Northshore. Maybe stay a few days, unless you need to be here in Boston."

She looked up in thought. "Believe it or not, I'm caught up on work and only have two clients right now."

"No one wants to get divorced?" I asked with a wink.

"Oh, trust me, plenty of people want divorces. Most are cheating bastard men who don't want a female divorce attorney."

I raised a brow. "What about the wives of these cheating bastard men?"

She smiled. "They're going for the more powerful, well-known attorneys."

"Well, they don't know what they're missing by not having you on their side."

Bree gave a one-shoulder shrug.

"How are your parents?" I asked. The fact that she hadn't told anyone about me—not her family or any of her friends—was a bit worrisome, but I tried not to let it bother me too much.

She lifted her gaze and met mine. "They're good. Busy with the bed and breakfast. I have a feeling Willa is pregnant, but she isn't spilling the beans quite yet."

I laughed.

"Luke...I know our relationship is wide open with your family, but I appreciate the fact that you haven't pushed me to introduce you to my folks."

"Or your friends," I teased.

She smiled softly. "I want to tell them, and I'm not ashamed of dating you or anything. Boggy Creek may be a small town, but the moment my mother finds out I've been dating a man longer than three weeks, she'll be contacting your mother and planning the wedding. I haven't ever really been super open with my folks about my personal life. I was engaged once, and my parents never knew it."

That had me sitting forward. I placed my glass on the table and frowned. "You were engaged? When?"

"Right out of college. It was stupid, I was young. I thought when he jokingly asked me to marry him that he was being serious. I ran out, bought a wedding dress...because let's be honest, the wedding is all about the dress."

I nodded and smiled. "Of course, it is."

"Anyway, I loved the idea of it, and by 'it' I mean the wedding and marriage. But when it came down to it, he didn't and he wasn't faithful, so we broke up. It was a good thing, because Willa had a quick wedding and I happened to have that dress in my closet, ready for her to use."

"Did Willa know why you had the dress?"

She shook her head. "I'm really good at deflecting questions. You should see me when I'm going head to head with opposing counsel."

Laughing, I pulled her to me, and she straddled my lap and wrapped her arms around my neck.

"I'm not upset or worried that you haven't told your family and friends about me, Bree. Only Hank and Jack know about you."

"And your folks and sister."

I rolled my eyes. "They don't count."

It was her turn to laugh.

I drew in a deep breath and let it out. "Someday, I think we'll look back on this and *wish* we had this privacy."

Bree threaded her fingers through my hair. "I like having you all to myself. The whole cloak-and-dagger thing is kind of sexy for now."

"Oh yeah?"

She nodded and ground down on me. "Didn't you say something about making love to me?"

Bree giggled as I stood and marched straight to my bedroom, where I did, indeed, make love to her.

Chapter Ten

Brighton

I stood at the window in my office and looked down at all the people moving about downtown Boston. It was August and hot as hell. Luke had gotten a call from his agent a few months back, telling him about an opportunity to star in a movie that another A-list actor had pulled out of. He had jumped on it and warned me he'd be gone for weeks at a time while filming in Victoria, Canada. That meant he was darting back and forth from Canada to Boston whenever he had a few days off, which wasn't often.

Now he was back in LA, finishing up a few things before the movie finally wrapped. I had missed him more than I thought possible. Going four or five days between seeing him hadn't been so bad, but going for weeks was a killer. It was my first real insight into what life would be like with him. Me in Boston, and him God knows where. We talked every single day, sometimes multiple times. I had tried to remain positive, but the truth was, I honestly wasn't sure how I felt about it all. I hadn't made the trip out to LA yet, only because I wasn't as sure as Luke was that we could keep our relationship on the down low in California.

The key was keeping busy and staying off the Internet and searching for his name, which was hard to do. In my searches, I'd stumbled upon old relationships and had gotten sucked into reading some comments. Lord, women were mean when they wanted to be.

I turned from the large windows in my office and sat down at my desk. A large bouquet of red roses was perched on my desk, and I couldn't help but smile each time I saw it. Pulling the card out, I read it once more.

I miss you more than anything, love.
Please think about flying out this weekend.
I love you,
Luke

I sighed and dropped back in my seat. I picked up a file and forced myself to open it. I was helping another lawyer with a case he was working, and I really needed to look up a few laws I was rusty on.

A light knock on my office door pulled me out of my thoughts. "Come in."

Wendy came rushing in. "Did you see this about Luke?"

Other than Luke's family, she was the only person who knew I was dating him. Every time I went back home to Boggy Creek and tried to work up the nerve to at least tell Willa, I would back out. I had no idea what I was afraid of. This was Willa. I knew she would never tell a soul, yet something kept me from confessing. Maybe it was because I was afraid she'd tell me I was insane for dating an actor. That long-distance relationships ultimately failed.

"See what?" I asked. Wendy looked worried. Really worried. I jumped up. "What's wrong?"

She handed me her phone and I scanned the headline.

Luke Walters seen leaving Hotel Bel-Air hand in hand with Kathleen Daughtry.

There was a picture of Luke walking out of the hotel, holding hands with Kathleen. He almost looked like he was pulling her out to a waiting car.

"*Fuck,*" I whispered. "She lives in Boggy Creek Valley."

"Wait, what!?" Wendy gasped as she sat down in one of the chairs opposite my desk.

I nodded. "Yeah, she built a house there. Aiden's—my best friend Willa's husband—construction company built it. Or is building it. I don't think it's done yet. He can't stand her, from what Willa tells me. She apparently came on to Aiden when they first met, and he quickly shut her down."

Wendy raised a brow. "She doesn't have a very good reputation. Sleeps with a lot of actors and is a royal bitch, or so I've read."

I stared at the picture as I attempted to clear my ramped thoughts. I wasn't going to jump to conclusions, because I wasn't that insecure.

Or was I?

I suddenly had the urge to jump on a plane and go scratch that bitch's eyes out. Or maybe I wanted to curl up into a ball, pull the covers over my head and cry.

Shit, what in the hell is wrong with me?

Handing Wendy's phone back, I smiled. Okay, it was forced, but I felt like it was believable enough.

"Are you going to ask him about it?" Wendy asked.

I shrugged and tried like hell to project an attitude that said I wasn't the least bit worried. "I'm sure it will come up in our next conversation."

Her eyes went big and round. "It sure as hell better, Brighton! I mean, I know a lot of times the media prints bullshit, but they are leaving a hotel together."

I cleared my throat as I attempted to make my next words seem like I believed them a hundred percent when I didn't. "It could have been a simple business meeting, Wendy."

"At a hotel?"

Okay, that one did bug me a bit. But I also knew meetings were held in hotels all the time, and I knew in my heart Luke wouldn't hurt me.

I gave Wendy a look. "Did you happen to pull up those older lawsuits I asked about earlier this morning? Or have you been too busy stalking my boyfriend on social media?"

"It was on *People's* website, and they're reliable."

I jerked my head up and met her gaze. "Uh-huh...that doesn't answer my question."

Wendy stood. "Deflection at its best. I'll have them in your email in less than thirty minutes. I need to pull one more."

Using a cheerful voice, I said, "Thank you, Wendy."

She turned to leave, then looked back at me. "Brighton, when will you guys go public? Aren't you tired of living this other life?"

Other life? If only it were that simple. I could handle not telling my family and friends I was dating Luke. I would tell them eventually. It wasn't like I'd never done this before.

What really scared me was what would happen once the world found out Luke Walters was dating a lawyer who worked for his father's firm. Not that Luke shared any information about his personal life. He was vague, stating he liked his privacy and his family liked theirs, and from what I could tell, the press mostly respected that.

Yet, at the same time, it was beginning to feel like I had been cast in a role I hadn't planned on auditioning for. I would never in a million years regret falling in love with Luke. Never regret the decision to run off to Maine with him, even after finding out who he was. But...Luke had hinted that once the world found out about us, our happy bubble would burst and things wouldn't be the same. And when I'd Googled him and read about some of his past relationships, I learned they'd never lasted for more than a few months.

Was it because once the world snuck in everything changed?

I shook my head. No, I would never regret falling in love with Luke. But how long could I honestly keep pretending we were in a normal relationship before it started to eat at me? I could feel the real world closing in on us—Lord, could I feel it. I had simply gotten really good at ignoring that it would eventually happen.

Wendy cleared her throat, drawing me out of my thoughts. I glanced at her, standing there with her hands on her hips and a look that demanded an answer to her question. With another practiced and forced smile, I replied, "When the time is right, we'll go public with our relationship."

"Will he move to Boston?" she asked.

Her question threw me, and I blinked a few times. With a curt laugh, I replied, "I don't intend on moving to LA."

She nodded, then gave me a weak smile before she softly shut the door.

My entire body shook as a chill raced through me. Why had I never thought that far ahead? Was this what our relationship would be like? Me in Boston, Luke in California?

I dropped back in my seat and massaged my temples in an effort to ease the sudden pounding in my head.

The sounds of the harbor slowly drifted up as I sat on Luke's balcony, a beer in my hand. Since Luke had been out of town for so long, I'd started to stay at his place so I could smell him on his pillows or slip one of his shirts on and feel closer to him. I had thought about staying at my house tonight, but I'd somehow found myself at his door, unlocking it with the key he'd given me. I'd ordered takeout and sat outside, thinking. And thinking, and thinking.

I wasn't even sure what in the hell I was thinking about anymore. A part of me longed to call Willa. To tell her everything, so I could get advice. Why was I so nervous to talk to Willa about Luke? She was my best friend. I tried to put on the front that I had my shit together. I always pretended that I was strong enough to handle everything. Yet, I was so tired and felt so alone. I wasn't even aware of anything anymore. The sudden weight of the world felt heavy on my shoulders.

I didn't want to be strong at that moment. I was confused and unsure of what exactly I had gotten myself into by falling in love with Luke. An actor. A very famous actor. And right now, all I wanted was for him to hold me in his arms and tell me everything was okay.

That made me feel weak, which in turn pissed me off, but it was okay to *not* be strong. To need someone else to comfort me.

I sighed as I glanced at my phone on the table. I had called Luke three times after seeing the picture on Wendy's phone. When he didn't return any of my calls, I texted him. When I got no response, I did what any other pissed-off girlfriend would do. I turned off my phone, ordered Chinese takeout, and then ate a pint of Ben & Jerry's Cherry Garcia ice cream while I pouted and drowned my sorrow in beer.

Pressing the bottle to my lips, I tipped it back and finished off the beer, then set it down on the table. I pulled my legs to my chest and rested my chin on my knees as I looked out over the dark water. Lights were scattered about, indicating boats coming and going. Or maybe they were anchored out there. Some only bobbed slightly, the waves moving them this way and that. I hadn't ever really paid attention to the water at night. It caused my tension to ease some as I watched the dancing lights, knowing that I wasn't the only one floating around, lost in the dark.

It was a cool night, maybe sixty-two. It wasn't cold by any means, but I couldn't seem to shake the chill I'd had all day. When I had gotten to Luke's place, I'd pulled on one of his Boston Red Sox sweatshirts and a pair of his sweatpants. I was swimming in both, but they made me feel closer to him.

I wasn't used to this feeling of uncertainty. In a normal relationship, one wouldn't ever see pictures of the man they loved whisking a woman out of a hotel and into a limo. Well, I guess one could, it just wouldn't be splashed across the media outlets. One wouldn't have to pretend it didn't bother them that their boyfriend kissed other women, even if it meant nothing. It was acting. I'd kissed a man before and felt nothing, so I knew it was possible. The damn nagging doubts about this was unsettling.

Yet, knowing Luke was the one doing it felt different. I couldn't fully wrap my head around it. But I did know that for the last seven months, I had been pretending. That Luke was off to California on a business trip, and I'd see him when he came home that weekend. When he did, we would lock ourselves away from the world and spend days in and out of bed. I pretended that meeting him at restaurants in dark corners or private rooms was romantic—and it was. But was it something I could keep doing for much longer? I wasn't sure.

And now? Now the ugly reality of what he did for a living was rearing its head, and I was utterly lost and confused about how I felt. How did wives of actors do it? Watch them pretend to have these relationships? Kiss other women. Touch other women.

"Ugh."

Sighing once again, I closed my eyes.

"I'm going to really feel like an idiot if you're sleeping with her," I whispered to no one but the wind.

After another thirty minutes of watching the stars on the water, I stood, grabbed the beer, and headed back in. I tossed the empty bottle in the recycle bin, took another one out of the fridge, then made my way to the large leather sofa and turned on the TV. I pulled up Amazon and hit Play on *Singing in the Rain*. As the movie stared, my eyelids grew heavier. My effort to keep them open failed and I slowly drifted off to sleep, finally allowing my mind to stop, if only for a little while.

I moaned when I felt a soft caress on my cheek. I knew that touch. Had dreamed of that touch so many times.

"Sweetheart."

Luke's voice. I was dreaming that Luke was home.

Letting out a contented sigh, I whispered his name. "Luke."

"I'm home, love."

I felt myself smile—then snapped my eyes open to see Luke sitting on the sofa, gazing down at me with his handsome face and that smile that left me utterly breathless. Dimple on full display.

"Am I still sleeping?"

He let out a soft chuckle. "No. I went to your place first to look for you. I've been trying to call you using Hank's phone for the last few hours, but you either turned it off or it needs to be charged."

I pulled myself up into a sitting position and wiped the sleep from my eyes. "Wait...you didn't answer my calls or texts."

He frowned. "I lost my phone. Or someone swiped it from me. Once I figured out it was gone, I had Hank call and turn it off."

I drew my brows together as I let that explanation sink it. "Someone stole your phone?"

"It's more likely I lost it. I must have set it down when we were filming on set, and who knows what happened to it. I've done it before."

All I could do was nod.

"I didn't even realize it until I was in the car heading back to my place when my agent called Hank looking for me." He took my hand in his and laced our fingers together. "She wanted to warn me about a picture that *People* had published."

And just like that, all the warm fuzzies over Luke being here washed away. "Yeah, I saw it."

For some unknown reason, I suddenly got very pissed off. All the confusion from earlier today turned into full-blown anger.

Luke nodded. "I thought that was why you weren't answering your calls."

I let out a bark of laughter. "Think pretty highly of yourself, do you?"

His expression turned to one of confusion.

Okay, chill out, Bree. You're not the jealous type. Or at least you need to act like you're not.

"Wendy showed me," I said when he sat there.

"It wasn't what they made it out to be, Bree."

I drew my legs around him so I could stand. "You think I flew into a rage of jealousy, turned off my phone, and fell into a pit of despair because I saw a picture of you leaving a hotel holding hands with another woman?"

Shit. That was exactly what I'd done.

He looked up at me. "I didn't think you fell into a fit of despair, but I wouldn't blame you if you were mad about it. I know I would be, if the roles were reversed. Then add in that you reached out but I never returned your messages."

I walked over to the kitchen and turned on the light, blinding myself for a moment before I opened the fridge and looked for something to eat. Anything. Something to make it appear I'd walked away from him for a good reason.

Christ, think, Brighton. What would you eat in the middle of the night?

Yogurt.

I grabbed a French vanilla yogurt and peeled off the lid before opening the drawer for a spoon. "If I was mad at you, Luke, why would I come to your place?" I asked as I turned and leaned against the counter.

He raised a single brow. "You seem mad."

"You woke me up. I had a long day of looking up boring law shit."

That made him smile. "I thought you loved all that law shit."

I shrugged. "Well, some days I don't. Today was one of them."

Luke stood and nodded before he walked over to me. "I was meeting Kathleen Daughtry at the hotel because we both signed up for a new movie we'll be co-starring in. The director was there and wanted to meet with us both. The movie will be filmed in the New York area."

I licked off the yogurt from my spoon and watched as Luke's eyes followed the action. They seemed to grow dark with desire for a moment, and a part of me liked that little bit of power I had. "That's nice. You'll be closer to Boston."

"And to you."

I nodded and smiled because that really would be nice. "And the reason you were holding her hand as you both left?"

"There was a lot of media present, and I grabbed her hand so we could get to the car faster. What you didn't see behind us was Donald Michaels, the director, slipping into the car as well."

And there you have it. The I-feel-like-a-jealous-idiot phase has hit.

All I could do was nod. I had been upset. Jealous, confused, call it whatever the hell you want to.

"This is all new for me still, Luke. Even after dating for nearly eight months, I'm not sure how to navigate all of this. Especially pictures of you with another woman, regardless if they're your co-star or not."

"It's not uncommon for actors to meet before shooting, especially when it's a romantic comedy. Kathleen and I auditioned together, but the director still needs to see if we'll have chemistry on screen."

I stared at him. "Chemistry?"

He nodded. "Yes."

"So when you're filming your love scenes it's believable?"

He rubbed at the back of his neck. "Yes."

I suddenly felt extremely tired.

He ran his fingers through his hair. "Bree, it means nothing. It's acting, that's all. When we do a love scene, we're covered and there's a whole fucking crew of people around us. It's far from romantic and—"

"Stop." I held up my hand to halt his explanation. "I don't want to hear about how you're going to be pretend-fucking Kathleen Daughtry." Shaking my head, I let out a growl. "Great, now I'm never going to be able to listen to Daughtry again because it will remind me of her."

Frowning, I pointed at Luke. "Thanks a lot, Luke! I really like Daughtry!"

The corners of his mouth twitched with a hidden grin.

I frowned. "If you so much as smile right now, I'm walking out and never giving back your favorite Sox sweatshirt."

He held up his hands as if promising he wasn't going to laugh. Then he dropped them and walked toward me. "Bree, I want you to trust that I would never do anything to hurt you."

I could feel tears prick the back of my eyes, and that pissed me off, too, because I vowed a long time ago that no man would ever make me cry.

"I love you," he said, "and I know this whole thing with us is ass-backwards. I hate that you would even think I'd do something like cheat."

"I didn't think that, Luke. At least, I tried not to think it. I won't lie and say a small bit of doubt didn't play in the back of my head. I'm just tired of..."

I had been about to say "never seeing you," but that wouldn't have been true. Luke had been busting his ass flying and back and forth to spend time with me. I knew what he did for a living. I knew he lived in LA. I knew our relationship would be a long-distance one from the start.

"You're tired of what, sweetheart?"

Shaking my head, I whispered, "Nothing. It doesn't matter."

Luke pulled me into his arms. I buried my face into his chest and drew in a deep breath. I loved his smell. It was natural and manly with something slightly citrus. It was...Luke.

"If it makes you unhappy, it matters," he says.

Drawing back, I smiled up at him. "I'm not unhappy."

He pushed a piece of hair back from my eyes and cupped my face. "Do you promise? Because if you want to take our relationship public, we can."

"No," I said, wrapping my arms around his neck. "I don't think I'm ready to let the rest of the world in yet."

A stunning smile broke out over his face. "Well, I'm done with the movie, and I'm all yours."

My heart did a weird little flip. "Until when?"

"November."

"What?" I said, nearly jumping for joy. "You'll be here in Boston until November?"

He laughed. "Yes. I have a few things I'll need to fly out to LA for, but they won't take more than a day or two at the most."

I reached up onto my toes and kissed him. My happiness at having Luke to myself for the next two months pushed me right back into my pretend world.

The world that would eventually spin out of control. I just didn't know when it would happen.

Chapter Eleven

Luke

Five months later — January

"**F**ix this now, Laura," I said to my agent as I stared at a picture of Bree and me walking into the front door of my building on our way home from lunch. The one time I had Hank drop us off at the front of the building so we could rush in because it had been so fucking cold. My agent had emailed it to me and asked if I wanted to make it public, to which I'd said no. I honestly never thought a photographer would be camped out there waiting for a chance to catch me. I hadn't made it known I was in Boston, and it was bitterly freezing outside.

Since I'd been staying in Boston for most of the fall, I'd noticed more and more paparazzi hanging around my building. They'd gotten a picture of us out to dinner once, but Bree's face was blocked. They never were able to figure out who she was. Still, word was getting out that I was seeing someone in Boston, and I knew the vultures could swoop in at any time.

I also knew Brighton was growing tired of the whole cloak-and-dagger game. She'd been going back to Boggy Creek a lot more often, even while I was in Boston. Seeing all her friends getting settled down and married was giving her a lot to think about. It was for me, as well. A hell of a lot.

"I'll take care of it," Laura said. "The photographer who sent it to me is one we can trust. I'll let him know you're not ready to go public, but once you are, he can have the first photo."

"Fine," I said in a clipped tone. "I need to go."

I didn't even give Laura a chance to say goodbye, I was in that shitty of a mood.

"Luke, you're growing increasingly unhappy. When are you going to admit to yourself that maybe this isn't the life you want anymore?" Hank asked after I hung up the phone.

I glared at him as he pulled into my building's parking garage. "If I wanted your advice, I would have asked for it."

When I opened the door, I was surprised to see Hank getting out as well. He normally pulled in and let me out. But now he walked around the car and stood in front of me.

"You're not asking for my advice, but as your friend, I'm going to give it to you," he said. "Brighton is not going to be there forever, and the longer you keep trying to live this double life, the harder things are going to get. And let's not even talk about how many roles you've turned down. I'm your assistant, remember? I'm the one responding to the emails."

"Not now, Hank."

But he kept going. "You don't find it strange that Brighton is going home to Boggy Creek more often? Or that she's working longer hours and can't meet you for dinner as much? Dude, I'm trying to get you to realize someone you love is slipping out of your hands—and you don't even realize it. Brighton is as lost as you. Even I can see it. She's scared, and the two of you can't keep ignoring this. You've been together for a year now. That's a long fucking time to have kept this secret, and I applaud you for doing so. But at what cost?"

I clenched my fists and took a step toward him, ready to knock the living shit out of him, which really wouldn't be helpful. Yes, he worked for me, but he was right. He was also my friend. My best friend, if I was being honest with myself.

I opened my mouth to speak, then quickly shut it. Taking in a calming breath, I said, "She'll leave once she finds out what it'll be like. You and I both know it."

Hank shook his head. "She loves you, and if you honestly think she'll leave, then maybe you don't know her as well as you think you do."

The conversation I'd had with another actor months ago replayed in my memory. He had only confirmed what I had feared. He had fallen in love with a woman who was not a part of Hollywood, and she ended up deciding it was not the life for her and they broke up. Hank was wrong. The moment we went public, everything would change. I just needed a little bit more time. One more movie. I only had to do this one last obligation and that would be it. "I don't have time for this. I've got an event to get to."

"Which Brighton declined, didn't she?" Hank tossed out.

I stopped for a moment. This time I *really* had to force myself not to turn and punch him. But he was right again. Bree *had* declined to go. I'd told her a friend of mine had invited me to a private function, and we could go together as a couple and not have to hide it. It would mean more people would find out about us, and the chances of her name getting out would be even greater, but the way her eyes lit up at the idea of us being together in such a public setting had thrilled me.

She'd still said no, though. She had a trial she was preparing for. And I'd been heartbroken. I knew the press would be vetted inside, so I wasn't worried about them digging up information or printing anything harsh about Brighton. This would have been the perfect place to appear together. Other actors would be there as well, and it wasn't like it was a huge secret anymore. A lot of people knew I was dating someone, just not *who* I was dating. But I had always been fiercely private, so it wasn't unlike me to hide information about the person I was dating.

Instead of punching Hank, I said, "Make sure you're here at four to pick me up. We have to get Kathleen on the way."

"Kathleen?" Hank repeated in a shocked voice.

I nodded. "Yes. Laura wants us to show up together, to promote the upcoming film."

Hank stared at me with a disbelieving expression.

"What is it?" I asked.

"I'm confused. What if Brighton had said yes?"

I shrugged. "I'd planned on meeting her inside. I'd do the walk in with the press with Kathleen and meet Brighton there. Even if we were public it would be that way, Hank. You know that. We're trying to promote the movie."

Hank stood there and blinked over and over before he slowly shook his head. "You really are a stupid son of a bitch."

Before I could say a word, he headed around the front of the car and slipped into the driver's seat, speeding off to park the car.

"What the fuck is wrong with you?" I called at the retreating car before I turned and headed in to change for the black-tie event.

The problem was, I knew exactly what was wrong. I was simply afraid to admit the truth.

Kathleen was being a little too friendly in the limo on the way to the event. I'd already lost count of how many times I'd moved her hand off my leg.

"So we won't be meeting this mystery woman of yours tonight?" Kathleen asked.

"No, she couldn't make it."

"Pity. I guess I'll have to play your date for the evening, then."

Turning to look at her, I smiled. "I don't think that's necessary, Kathleen. We walk in together and then go our separate ways."

"We're filming a movie together, Luke. The more publicity we get, the better."

I sighed. "I'm not looking to get that kind of publicity."

She laughed, and it was fake as hell. "Everyone wants that type of publicity."

"Not me."

We'd already started to film the movie, shooting a few scenes back in LA. Official filming wouldn't begin until next month, since Kathleen had another movie she was finishing and I was about to co-star in a project that was being filmed in Australia. I had already asked Brighton to come with me, since I'd be there for two or three weeks, and she'd said yes. The press in Australia was nothing like here in the States. We'd be free to be ourselves, go anywhere we wanted, do everything together. It would be heaven.

I planned on telling Brighton my decision about my future, *our* future, then.

Kathleen snapped her fingers in front of my face. "Earth to Luke. Hello? We're here. Are you going to make me get out first and help you out?"

I forced a smile. "Of course not."

She lifted her chin and grinned. "Remember, stand on my left so I can show—"

"Your good side. I know, Kathleen."

Not many actresses I'd worked with were such superficial bitches like Kathleen. But there were a few of them out there...and this one was the queen of the pack.

"Okay, Hank," I said, indicating we were ready.

Hank got out and made his way around to open the limo door. I'd wanted to arrive in the Mercedes, but Kathleen wouldn't think of showing up in anything less than a limo.

As I stepped out, I smiled and waved at the fans and press there. Hank stood off to the side, scanning the area. I saw him frown as he focused on something behind me.

"Luke, Bri—"

"For fuck's sake, Luke!" Kathleen whisper-shouted, cutting off whatever Hank was going to say. "Take my goddamn hand, will you?"

I reached my hand into the limo and helped Kathleen out. She instantly pressed herself against me, and I put my hand around her waist as we walked toward the entrance. Reporters from different outlets called for us to look at them for pictures. Every now and then, Kathleen would reach up and whisper something dirty in my ear.

"I want to fuck you in the back of that limo."

I had to force myself to laugh, pretending she was saying something altogether different. When what I really wanted to do was gag. At one point, I leaned down and whispered back, "Knock it the fuck off *now*, Kathleen, or I'll walk away and leave your ass out here alone."

She laughed and leaned her head against mine while someone snapped a picture.

"Has filming started yet on *Love Rebound*?" someone called out as we walked up the steps.

"Kathleen! Luke! Does this mean you're dating? What's it like to date your co-star?"

Kathleen snickered. "Like I said. Publicity, Luke."

I rolled my eyes and motioned for her to walk in first. Reaching into my jacket pocket to text Hank, I cursed.

"Fuck."

"What's wrong?" Kathleen asked.

"I must have left my damn phone at home. I was in a rush to get dressed and out the door."

She patted me on the chest. "Don't worry, darling. The only person you need to pay attention to tonight is already on your arm."

If people weren't staring at us as we walked into the ballroom, I would have rolled my eyes again.

We mingled for a bit, and Kathleen kept her arm draped in mine, even though I tried twice to untangle myself from her. From across the room, I saw Hank. He motioned for me to come to the side to talk to him, but Kevin Courter stepped up and started to chat with me. He was a seasoned vet with two Oscars. It would have been rude to snub him.

He reached his hand out for mine, and I was finally able to get Kathleen off of me. "Luke, such a pleasure to see you here. I really enjoy this event that Bryce puts on."

I nodded. "It's for a good cause, that's for sure."

"What's it for again?" Kathleen asked as she beamed up at Kevin. He laughed, thinking she was kidding.

"At ten-thousand dollars a plate, I'd think you'd remember, Kathleen," Kevin joked.

"Battered Women of Boston," I said, glancing at the clueless woman next to me.

"Oh." She waved her hand in the air. "That's right. I knew it had to do with women's rights."

Kevin's smile faded as he looked at me with a befuddled expression. This time I *did* roll my eyes.

The music started, and Kathleen took hold of me again. "You promised me the first dance, Luke."

"I don't remember that," I said with a fake-as-hell smile.

Kevin slapped me on the back. "Son, never turn down the opportunity to dance with a beautiful woman."

"It's just—"

Before I could finish, Kathleen was tugging me to the dance floor. Since there was press here, I wasn't about to make a scene, even if they had been vetted and wouldn't publish anything untoward. It was easier to dance with Kathleen and then send her on her merry way.

I glanced back over at where Hank had been and found him making his way toward the other side of the room. He wound his way through couples and groups of people talking. He clearly had someone or something he was attempting to reach. Letting my gaze wander over to see where in the hell he was rushing off to, I nearly tripped.

"Bree," I whispered.

Kathleen tensed in my arms. I was about to excuse myself when she ran her fingers through my hair, causing me to look at her with what I was sure was a confused expression.

"What are you doing?" I asked.

"We were good together, Luke. We still can be." And before I even saw it coming, Kathleen pressed her lips to mine.

I quickly placed my hands on her upper arms and pushed her away. She pouted—then a loud crash caused her to turn.

When I looked at where the noise had come from—where Bree had just been—I saw that she'd run into some waiters. Hank was almost there. He called out her name, but she ran so fast for the back exit, I didn't even have time to think. I took off after her.

"Bree! Brighton!" I shouted as I made my way through the crowd. *Fuck. Fuck. Fuck!*

She'd seen Kathleen kissing me. How long had she been here? Had she seen us walking around the room? It probably appeared we were posing as a couple—exactly as Kathleen had intended. But surely Brighton would know it was all an act?

"Brighton!" I called out.

I saw her burst through the doors and run down the steps. How in the hell she could run in heels was beyond me. I could barely run in these damn dress shoes. A taxi happened to be parked outside the hotel where the event was being held, and Bree made a beeline right for it.

"Bree, wait!" I shouted. She slipped into the taxi, and it quickly sped off.

"Fuck!" I threw my hands in the air. Hank appeared next to me.

"I saw her earlier," he stated.

Turning, I looked at him. "What do you mean?"

"I saw Brighton walking up when you got out of the car. I tried to get your attention, but Kathleen made that impossible. When I looked back at her, she was gone. I didn't see her again until a few moments before she turned and ran into the waiters."

"Son of a bitch. Why didn't you tell me you saw her outside, Hank?"

"I tried."

"Not fucking hard enough. Did she see the kiss?" I asked.

Hank shrugged. "I was on my way toward her, so I wasn't watching you. From her reaction, I would say yes, she saw it."

I pushed my hand through my hair in frustration. "How in the hell would Kathleen know Bree was there?"

Hank handed me my phone. "It was pushed down between the seats. *Way* down. I heard it buzzing when I parked the limo. Brighton texted you. Kathleen must have seen it and stashed your phone."

"Goddammit. I should have known Kathleen was up to something. She was acting weird and hanging onto me inside."

I pulled up Bree's number and called it. It went right to voicemail. "Bree, call me. Please. I need to talk to you. Whatever it was you think you saw, it was nothing. Please...just call me."

"Luke?"

I heard my friend Bryce, the host of the private event, calling out to me. It was only then that I noticed the press standing around. A lot of them had left, but some had stayed behind.

"Shit, how much of that do you think they heard?" I asked Hank.

"We're too far away and security is keeping them behind the barricades, so I doubt they heard anything. Brighton ran out too fast and slipped into the taxi quickly. I'm sure they didn't have a chance to even photograph her."

"Luke, is everything okay?" Bryce asked as he walked up to us. "What in the hell was that all about?"

"I'm sorry if we caused a disturbance, Bryce. I'm going to have to leave. Something came up." Turning to Hank, I said, "Stay here and make sure Kathleen gets back to her hotel."

"I can make sure she gets back okay," Bryce offered.

"You're sure?"

He nodded and clapped me on the arm. "Go get the girl, Luke."

Hank took off toward where he'd parked the limo.

"Thanks, Bryce. I'll be sure to make an additional donation." Not wanting to waste another minute, I jogged and caught up with Hank.

"Where to?" he asked.

"Her place."

I tried to call Bree at least a dozen more times. But it went straight to voicemail each time. After the seventh call, I stopped leaving messages. Hank pulled up to her building, and I jumped out and started toward the door when Lewis, one of the doormen, stopped me.

"Mr. Morrison, I'm sorry, but I'm not allowed to let you into the building."

"What?" I asked, stunned.

"Ms. Rogers has stated that you are not to be allowed into the building. And if you show up, I'm to tell you, and I quote 'Go fuck yourself...um...you, um...asshole.' Yeah. I'm pretty positive that was what she asked me to relay. I still like you, though, sir."

I was positive I was standing there with an absolutely befuddled look on my face, because Hank cleared his throat from behind me.

When I glanced back, Hank was waiting outside the limo. He must have had an idea I wouldn't be staying.

"I appear to have made Ms. Rogers angry," I calmly said as I looked through the doors into the lobby.

Lewis nodded. "It appears so, sir."

"Thank you, Lewis."

I slid back into the limo and tried to call Bree once more, with no luck.

"Where to now?" Hank asked.

"Home."

"You don't want to go back to the event?"

I lifted my eyes and met his in the rearview mirror. "No, Hank, I want to go home. And not to my condo. My parents' house. I need to talk to my mother and figure out what in the hell to do now."

The moment I stepped off the elevator and made my way through the offices of Morrison, Becker, and Gline, I heard the whispers. I did what I had to do and smiled politely as I made my way to Bree's office. I knew the gasps were most likely coming from people who recognized me.

My father had fully backed the idea of me showing up at the office since Bree refused to take any calls from me, my mother, or my sister, Jenn. I had even asked Lou to try to contact her. Lou had had more success, since Bree at least texted back. Lou had sent Bree a message asking what in the fuck I'd done to mess things up and then had screenshotted Bree's reply for me. It said: "Please tell Luke to leave me alone." That was it.

Now, as I approached Bree's assistant's desk, I saw her look up and then do a double take. She immediately jumped up and rounded her desk.

"Um, Mr. Morrison, er...Walters, um...whoever you are this morning, Bree is in a meeting."

I raised a single brow. "Is that so? I just came from my father's office, and he informed me she's available."

It was a lie; I hadn't been up to his office. The fewer people I ran into while I was here, the better.

"Oh, well, um, she's on a conference call, and I, um..."

Her eyes darted to her phone, then to Bree's door, then back to her phone. I could almost hear her thoughts.

I need to alert Brighton!

With a smile, I leaned in and said, "This will only take up a few minutes of Ms. Rogers's time, Wendy."

I headed to the door and heard her whisper-shout, "Oh, she really doesn't want to see you! If you value your life, don't open that door."

Before I opened it, I looked back at her and winked. "Are you worried about me?"

She stood there, stunned into speechlessness, then shook her head and scoffed. "Hardly." At least I knew she wouldn't rush in ahead of me. I took advantage of her shock and opened the door and quickly slipped in.

My heart felt like it skipped a beat in my chest when I saw Bree standing at the large windows overlooking Boston.

"Wendy, I thought I said I needed to be alone," she said without turning.

"She tried to stop me, but I managed to get around her."

Brighton spun around and stared at me. For a moment, I saw it on her face. That brightness she always got when I walked into a room, or showed up to her place after being gone for days or weeks at a time. It vanished as soon as it appeared, and a cool expression replaced it.

"It seems like you know your way around women." She folded her arms across her chest and shot me a glare that made me take a step back as a chill ran down my spine.

This was a very pissed-off Brighton. I had yet to meet this version of her.

"Why won't you return my calls, Bree?"

She gave a nonchalant shrug. "I figured we didn't have anything to talk about. What I saw at the event Thursday night gave me a very clear picture of where we're at in our relationship."

"The fuck it did," I said with a shake of my head. "Bree, there is nothing going on between me and Kathleen."

"So you say, but you looked awfully comfortable with one another. The little whispers to each other...was that for show, as well, Luke? It almost seemed like you had a history."

I sighed in frustration. "We're filming a goddamn movie together. Our agents wanted us to show up to the event as a pair. Kathleen loves the spotlight and loves for people to gossip about her. She wanted people to think there was something going on between us other than being co-stars. She thinks it drives people to want to see the movie more."

Bree snarled her lip. "These are the type of women you work with? They not only like to pretend on screen, but in real life as well? What would have happened had I agreed to go? What would Ms. Daughtry have done?"

"The plan was for me and Kathleen to walk in together, mingle a bit, then for me to meet you there."

Her mouth fell open. "*Again.* Again with the meeting you there. You had no intention of bringing me with you as a date?"

I frowned. "I told you the press outside the venue weren't vetted. If the story of us is going to come out, I want to control who releases it."

She slowly shook her head. "And the kiss?"

I exhaled. "There *was* no kiss. I mean, yes, she tried to kiss me, but I pushed her away. Kathleen knew you were there. I must have set my phone down on the seat of the limo, and she picked it up. She saw your text saying you'd be coming. I never saw it because my phone was on silent. I honestly wasn't expecting to hear from you, since you said you'd be working late on a trial."

Tears formed in Bree's eyes, and it nearly broke me. Brighton was one of the strongest women I had ever met, and to know I was causing her pain nearly killed me.

She slowly shook her head. "Why would she want to make me jealous, Luke?"

"I don't know."

One of her brows rose. "Try again."

I rubbed at the back of my neck. "She's twisted...and I think she wants to start another affair."

Bree stumbled back. "*What?* You've slept with her before? When?"

I swallowed hard. "It was a long time ago, Bree. Years. We were both new on the scene and extras in a movie. It was short-lived, and it meant nothing."

She blinked at me. "And you didn't think to tell me this last summer, when you were seen leaving a hotel with her?"

"Because it was history. It happened *years* ago."

"Yet you're about to film a romantic comedy with this woman? A woman you've slept with? You didn't think I should know?"

"Would it have made it any easier for you?"

She closed her eyes and whispered, "No."

"That's why I didn't feel the need to tell you."

Her eyes opened again, and she exhaled. "And she wants to have another affair?"

"She hinted at it, but I'd never do that. Bree, I love you, and I would never do anything to hurt you. It was better to humor her and get the whole fucking night over with."

"You thought it would be okay to humor her? To pretend that you're a couple when you're really dating someone else? How do I know it's all an act?"

I threw my hands up in the air and dropped them at my sides. "For fuck's sake, I told you the truth! Why can't you trust me? Nothing is going to happen between us."

She wrapped her arms around her body as if suddenly overcome with a chill. Her eyes got wet with tears again but she squeezed them shut, then drew in a deep breath before she whispered two words that nearly knocked me completely off balance. "Get out."

My reply came out strained. "What?"

She opened her eyes and stared at me, not a single tear in sight. This was the trial lawyer in her coming out. No emotions on her face or in her voice. Stone cold.

"I can't do this," she said. "I cannot stand by and watch the man I love pretend to be with other women for the sake of a fucking movie. It's a romance, this movie you're filming with her. *Love Rebound*. It's supposed to be a 'sensual romantic comedy' about two long-lost lovers who are reunited by luck. What a coincidence, how it mirrors real life."

"Bree, it means nothing to me, and it doesn't mirror real life."

She slammed her hands down on her desk. "It *does* mean something to me! I cannot—no, I *will not* do this. I deserve more. I deserve more, and I *want* more. I'm tired of the part-time charade, this let's-sneak-around-and-not-tell-anyone game."

My anger quickly boiled up to match hers, and my words spilled out freely. "This coming from the woman I've been dating for a year who still hasn't told anyone about me—including her own family."

Her face turned red with anger.

"Yet you stand here and preach to me about sneaking around," I said. "Why don't we start with why you haven't even told your best friend about me?"

"I think it's time you left, Luke. Go to your pretty little actress, because I'm done waiting on the sidelines." She sniffled, and I could tell she was hanging on by a thread. "I can't do this anymore. I'm sorry...but please get out of my office."

It took a moment or two for her words to settle into my brain. I wanted to drop to my knees and beg her not to do this. But Hank's words from the other night came back to me—and I knew exactly what I had to do. Until I could get my own fucking future settled, I couldn't keep Brighton in the dark, waiting.

So I did as she asked. I left. And it was one of the hardest things I have ever done in my entire life. Especially when I softly shut the door and heard her start to cry.

Wendy stood there shooting daggers at me. "I knew you'd hurt her. It was only a matter of time."

I swallowed hard. "I never meant to hurt her. And I love her. I just have to prove to her how *much* I love her."

Wendy looked at me with an expression that said she highly doubted it.

Without another word, I turned and headed out of the building. I needed to get back to LA to talk to Laura. The sooner the better.

Chapter Twelve

Brighton

Present day — May

I wiped angrily at my tears and pulled myself back up from where I had slid to the floor after seeing Luke in the bed and breakfast. What in the hell was I doing, sitting on my parents' kitchen floor in their bed and breakfast, once again crying over this man?

Drawing in a deep breath, I walked over and looked at my reflection in the window. Good God. I looked like hell. No makeup, sweaty hair, and a long-sleeve T-shirt and yoga pants. Not to mention the bloodshot eyes.

After taking in a few deep breaths, I got myself together and headed back out to the front desk area. Luke was, of course, still standing there. The bastard was eating cheese from the board I'd made for him.

"Sorry, there was something I needed to take care of for my mother," I said.

He smiled, and I hated that it made my insides feel like warm butter. "I was stunned when my father said you quit at the end of January."

"When did you find out?" I asked.

"February. When I was home, I asked about you. He told me you said you were moving back to Boggy Creek. Are you—" he glanced around the bed and breakfast—"working for your folks now?"

"Some. I'm trying to decide what I want to do. I've tossed around the idea of opening my own firm in town, but I'm not sure."

He smiled again.

Asshole jerk. God, if only I could punch him right in the face.

"Why did you leave Boston so quickly?" he asked.

I lifted my chin. "I figured it was time when a reporter showed up at my apartment to ask me about Luke Walters."

His eyes went wide. "What?"

"Why are you here, Luke? And why the fake name?"

He frowned, not liking that I had brushed over a subject he clearly wanted answers to. He cleared his throat before speaking. "We're filming close by, just up the valley at Lakewood Country Club. Everyone else is staying at the resort up there, but I decided not to."

"Where are you staying if not there?" I asked, not sure why. Morbid curiosity, maybe. Every part of me expected him to say Kathleen Daughtry's house.

"I want privacy, and I need to talk to you. So, I figured the best place to stay was here, at Willow Tree Bed and Breakfast."

I was sure that if it were humanly possible, my jaw hit the floor. "Here? You're planning on staying here? Why?"

"Like I said, the privacy for one, and I wanted to be able to see you. Talk to you."

I felt my body go stiff, so I stood taller. "I thought we said everything we needed to say, Luke. I'm not interested in a relationship with an actor."

He leaned against the counter and smirked. "So you said."

"I'm not going to be on the sidelines waiting for anyone anymore. I'm ready to settle down and start a family, and I don't need a part-time husband or father."

His brows shot up.

Holy shit balls, where in the hell did that come from?

I was positive my breathing had quickened and my heart was beating three times faster than normal. I couldn't tell if my jab had surprised or hurt him. Probably a bit of both.

Then again, maybe I *was* ready to settle down. All of my friends were getting married. The only single ones left were me and Kyle Larson, Greer's brother. Greer was one of my best friends and owned the bookstore in Boggy Creek. She was to blame for the countless dildos I'd invested in after she got me hooked on romance novels when I tried to hide my heartbreak in fiction.

"Settle down?" he repeated.

All I could do was nod. Then the front door opened and, as if he was summoned here, Kyle walked in.

He took one look at me and frowned. "What's wrong?" he asked.

Kyle and I had a love-hate relationship. We loved to hate one another. He annoyed the hell out of me, and I was pretty sure he'd wanted to stick my head in Boggy Creek and hold it under the water a time or two. The only thing stopping him was the fact that he was a cop. Just like Willa's brother, Hunter. Both of them had K9 partners, and Kyle's was right next to him now. Her name was Cat, short for Catherine. No one could figure out why in the hell Kyle would name his K9 partner that, let alone call her Cat for short.

Even though Kyle was a pain in my ass, he was a friend. A friend who I knew would do anything for me. That was clear from the look on his face—and the fact that he knew I'd been crying.

"Nothing, Kyle. You're here!" I said with a forced glee I normally didn't reserve for him.

He turned and saw Luke, and I knew the moment it dawned on him who he was. But thankfully, he didn't react. Or at least he tried not to react.

Before Kyle could utter another word, I walked around the desk and threw myself into his arms, hugging him.

He tried to back away as he looked down at me like I was attempting to murder him. Cat barked and tried to move in between us.

I laughed and reached down to pet her. "Jealous girl!"

Pulling Kyle away from Luke and to the opposite side of the room, I looked up at him and whispered, "I need a favor from you."

He looked suspicious. "What kind of favor?"

Quickly glancing back across the room to Luke, I saw he was glancing at his phone. "I need you to kiss me."

That made his eyes nearly pop out of his head. His voice was low as he asked, "Kiss you? Does the fact that Luke Wilson is standing here have anything to do with this?"

"Yes, and I promise to tell you all about it later, when you take me out to dinner for my birthday."

"That would be two favors, Brighton. I like you, but I'm not sure I like you *that* much."

I silently pleaded with him with my eyes. "Kyle, please."

He sighed and said, "Passionate kiss like we're dating or peck on the cheek?"

"Passionate. I'll try not to throw up."

Laughing, he cupped my face with his hands and kissed me.

Okay, I'm not going to lie, the man could kiss. He could *really* kiss. And when his tongue slipped into my mouth, I had to fight the urge to give in to it. Props to Kyle Larson. I could see why women melted in his arms. Too bad I really *was* fighting the urge to puke. I was going to deserve an Oscar of my own after this kiss was over.

When he pulled away, he looked down at me with a smirk and whispered, "How was that?"

"A five, maybe. A little too much tongue action."

The corners of his mouth twitched. "Should I try again?"

"No, I'm barely able to keep my food down as it is."

Kyle laughed again and quickly slipped into the role like the pro he was. He put his arm around me and then turned back to face Luke. Who, I might add, looked like he was ready to hit Kyle. Had he not been in a police uniform, he might have. I had to hand it to Kyle, he was good at this. And I was going to owe him big time.

It dawned on me then that Luke had used another name to register his room. Walter Cunningham. How should I introduce him? Shit. He had three different names.

"I'm sorry, I'd introduce you to my boyfriend, but I'm not sure what name you're going by right now."

Luke forced a laugh and walked toward us, his hand extended toward Kyle. "Luke Morrison."

Kyle lifted his brows. "Didn't you work for a Morrison, sweetheart?"

A nervous bubble of laughter escaped from my throat, and I cleared it. "Yes. This is his son."

They shook hands, and Kyle turned to face me. "I can't stay. Just stopped by to wish you a happy birthday, and to make sure we're on for dinner at Bella's tonight."

The fact that Kyle had remembered Bella's was my favorite place to eat—besides The Coffee Pot, which was our local café—touched my heart. As much as I gave him a hard time, I knew deep in my soul that Kyle Larson would do anything for his friends. The fact that he was playing along with this, no questions asked, told me one thing.

Okay, two things: One, he was going to make me pay him back tenfold. And two, I was lucky to call him a friend.

"Yes, that sounds amazing," I said. "Seven?"

He winked. "Yep. Well, I need to run."

And before I could say another word, he pulled me in for a second kiss. I reached around to his side—the one that Luke couldn't see—found the area his bulletproof vest wasn't covering, and pinched the living shit out of him.

Kyle pulled back and laughed. "I always knew you'd like it rough." He stepped back and looked at Luke with a wide grin. "It was nice meeting you. Enjoy your stay in Boggy Creek."

Luke forced a smile. "I will, thank you."

I let out a yelp when Kyle slapped me on the ass and headed toward the door. Cat was right by his side, but not before she shot me a dirty look.

"I'll be right back," I said. "I'm going to walk him out. My boyfriend. Who is a cop."

Luke nodded. "I'll take my cheese board and head on up to my room, since this doesn't seem to be a good time for us to talk."

Why his words sent a rush of disappointment through me, I wasn't sure. Hadn't he said he wanted to talk to me? Now he was going off to his room? *Of course, he is, Brighton.* Ugh...I was being childish and that pissed me off.

But I didn't have time to question him if I wanted to catch up with Kyle before he left.

"Enjoy it," I said over my shoulder and headed out the front door, down the steps, and jogged over to Kyle's SUV. He opened the back door and Cat jumped in. She turned and looked at me, and I had to stop for a moment.

"Does it look like she's scowling at me?"

Kyle glanced at his partner and laughed. "She doesn't like to share." He reached in to give her a kiss and a quick pet on the head and all seemed to be fine.

"Man, she's sure getting big," I said as I reached in and gave her some pats. She may be a police dog, but she was so damn cuddly. A strange thought entered my mind. Maybe I should get a dog to snuggle up with at night. Before I could debate the idea in my head, Kyle pulled my attention back to him.

"Okay, what in the hell was that all about, Brighton? That was Luke Walters. The actor."

I chewed nervously on my lip while I kept stroking Cat. "It was, yes. He's staying here while he films a movie up the valley with that vile Kathleen Daughtry."

"Dude, why do you hate her so much? You've mentioned her before and..." His voice trailed off, and he stared at me for a moment. As if a light bulb went off in his head, he slowly closed his eyes, then snapped them open and met my gaze. "You dated him."

With a long sigh, I stepped away from Cat and glanced at the house. Luke's room faced the backyard, so I wasn't worried about him seeing us, unless he made his way to the living room and peered out. I looked that way but didn't see anyone standing there.

"Yes," I said. "I dated him for about a year."

"A year!" Kyle shouted. "What the fuck? When did this happen, and why did you keep it a secret?"

I smacked him on the chest. "Shut up! This past year. I met him a year ago last Christmas, and we broke up in January."

Kyle stood there, blinking as if he couldn't process the words I'd spoken. "*You*. You dated. Luke. Walters? You dated him—for a year?"

I placed my hands on my hips and glared at him. "Yes. Why do you seem so shocked?"

"How did you keep that a secret, Bree? Does Willa know? Greer? If my sister knew, I'm going to kill her. Do you know how good he was in the movie *Till Death Do Us Part*? I mean, the man can play an action hero better than Jason Bourne."

My jaw ticced as I fought against clenching my teeth. "You do know that Jason Bourne is not a real person."

He rolled his eyes. "Yes. But Mark Johnson, played by your ex in that movie, was fucking amazing. He won an Oscar for that, Bree. The man won an *Oscar*."

"So I've heard," I replied dryly.

"Okay, so the ex shows up, and the first thing you do is pretend to be dating someone? Was the breakup mutual?"

I dropped my head back to study the clear blue sky. "Ugh, Kyle. It's so complicated." Looking at him, I asked, "Can I tell you all about it tonight? It'll honestly be good to finally tell someone other than Bella."

Kyle's mouth dropped open. "Bella knows? Hunter is going to be livid!"

Bella was another one of my best friends. There was a group of us. Me, Willa, Greer, Abby, Bella, and Candace. Bella and Hunter had only recently gotten married after being separated for a number of years. I was so happy for them both. It also happened to be Bella whom I'd finally told about Luke after I'd moved back to Boggy Creek.

"Listen, you can't tell anyone Luke is here," I said. "He's staying under a false name and he really does like his privacy."

Kyle looked up at the house. "I'll say. The dude kept you a secret for a year."

I shot him a dirty look. "I'll see you tonight. Oh, by the way—why did you stop by?"

He gave me that boyishly handsome smile that I was positive had gotten him laid plenty of times. It had zero effect on me, but I could see why women flocked to the man. "To wish you a happy birthday."

Well damn. I honestly hadn't been expecting that. I reached up and kissed him on the cheek. "You really are an amazing guy, Kyle. And if you tell anyone I said that, I'll deny it."

He shrugged, shut the door to the back where Cat was, and walked around to the driver's side. Before he got in, he said, "I mean, you must think so if you're dating me."

I couldn't help but laugh as I waved him away. He started up the truck and drove off.

"What in the living fuck? You and Kyle are dating?"

Spinning around, I let out a groan when I saw Candace standing there with a stunned expression on her face.

"Has hell finally frozen over?" she asked while making the sign of the cross on her chest. "I thought you two couldn't stand each other. Was it all an act? Oh my God, I'm losing my touch. I didn't see this coming. At all."

I laughed, walked up, and hugged her. Then I stepped back and gave her a good looking over. She was stunningly beautiful. Warm brown skin that was flawless and made me jealous as hell. Her curly hair was up and piled on top of her head, and those brown eyes of hers sparkled with curiosity. There was something else in them that put me on guard, though...

"Have you been crying?" I asked.

With a furrowed brow, she replied, "I could ask you the same damn thing."

"I haven't been crying."

She raised one knowing brow.

"Fine, but why have *you* been crying?" I asked.

She waved me off. "No, I'm just tired. I mean, I might have had too much to drink last night and then I dug up this old spell book Greer and I found in college. I might have stayed up until four in the morning trying to put a curse or two on Rick's dick, so it would rot and fall off. Other than that, I think it's lack of sleep. I need a good cold eye mask, and I'll be fine."

I stared at her, my mouth opening and closing. Then opening again. "Wait, you put a curse on Rick's dick? Rick? Your boyfriend? Care to share why?"

With a shrug, she replied, "He cheated and then proceeded to say it was my fault. So yes, I hope he rots in hell. But apparently that's not going to happen because it hath already frozen over. You and Kyle are dating?"

"No. Yes. No." I shook my head and sighed. "It's complicated. Are you free for dinner tonight?"

She nodded. "I came by to see if you wanted to go out for your birthday since I'm single now."

"Kyle and I are having dinner at Bella's at seven. I'll explain it all then."

Candace nodded, then said, "I brought you a birthday basket."

I kissed her cheek and took the basket. "Come on, I'll make us some tea. Just promise you won't ask or say anything about Kyle."

Crossing her heart with her finger, she said, "I promise. I'm a patient girl, I can wait."

We walked up the steps right as the door opened. Luke stepped out—and Candace let out a scream so loud, I was positive my eardrums burst.

She pointed at him while her other hand went over her heart. "Holy mother of God. You're Luke Walters!"

Then she ran forward and threw her arms around him. He stumbled back, his arms pinned at his sides. I wasn't the least bit surprised Candace would do something like that. When she fangirls, she apparently gives it a hundred-and-ten percent—like with everything she does.

Luke looked at me for help, and I casually glanced down at the basket she'd brought me. It was full of beauty supplies...and an apple. What was up with the apple?

I took it out and bit into it. "Don't worry. She's harmless. She'll get over the shock in..." Glancing at my Apple Watch, I counted down, "Three, two, one."

Candace let go of Luke and took a step back. "I'm so sorry. Oh my gosh, I don't know what came over me. I'm so sorry!"

Luke smiled and held up his hands. "No worries at all." Then he looked at me. "I need to head out; I've got to be on set. I don't have to worry about..." He looked at Candace.

"No, she won't say a word," I said, trying to sound like him being here wasn't throwing me for a damn loop. "Don't worry. Have fun."

I grabbed Candace by the hand and pulled her into the house.

"Bye, Luke! Have fun! Will I see you again?" Candace cried out. "I hope I see you again! By the way, I loved Mark Johnson!"

I kicked the door with my foot, slamming it shut before Luke could say anything. I dropped Candace's hand and made my way to the kitchen.

"Holy shit. Bree! *Bree!* Did Luke Walters really just step out of the bed and breakfast?"

"He did," I replied as I set the basket down and took another bite of the apple.

"Holy shit. Is he...is he staying here? You know he's filming a movie not far from here."

Turning to look at her, I asked, "How did you know that?"

She laughed. "Please, I keep up with fine-ass actors like that. Last year it was rumored he had a girlfriend, but no one could figure out who it was—only that she lived in Boston because he was there all the time. Lucky bitch."

I stiffened, my eyes darting around the room before I looked at her again.

Candace leaned against the counter and looked at me with an appraising eye. "Wait a minute."

"What?" I asked.

"Why don't you seem the least bit fazed by him being here? How long has he been here? Did you already fangirl over him?"

"Please, I do not fangirl over anyone, *especially* him."

Candace tilted her head. "He kind of looks like that old actor you like. What's his name?"

"Gene Kelly," I stated with a sigh. I poured a glass of tea for both of us and handed her one. "And if Gene Kelly walked in here, I *would* fall all over him. But he can't because life is not fair, and he's dead."

She nodded and took a drink. "True. Still, you aren't acting how you should. It's almost like you...already know him."

Her brows rose in a questioning way, and I felt like I was about to cave under her intense stare. Nothing got by Candace, and she wasn't going to let this drop. I knew that.

"I'll tell you at dinner," I said. "Right now, I want to hear what happened with you and Rick."

She waved her hand in front of her as if that conversation wasn't the least bit interesting. "He cheated. I broke up with him. He said I was spending too much time at The Queen Bee."

The Queen Bee Café was Candace's dream and one she was able to make happen with Arabella as her partner. Candace had originally moved to Boggy Creek to help Greer with her bookstore, Turning Pages. But her real dream was cooking and baking. At the time, Arabella was running a small café at the apiary her family ran, and Candace had helped her there off and on. Then Bella and Candace decided to form a partnership and rented a building on Main and Althorpe. Candace was going to run the café and bakery while Bella had a retail side where she featured items from the apiary, as well as other local businesses.

Bella's main focus was the apiary, especially now that she and Hunter were married. I loved that they were featuring items from local folks. Like honey from Bella's apiary, flowers and seeds from Abby's parents' flower farm, and Christmas items from Abby and Bishop's Christmas tree farm, Wonderland Trees.

"Does he understand what it means to take on something like this?" I asked. "I mean, you guys had to nearly gut the place and start over."

Candace shrugged. "He says I've been spending all my time there, and I have, but this is my dream. I've never been so happy, and I really thought he was going to be supportive. But it turns out he likes having me tucked away in the bookstore. Well, no one's putting Candace in a bookstore corner."

I crinkled up my nose in an attempt not to laugh. "You better not let Greer hear you say that."

She smiled, and I was happy to see a bit of spark come back into her eyes.

"It looks beautiful, by the way," I said. "You've done an amazing job."

Candace reached for my hand and squeezed it. "I couldn't have done this without the love and support of all my friends. I know Bella is a partner, but she's more of a silent one, and she truly has given me full control over it all. I'm just...I'm so happy, if I'm being honest with you. I don't know if I was crying because Rick cheated on me, or if I was crying because I knew deep down he wasn't the one. I feel such a lightness in my heart. That clearly has to mean he wasn't the one, don't you think?"

A sharp pain squeezed my chest. I hadn't felt that way when Luke walked out of my office. In fact, I felt like I'd given up half of my heart. Half of my soul. What did that say?

Candace felt light and free after breaking up with Rick, as she should. Deep down, I knew in my heart that Luke hadn't been sleeping with Kathleen. My pride wouldn't let me admit it, and the fear of the unknown had been more of my pushing him away than anything.

I moved around the counter, took Candace into my arms, and hugged her. When I stood back, I looked into her deep brown eyes.

"I'm glad you're happy, Candace. You're better off without him, if you want my two cents. You deserve someone who wants the same dreams *you* want."

Ahhh...there it was. Luke would never want the life I longed for. Not when he had people reacting to him the way Candace had. Not when he'd worked so long to make it all happen. And what type of woman would I be to ask him to give that up?

No, I would never ask anyone to give up their dreams. Especially the man I loved.

I smiled. "What man wouldn't take one gander at you and want you? Not only are you beautiful on the outside, but the inside as well. You've always been there for Greer, Abby, Willa, Bella, and me."

"And Kyle. Don't forget him."

I lifted a brow. "What did you do for him?"

A wicked smile appeared on her face. "He'll kill me if he knows I told anyone else, especially you. He wanted moisturizer for his face because he said it was feeling 'a little off.' His words, not mine. I went to his place, gave him a full facial mask, *and*—are you ready for this?—I gave him a manicure."

My mouth fell open. "Define manicure."

"Trimmed his cuticles, filed his nails all nice and pretty, and buffed them. I nearly had him talked into a clear nail coat, but he backed out at the last minute."

I blinked a few times as I tried to absorb that information.

"Oh, and I got him addicted to this hand cream that he's already asked me to buy for him again. The man is a skin care addict, Bree. Who knew?"

"No!" I gasped.

She nodded. "I tried to talk him into some lip care that would plump up his lips, but he drew the line at that."

"Trust me, his lips do not need to be any softer than they are." I pressed my mouth into a tight line when I realized my mistake.

Candace narrowed her eyes at me. "How do you know what his lips feel like?"

All I could do was stare at her and hope that she'd somehow forget I'd said that.

"You kissed him." She gasped. "You *are* dating!"

"No, we are not. Yes, we kissed. It was an emergency, though. It meant nothing."

Candace drew back and studied me for a moment. "The only reason you might kiss Kyle is to..." She covered her mouth with her hand. Her mind was clearly in overdrive, and I could see when she put all the pieces together. "Holy shit. His name was Luke. The guy you met at the Christmas party. Oh. My. God!"

"Candace—" I started before she threw her hands up and placed it over *my* mouth.

"You bitch! You dated Luke Walters, and you didn't tell me!"

I tried to speak, but everything was muffled by her hand still pressed to my mouth.

"Nod if you dated him."

Giving her an eye roll, I nodded.

She let out another scream.

I heard my mother calling my name and asking if everything was alright, and my heart started to race. I grabbed Candace by the shoulders and gave her a quick shake. The curls on the top of her head bounced as I attempted to bring her back to me and out of the daze of finding out I had dated Luke Walters.

I lowered my voice and gave her a deadly glare. "Listen, not a word to my mother about any of this! Yes, I dated Luke. I'll tell you all about it tonight at dinner if you promise not to say another word."

Her eyes widened. I heard my mother walking around outside the kitchen, and I took a step back and plastered on a smile as she stepped into the room.

She glanced between us, frowning, before she focused on Candace. "Candace, darling! How are things going at The Queen Bee?"

I had to hand it to her, Candace was a pro. She spun around and launched right into a conversation, not even hinting that I'd dropped a huge bomb on her.

"Things are amazing! I'm so pleased. I'm hoping to have a soft opening on May 20th. It's National Bee Day."

"How fun!" my mother said with excitement in her voice.

Candace gave a nod. "We're on the hunt for a carpenter. Bella and I need to have some shelves built for the retail part of the store."

That caused my mother to perk up even more. "A carpenter, you say?"

"Oh Lord," I whispered. I knew that tone in my mother's voice, and I vaguely remembered her trying to introduce me to a guy named Jason. He was a carpenter. A single one.

I leaned over and whispered, "Watch out, she's getting ready to hit you with a single guy."

Candace turned and said over her shoulder, "I am single and ready to mingle."

"Don't let her hear you say that!" I whisper-shouted, clearly knowing my mother could hear every word we said. She pretended to ignore us as she put her things down on the counter.

"What are you girls going on about?" My mother pulled out a few bowls from her bag and placed them in the sink.

"How are Milo and Jenny?" I asked, hoping to change the subject.

"They're doing wonderfully. Now, Candace, about this carpenter I know. Let me get his number from my desk. He's done some work around the bed and breakfast."

"He did?" I asked, knowing damn well my father did everything around the house.

My mother glowered at me. "He did. You just haven't met him yet, by your own doing. I was hoping to introduce you two, but I think Candace here is the better choice."

Candace looked at me and stuck her tongue out before my mother turned back to her.

"Is he that handy with his tools, Mom?" I asked.

Candace laughed, then coughed to cover it up.

If looks could kill, I would have been on the floor. Ignoring me, my mother wrapped her arm around Candace's and led her out of the kitchen and to her office. As they walked away, I heard my mother say, "You're going to love Jason Burns. He was born and raised up the valley in Hopetown."

Sighing, I shook my head. "Well, she went willingly, so the best of luck to her."

Chapter Thirteen

Luke

Donald Michaels, our director, was barking orders for someone to get the princess out of her tower.

"What's going on?" I asked as Hank handed me a cup of coffee.

"From what I can gather, Kathleen is upset that no one told her the big love scene was cut out of the movie and she's refusing to come out of her trailer."

I tried not to smile and took a sip of my coffee. That had been my doing. I was ready to walk away from the movie and had every intention of paying back the money I'd gotten upfront from the studio unless they cut the love scene. If it had been filmed, the movie would have certainly gotten an R rating.

Normally I wouldn't give two shits. A love scene didn't usually bother me in the least. But having Kathleen straddling me, pretending to come as I called out her name, was *not* something I was about to do—with any actress—and I told my agent it was a deal-breaker. After going back and forth, they agreed to take it out of the movie.

Apparently, no one told Kathleen. Or if they did, she figured she could get it put back in.

"You seem pleased with yourself," Hank commented. "Did you see Brighton?"

I nodded. "Yep."

"Was she surprised to see you?"

Looking at him, I replied, "You could say that. I think surprised and then pissed off. She even pretended to have a boyfriend. Kissed him in front of me and everything."

Hank's eyes widened. "Are you sure he's not her real boyfriend?"

"I'm positive. It's Kyle, one of the cops."

"The one she used to say drove her to near insanity?"

I lifted my cup at him. "That's the one. He also recognized me, but I have to hand it to him, he played it off well. Dude could have an acting career if the cop thing doesn't work out."

Hank chuckled. "How long are you going to let her think you believe it?"

I lifted one shoulder. "I'm not sure. It could be a lot of fun."

"You do remember this is Brighton, right? She could chew you up into a million pieces, spit you out, and not give two shits."

"No," I replied, shaking my head. "You didn't see the way she looked at me, Hank. I know she still loves me, and I'm not giving up."

"I hate to break this to you, Luke, but you walked away from her. She left Boston and moved back home. I don't think she's going to welcome you back with open arms. And the look she gave you...how fast was it before it turned to something else?"

I laughed. "Two-point-five seconds. Then she looked like she wanted to rip my balls off and shove them down my throat."

"Hope you have a plan, friend."

Turning to face him, I said, "You know I had things I needed to take care of first."

All he did was nod.

"She wants a life away from all of this," I continued as I motioned toward the outdoor set. "I needed to make sure—a hundred percent sure—I could do that."

"And this is what you want, Luke? To walk away from a career you've worked hard to build?"

"If it means having Brighton in my life, then yes. I'd gladly leave it all behind for her. I wasn't happy until she walked up to me at that

Christmas party. The moment she smiled at me, it was like she took a match right to my heart and lit it on fire. I knew my life would never be the same. It gave me a high I've never experienced before, and I doubt I ever will again. Loving her is like discovering something beautiful every single day. And ever since she told me to leave her office, my world has felt black."

"It's been what...four months? Are you sure she feels the same way about you?"

I thought about his question for a moment and then looked toward the mountains in the distance. "I can only hope that the love she felt for me was as strong as mine still is for her. And for the briefest of moments, I saw it in her eyes. She still loves me."

"Back to my other statement: I hope you have a plan."

Laughing, I shook my head. "I have no fucking clue what I'm doing."

Hank hit me on the back. "You already know how I feel about her, so the best I can do is wish you luck. You're gonna need it."

Kathleen came storming out of her trailer and looked around. The moment she saw me, her face drew into a frown. She stomped her way over, and I heard Hank whisper something under his breath. Her assistant, Lanny, was trying to keep up with her while holding Kathleen's little dog, Sweet Pea, in her arms.

"Ms. Daughtry, I haven't taken off the—"

"Not now, Lanny! Go take Sweet Pea for a potty break."

"But, Ms. Daughtry!"

Kathleen came to a halt, turned, and pointed for Lanny to walk away. The poor girl shrank and quickly headed off in the opposite direction. Kathleen drew in a deep breath, then continued to march toward me.

Hank hit me on the back again. "And this is where I'm tapping out. Good luck."

Kathleen came to an abrupt halt in front of me. "Who in the fuck do you think you are?"

I did a quick sweep of her. Her clothes looked as if she had quickly thrown them on and she had white shit smeared all over her face. She had clearly rushed out of her trailer without so much as a glimpse in the mirror. "You seem...out of sorts, Kathleen."

She folded her arms over her chest and shot daggers at me. "They just informed me that the one and only major sex scene in the script is no longer happening. And the worst part is that it was decided three months ago!"

I tilted my head and smiled. "Four, to be exact. At the end of January. It's May now."

She stomped her feet, causing the mask on her face—that she clearly forgot was on—to crack slightly. "I know what fucking month it is, Luke! Why was I not told?"

Lifting my hand, I pointed to her face. "Do you not feel that thing cracking?"

Her eyes went wide as she pressed both hands to her cheeks. She let out a horrified gasp and spun around, practically sprinting back to her trailer. All the while, she screamed for her assistant Lanny and added, "You are fired after you get this off my face!"

I heard a long sigh from behind me, and I turned to see the director, Donald, standing there. "I told the studio that keeping it from her would be a disaster. They wouldn't listen."

I smiled. "Look at it this way, Donald, if she'd been told, she would have complained constantly for the last few months and driven us all insane."

He nodded as he let that sink in. "True. She does seem overly upset about it. I think she was really looking forward to that scene with you."

Our eyes met, but neither of us said a damn word for a few moments.

"You could always get a stunt double to play me if she wants the scene in there so badly..." I said.

"You know as well as I do the scene has been removed from the script."

"I do know that."

A wicked grin appeared on his face. "Oh, but to see her face when I suggest a stunt double. I'll need to make sure someone's filming it."

And with that, Donald headed off in another direction, clearly plotting. He wasn't normally petty like this, but something about Kathleen brought out the devil in a person.

"Mr. Walters, wardrobe is waiting for you."

I finished off my coffee and tossed it in the trash before I headed to wardrobe. I whistled a happy little tune the entire time, knowing this would be one of the last times I'd make this walk.

As I strolled into the Willow Tree Bed and Breakfast hours later, I came to an abrupt halt. Bree was standing there, dressed in a snug-fitting black dress that fell above her knees. Her brown hair was pulled up and piled on top of her head, with a few curls hanging down her neck.

I swallowed hard and let my eyes move down her body until I saw the black high heels she was wearing. She looked beautiful, and every hair on my body rose when she slowly turned and met my gaze.

"Mr. Cummington," she said.

"Cunningham, Brighton," her mother corrected as she came around the small desk area in the foyer. "How was your day? Did you get to drive around the valley like you mentioned?"

Bree lifted a single brow and waited for my answer.

"I enjoyed the drive up the valley," I said, "and even stumbled onto a movie set."

Folding her arms over her chest, Bree fought to keep the corners of her mouth from tipping up into a smile.

"Oh! How lovely," her mother replied.

"Thank you for the tray earlier today, Mrs. Rogers."

Bree's mom waved her hand. "Please, none of that here. You can call me Joanne and my husband Ron."

I nodded. "Will do."

Joanne turned and looked at Bree. "I'm guessing you've already met my daughter, Brighton. Today is her birthday, and she's going out to dinner—"

Bree quickly cut her mother off. "We met earlier, Mom. I really need to get going."

"Is Kyle not picking you up?" I asked.

Joanne frowned and looked at Bree. "Why would—"

"He's working late," Bree said, interrupting her mother again. "But don't worry, it's not the first time a man has asked me to meet him at a restaurant."

I felt the hit right in my gut. My smile faded slightly before I cleared my throat. "I hope you enjoy your birthday this evening."

"Oh, I will. Trust me. I plan on enjoying it over, and over, and over."

Joanne stared at Bree with a look of utter confusion.

I nodded, then looked at Joanne. "If you'll excuse me, I've got to get ready as well. I have plans this evening."

The smirk on Bree's face disappeared, and she turned away from me as I walked by and headed up the stairs to my room.

"Enjoy your evening, Mr. Cunningham!" Joanne called out.

The moment I got to my room and shut the door, I let out a string of curses. I hadn't come to Boggy Creek to play these fucking games. I wanted to talk to Bree, but she clearly preferred to pretend she was going out to dinner with her fake boyfriend and that they'd be having sex all night.

Sighing, I pulled my wallet and keys out of my pockets and tossed them onto the small table in the room. I looked at the little basket that had been here when I'd checked in. There were shortbread cookies inside, along with a notepad and pen, mints, a chocolate bar, and a handwritten note from Joanne.

The room was a bright, cheery yellow, with a light blue comforter and blue sheets. On the bedside table sat a small bottle of lavender spray with a note that suggested I spray my pillow for a good night's sleep.

The rest of the room was decorated in soft blues and yellows, with an antique dresser and writing desk. The queen-size bed also had an antique frame and the most amazingly intricate carvings I had ever seen in wood. It was beautiful. I imagined all the rooms in the bed and breakfast were decorated in a similar fashion. A large picture window with a cushioned seat overlooked the huge backyard. A small pillow sat on it that read "A Bushel and a Peck." That seemed to be Joanne's favorite saying. I had seen it numerous times already, and I'd only checked in this morning.

I sat down on the bed and rubbed at the back of my neck. Kyle had mentioned where he was taking Bree to dinner tonight, and part of me wanted to show up, just to see what Bree would do. It was obvious to me that the two of them weren't a couple. I was an actor, and I could spot an act a mile away.

"Christ, you can't show up alone, Luke," I said to myself. Standing, I started to pace...then smiled. I reached for my phone and pulled up Hank's number.

"You couldn't possibly need me already," he answered, sighing heavily into the phone.

"I don't need you. I need Arianna."

There was a short pause. "Why do you need my sister?"

"I need a date."

"A date?" Hank asked, surprise in his voice.

"Yes. I mean, with Brighton acting like she's dating someone, I can't show up alone."

"So you want to use my sister in this little game?"

"Brighton started it," I said.

"Really, Luke? That's the best you can come up with? Hold on. Arianna wants to know what's going on."

The phone was muffled, and I could barely hear Hank talk to his sister. When he came back on the line, he was clearly agitated.

"I think this is a mistake, but it seems like Arianna is into the deception."

I cackled. "Deception? I'm not going to hang on her like she's my date. I simply need her to show up with me."

"To make Bree *think* you're on a date."

I sighed. "I guess it is rather childish."

"Thank God you see the light."

I stood and started to pace around the room. The image of Bree in that black dress had my body tightening up like a damn coil. "Tell Arianna thanks, but I think I've come to my senses."

"No thanks to me, huh?" Hank stated.

"I'll give you a raise."

He laughed. "May I suggest you get the woman you love back and do it the right way. Not with childish games."

Arianna called out in the background, "He's a killjoy!"

It was true, Hank was, but he was also the one person who always knew how to bring me back to my senses. And the only reason Arianna was up for it was because it would give her a chance to practice her acting. She had a small role in the movie, but Hank was trying desperately to talk her into staying in nursing school. I couldn't blame him.

"I think I'll head down and have dinner with the rest of the guests," I said.

"What if someone recognizes you?"

Shrugging even though he couldn't see me, I replied, "It's worth the risk. I don't think I can eat any more takeout, and the menu in the room says it's meatloaf tonight."

Hank laughed. "Enjoy your evening, boss."

"Hank?"

"Yeah?"

"Thank you for not letting me fuck this up on the first day."

I could hear the smile in his voice as he replied, "That's what friends are for."

Chapter Fourteen

Bree

The moment we walked into Bella's, I let out a curse.

"What in the hell?" I stopped and turned to Kyle.

He held up his hands and smiled. "It wasn't me, Bree, I swear. I didn't tell anyone about Luke or dinner tonight."

I slowly turned back around and scanned the large table to count seven of my closet friends sitting there. None of them had noticed us walk in yet, their heads bent in conversation. And sitting at the very end of the table was Candace.

"Candace," I whispered, clenching my fists.

"Always knew she was the troublemaker out of the two of you," Kyle said with a shake of his head.

I shot him a look, then focused back on our friends. "Did you bring your handcuffs, by any chance?"

I could see Kyle's confused expression from the corner of my eye. "Um, no. I didn't think it was that kind of date."

I growled. "You should have, because I may kill Candace Reynolds by the end of this dinner." Even though a part of me was grateful that I'd finally be able to get the story out once and for all.

Before he could say a word, I marched—well, attempted to in my high heels—to the table and stood there, my hands on my hips as I glared at Candace. She met my eyes and smiled. She actually smiled.

"Do you want to tell me why everyone is here?" I asked.

"It's your birthday!" she declared.

I slowly shook my head. "I can't believe you told them about Luke, Candace."

She quickly stood and started to wave her hands. "I didn't—"

"You promised me! I wasn't ready to tell everyone I'd dated him."

"You've got it all wrong," she said, looking around at everyone and then back at me. "They don't—"

"Don't even try!" I turned to Willa. "She told you I dated Luke Walters, and you all came to hear the story."

Willa's eyes went wide as Hunter and Hudson both said, "Holy shit!"

Aiden looked around. "Who's Luke Walters?"

"You don't know who Luke Walters is?" This came from Kyle. "Dude, he was in that movie—"

"*Till Death Do Us Part*," Hudson, Hunter, and Kyle all said in unison.

Aiden shrugged. "No clue."

Bella added, "Me either."

"I don't know who he is either," Greer said.

Candace laughed. "That's because your nose is always in a book, Greer. And Bella, you're too busy with the bees and Hunter."

Bella's cheeks turned a bright pink, and Hunter leaned over and kissed her softly.

"When was the last time either one of you even watched a movie?" Candace tossed out to Bella and Greer.

"Really, sweetheart? You don't know who Luke Walters is?" Hudson asked his fiancée. Greer shook her head.

"I know who he is," Willa said, her eyes boring into me with such anger, I stepped behind Kyle. "How could you not tell me he was *the* Luke?"

Suddenly, Greer gasped. "Luke? *Luke* the blind date last Christmas?"

"Bree was home last Christmas," Bella said.

"No, not this past Christmas. The one before that. After Willa and Aiden got married," Greer clarified. "She had a blind date with her boss's son."

"I'm so confused," Aiden mumbled.

Candace sighed and dropped back down into her seat. "I mentioned to Greer I was meeting you and Kyle for your birthday tonight, and before I knew it, everyone wanted to come."

Kyle placed his hand on my lower back and guided me over to the opposite end of the table. "You should take the other head of the table, so you can tell everyone about how you've been lying to us the last year or so."

Before he could pull the chair out for me, I stepped on his foot with my heel.

He started to let out a curse but held it in.

"Oh, so sorry, darling," I purred as I sat down and Kyle sat next to Hunter.

"Darling?" Hunter asked Kyle.

Kyle shrugged. "We're fake dating."

Three female voices cried out, "What?"

Candace grinned, lifted her wine glass, and took a sip.

Directing my attention down the table toward her, I said, "I'm sorry I accused you of blabbing your mouth."

"It's fine. I'll need to borrow that green velvet dress you have."

I gasped. "No, not the green velvet."

Everyone swung their gazes from me to Candace. "Yes, that one."

All eyes were back on me. "That is a two-thousand-dollar dress, Candace."

A wicked smile appeared on her face. "I know...*darling*."

"Okay." Willa tossed her hands up in the air. "Enough of this."

It was then I noticed the two empty chairs. "Where are Abby and Bishop?"

"Here we are!" Abby's voice called out. She looked adorable in a cream-colored dress that showed off her little pregnant bump.

Bishop glanced around as he held the chair out for his wife. "What did we miss?"

Everyone turned to look at me.

Twenty minutes later, all of my friends were caught up. I had also informed them that Luke had indeed tried to reach out numerous times after I'd fled from the...scene of the kiss.

"But he hasn't contacted you since you told him to leave your office?" Abby asked while she ran her hand over her tummy.

Taking a sip of my third drink, I shook my head. "No."

"And he showed up out of the blue today on your birthday?" Bishop asked.

Nodding, I replied, "Yep."

"What a douche," Hunter said. "I'm never ever watching another one of his movies."

I couldn't help but smile at him. I loved my friends. Sighing, I replied, "It's for the better. It would have never worked."

"Why not?" Willa asked. "You said you loved him, and now that you've reflected on things, you don't think he cheated. So why do you think it wouldn't work?"

Hudson caught my eye. He was a writer—a famous writer. Not as famous as Luke, but there were moments when someone recognized him. Greer had even admitted to me once that when they were in Boston at one of his book signings, she was stunned by the number of women who paid him so much attention. I had assured her it was because he wrote good books and not because he was handsome. She didn't call me out, but I was pretty sure she knew I was feeding her a line of bullshit.

"He wasn't going to leave his career, and I would never ask him to," I said. "I wasn't going to move to LA, and the back-and-forth, long-distance relationship couldn't last much longer. Not to mention having to watch him have pretend sex with other women. I don't want that. I mean, I know I dated him, and I let myself believe it would all be okay. But I was also living in a world of make believe. I guess I was doing a bit of acting myself."

"How do you know he won't give up acting? Did you ask him?" Kyle asked.

I chewed on my lip. "No. The last time we talked was that day in my office."

"No," he said with a laugh. "It was earlier today, when he was standing in the lobby of the Willow Tree."

Gasps echoed through the restaurant, and other tables turned to look in our direction.

"Oh yeah, I forgot to mention, he's in Boggy Creek," Candace stated.

Hunter nearly jumped up out of his seat. "Mark Johnson is here? In Boggy Creek?"

Kyle nodded in excitement. "Dude, right?"

"Wait, I'm still confused. Who's Mark Johnson?" Aiden asked.

"Luke Walters," Hudson said with a laugh. "It's the character he played in *Till Death Do Us Part*."

Bishop cleared his throat and raised his hand as if seeking permission to speak. I rolled my eyes and said, "Yes, Bishop?"

"So this guy you dated for a year suddenly shows up at your folks' bed and breakfast, and you don't find that odd?"

"Of course I find it odd! I'm confused, angry, confused."

"You said confused already," Kyle whispered.

I glared at him. "I wasn't expecting it, and when he showed up, I panicked. Then Kyle walked in, and we kissed."

Everyone's eyes went wide with either confusion or shock.

"Wait, wait," Willa said. "You kissed Luke?"

I sank down in my chair while Kyle started to look everywhere except at me or our friends.

"Holy shit," Bishop said.

"What? I'm missing something," Bella said.

Hunter turned and looked at Kyle. "You?"

Kyle frowned. "Don't sound so surprised."

Hunter, Bishop, Hudson and Aiden all busted out laughing.

"What's so funny?" Kyle asked, his voice a few pitches too high.

Greer covered her mouth to keep her own laughter at bay, then looked at me. "Bree, you honestly kissed my brother?"

"It was an emergency!" I said, reaching for Kyle's beer and nearly downing it in one drink.

"Hey, we may be fake dating, but that doesn't mean you get to drink my real beer."

Willa placed her finger and thumb on the bridge of her nose. "Let me get this straight, because I feel like things are spiraling out of control."

"You think?" Candace mumbled.

Willa shot Candace a look that said zip it, then focused on me. "Luke showed up at the bed and breakfast this morning?"

"Yes, he checked in while I was out on a run."

"Then you found out he was there, and Kyle showed up...why did Kyle show up?" Willa asked.

Kyle frowned. "To wish her a happy birthday! Geesh, I'm not *that* much of a dick. Plus, I wanted to see if Joanne had made any of those lavender cookies she puts out every day."

I slowly turned and glared at him. "You stopped by looking for cookies?"

"And to wish you happy birthday, *darling*."

Willa cleared her throat. "And while Kyle was there, what prompted you to...kiss him? I'm guessing Luke was there to witness said kiss?"

Kyle and I both nodded.

"I panicked, okay?" I said. "He was there, standing in front of me, and all these emotions and memories came flooding back and I wasn't ready to face him. So when Kyle walked in, I said he was my boyfriend."

"Holy shit, this is better than a book," Candace said to Greer.

Hudson nodded. "I wish I'd brought my notebook, dammit."

157

I shot Hudson a look, and he held up his hands. "I'm kidding. Sorta."

"Brighton," Willa said in that mom voice she'd perfected. "What were you thinking? Now you've dragged Kyle into this."

Candace lifted her hand. "By the way, how was the kiss? Curious minds want to know."

Abby and Bella both giggled and looked at me. Everyone was looking at me, including Kyle, who wore a smirk as he waited for my answer.

My head pounded. I wanted to rewind the clock and start this day over.

"The crowd is waiting," Hunter said with a laugh.

I stalled, hoping the waitress would walk up with our food. After one quick glance around the restaurant, I let go of that dream.

Kyle cleared his throat, and I turned to look at him. Through gritted teeth, I forced a smile, looked down at the table, and said, "It was a good kiss."

"Tongue?" Bishop asked, and Abby hit him on the shoulder.

I felt my neck go hot and then my cheeks.

Bella sucked in a breath while Willa stared at me. When I looked at Greer, she looked like she might throw up. Candace smirked, and Hudson, Aiden, and Hunter all waited for my reply.

"Yes. Tongue," I blurted out. "We had to make it believable!"

Kyle let out a dramatic sigh. "It was a sacrifice, but I was willing to do it for a friend."

I nearly growled as I shot him a dirty look and whispered, "I really hate you."

He winked. The bastard actually winked.

"Can we all agree that I made a poor decision?" I raised my wine glass when I saw the waitress. "Another one, please!"

She nodded and spun around to head to the bar.

"Which one?" Abby asked.

I felt my entire body go stiff and a cold sensation rush through my veins. "What do you mean, which one?"

She wasn't pulling any punches, and I wasn't sure if it was her pregnancy hormones or what. But she said without a bit of malice in her voice, "The pretending Kyle was your boyfriend, or the one where you told Luke to leave?"

A sudden sting of unshed tears made me blink rapidly. I had to force my throat to swallow the sob lodged there. Abby wasn't being unkind; she didn't have a mean bone in her body. She was being honest.

I felt Kyle reach for my hand and give it a squeeze. I pushed down my emotions and was about to put a fake smile on my face when something inside of me cracked.

I realized then that these were my friends. My people. My tribe. I had spent the last year keeping a huge part of my life a secret from them—and I was tired of doing it. I was tired of always having my shit together, or at least acting like I did.

My mouth opened, and what came out next should have surprised me, but it didn't. "Both," I answered softly as a single tear slipped free and ran down my cheek.

Chapter Fifteen

Bree

After everyone at the table saw that tear, Hunter and Bishop offered to rough up Luke. Kyle said he'd arrest him on set for some made-up offense that would embarrass him and be in the tabloids before his fingerprints dried. Hudson declared he would name his next fictional villain Luke—and kill him off. I had the best friends.

Abby, Bella, Willa, Greer, and Candace all took turns hugging me and telling me it would be okay. Our food came, and I smiled and said we needed a change of topic. So, Greer asked Bella and Abby how they were feeling. Baby shower talk started, as well as a discussion about whether we should have Greer's bachelorette party before Abby got too big to grind on a male stripper, which Bishop didn't think was funny.

Candace talked about The Queen Bee, which was having a soft opening next Wednesday. I tried to keep up with all of the conversations, but all the alcohol I drank and the urge to crawl into my bed and hide there for days kept my mind distracted. Still, I smiled, laughed, nodded, and contributed when I needed to.

The only person who saw through my bullshit was Kyle. And God, that annoyed the hell out of me. I liked our pretend hate for one another, and him being kind and sweet to me was throwing me off. So when he tossed his napkin on the table and declared he needed to get home, I jumped at the chance to leave with him. After all, it wouldn't look right if someone else brought me home. When Luke heard I was meeting Kyle at the restaurant, something in me had snapped and I'd quickly texted Kyle to pick me up, and of course, he'd agreed.

"I can give you a ride home later," Candace offered.

I shook my head and waved her off. "No. Thanks, but I'm tired."

Kyle had already slipped his credit card to the waitress and taken care of everyone's dinner.

"Thank you for the amazing birthday dinner, you guys. I'm so glad we were all able to get together," I said, standing when Kyle pulled out my chair.

Everyone thanked Kyle and wished us both a good night, and we hurried out of the restaurant.

Kyle pulled his SUV up to the small cottage I was staying in at my folks' place and parked. I remained in my seat, feeling numb, unable to make myself get out.

"Do you want me to come in for a bit?" he asked.

I turned and looked at the firepit. My father had started a fire, and my breath caught when I saw Luke sitting around it with the other guests who were staying at the bed and breakfast. I couldn't help but wonder if anyone knew who he was. He hadn't seen us pull up, or if he had, he didn't seem to care. He was talking to a younger couple who were roasting marshmallows over the fire.

"Bree, I know I don't have any room to give dating advice, but don't you think you should at least talk to him? I mean, he's here, so that must mean something. Right?"

Drawing in a shaky breath, I looked over at Kyle. "The sensible part of my brain says yes. The other part, the scared part, says no."

"What are you scared of?"

I dropped my head and looked down at my hands where I was twisting them in my lap. "I wish I knew. Maybe I'm scared that if I let him in, he'll break my heart."

"It seems to me, Bree, that your heart is already breaking."

"Then I'm afraid he'll shatter it. I've never felt this way before, Kyle. What I mean is...when I was with him, I felt so alive. Like everything in my life was complete. It was full. I'd never felt that way before about anyone. I started to dream of what a future would be like with him. Even while I was living in that stupid make-believe world. I know I can't have that dream, and allowing him back in would only prolong everything."

"Prolong what?"

My eyes burned from attempting to keep my tears at bay. "The end, Kyle. It will only prolong the end. I know what I want, and I can't have the kind of life I want if I'm with Luke."

His brows pulled in. "So it's all or nothing for you? What a selfish thing to say."

I jerked my head back up to look at him. My next word was barely above a whisper. "What?"

"I may not know a whole lot about relationships from personal experience, but I can tell you I've seen what happens when two people love one another. They sacrifice for each other. My mother and father... Do you know how many nights I remember watching my mother sit in the living room, crying because she was afraid something had happened to my father? I don't think for one moment she ever enjoyed those nights. But she stayed by his side because she loved him.

"And my father gave up the chance to be police chief in Boston because he knew it would only cause my mother more worry and stress. It had been his dream since he was a little boy to be a police chief in a city like Boston, but he didn't think twice about not taking the job. And look at Greer and Hudson. He moved to Boggy Creek for her.

"Sacrifice. That's what I think of when I look at people in love. Nothing in this fucking world is supposed to come easily, Bree. Did you ever tell Luke you didn't want to move to LA? Did you ever talk about a future with him or tell him what your dreams were? How do you even know what his thoughts might be on all of this? How do you know he wouldn't walk away from it all for you unless you talk to him about it?"

My chin trembled, and I ran my tongue over my suddenly dry lips. I reached up and felt the wet tears on my cheeks. "I'm crying. What the fuck, Kyle!"

He let out a soft laugh as he shook his head. "Bree, I get being confused. I get not knowing what's up or down. But if you really love this guy, and if you think for one moment he's here in Boggy Creek to prove that he loves *you*, then don't throw it away. I have a feeling love—true love—the kind of love that makes your breath catch in your throat and your heart feel like it's in a free fall, only comes into our life once. Don't let it slip through your fingers. You've been running for four months, Bree. It's time to stop now because he's caught up with you."

I sniffled and looked around Kyle's car. A Kleenex suddenly appeared in front of me. I took it and blew my nose. "What in the hell is happening? When did you become so good at advice? You're supposed to be handsome and dim-witted."

He smiled. "I knew you thought I was handsome."

I laughed. A good old-fashioned, belly laugh. Of course he would pick up on that word and not the dim-wit part.

"I've said this before: I can be deep," he said. "I've seen things."

My eyes met his, and I couldn't help but smile. "If you tell anyone I cried, I'll deny it. Then I'll tell everyone you like to give yourself facials."

Kyle's smile instantly faded. "Candace promised she wouldn't tell anyone!"

I chuckled again and leaned over and hugged him. "Thank you so much, Kyle. I needed someone to hit me with the cold, hard truth."

"So you'll talk to him, then?" he asked with a hopeful expression.

Sitting up straighter, I glanced back toward the firepit where Luke still sat. With a nod, I stated, "I will, but I am *not* going to make it easy for him. He's going to have to work for it."

Kyle sighed. "Why doesn't that surprise me?"

I glanced back at him and smiled. "I think we're going to have to break up now."

He mocked sadness by clutching at his heart and pretending to wipe away a tear. "And to think I had tickets to see BLACKPINK, and I was going to take you."

"What? Shut up! You have tickets?"

Laughing, he said, "I do, but don't worry—I bought four tickets. I only wanted three, but the damn site made me buy them in pairs. I thought you, me, and Willa could go. The concert's in Boston."

"Yes! I know!" I said, bouncing in my seat. "The sixth of November. Who's the fourth person going to be?"

He shrugged. "We've got plenty of time to figure it out, since it's only mid-May."

"Right."

He looked past my shoulder, and I turned to see Luke walking up the pathway toward the main house.

"You going to talk to him tonight?"

With a shake of my head, I said, "No. I'm exhausted, and I'm going to watch a movie and get the hell out of this dress. It's so uncomfortable."

"Well, you look amazing in it."

Smiling, I replied, "Thank you. What are you going to do? The night's still young. Go find a pretty little thing to spend the evening with?"

His laugh came out devoid of any humor. "Nah. I'm going home to snuggle up with my girl and probably watch a movie myself."

Frowning, I tilted my head and regarded him. Now that I thought about it, Kyle hadn't mentioned going out with anyone in a long time. I wasn't even sure if he went out at all anymore. With Aiden, Hudson, Hunter, Kyle, and Bishop all either happily married or about to be, he was the only single one left in the group. Well, single male.

"When was the last time you went on a date?"

He winked. "About thirty minutes ago, if you could call tonight a date."

"Okay, before tonight?"

Kyle shrugged. "I don't know. It's been awhile."

I fully turned in the seat and looked at him. "Why?"

He glanced away, but not before I saw something cross over his face, though I couldn't exactly read his expression in the darkened vehicle. "I've been busy at work and training Cat."

A strange pang of sympathy hit me right in the middle of the chest. Good Lord, was I feeling sorry for this man? Of course, I was. He could be a pain in the ass sometimes, but when it came down to it, he was my friend, and I knew there wasn't anything he wouldn't do for me.

"Who is she?" I asked softly.

He drew in a slow, deep breath before he let it out and looked back at me. "Someone I let slip away. So don't make that same mistake, my friend."

All I could do was nod.

The next morning, I walked into the dining area and came to an abrupt halt. Sitting at the large table for twelve was Luke. He looked devilishly handsome. I stared at him for a beat too long, because when I finally managed to drag my eyes off of him and look around the table, everyone else was staring at *me*. Including my father, a deep crease between his eyes.

"Good morning, Brighton!" my mother said as she walked in and set a large plate of biscuits in the middle of the table. "Darling, will you help me with the gravy?"

All I could do was nod, then smile at the rest of the guests before I gave my father a look. He was still frowning.

Once we were in the kitchen, I asked, "What's wrong with Dad? He looks pissed at me for some reason."

My mother handed me the gravy bowl and smiled. "He's not mad at you, darling."

"Then why is he giving me a death stare?"

"He heard about your date with Kyle."

I rolled my eyes. "It wasn't a date. Everyone was there. Kyle simply picked me up."

She paused what she was doing and looked at me with a confused expression that appeared to be fake. "Why, Luke told us you were dating."

Sighing, I said, "I only told Luke that…"

Mom tilted her head and lifted her brows. "Go on."

"Wait. How did you know his name was Luke?"

"He told us."

I blinked. A lot. As if there was something caught in both eyes and the only way to get it out was to rapidly blink like an idiot. Somehow, I was able to stop *and* find my voice at the same time. "He told you *what*, exactly?"

She nodded and reached for a plate of freshly cut-up fruit. "Your father said he looked like a younger version of Gene Kelly at the dinner table last night. Then, one of our other guests laughed and said he looked a lot like Luke Walters, the actor, and he admitted he was him. I thought the poor guy, who was clearly a fan, was going to pass right out into the fire! Your father thankfully kept him from doing so."

I exhaled and leaned against the counter. "Did he tell you everything?"

She stopped what she was doing. "Everything? What else would he need to tell us?"

Oh. Shit. Open mouth and insert foot.

"Nothing," I said entirely too quickly. My mother wasn't a fool, and she immediately knew I was lying.

She gently set down the plate of fruit, crossed her arms, and stared at me. I could hear her foot tapping on the old wood floor. "Brighton Willow Rogers. You're not telling me something."

166

I nodded. "You're right. I'm not, and now is not the time to talk about it, Mom. I'll tell you and Dad everything after breakfast."

She narrowed her eyes at me. After what felt like an eternity, she replied, "Fine. Let's go join everyone else for breakfast."

"I wasn't—"

She snapped her head up and shot me a look that warned me not to finish what I was going to say. So, like any smart woman who knew when her mother was giving her *the look*, I smiled and held up the gravy bowl. "Let's eat."

As we made our way back into the large dining room, I saw that small conversations were happening at the table. Luke was talking to a man who appeared to be about the same age as him. The man's wife or girlfriend smiled up at me as I walked in and placed the gravy in the middle of the table.

"My mother makes the best gravy you'll ever eat," I said in an overly chipper tone.

"You must be Brighton," the young woman said. "Your mother and father told us all about you last night when we were out by the fire. You're a lawyer! How exciting. I thought I wanted to go to law school, but it wasn't for me."

"Are you still in school, then?" I asked.

She laughed. "Oh gosh, no. I graduated about six years ago."

Okay, she looked young for her age.

"Will and I are on our honeymoon!"

Smiling, I looked at the guy sitting next to her who was still talking to Luke.

"Congratulations to you both," I said. "We have a lot of newlyweds who stay with us."

"So I heard. There was a beautiful basket up in our room filled with such lovely things when we checked in," the young woman said.

My mother joined the conversation then. "Brighton made that basket."

The woman turned in her chair and beamed at me. "Thank you so much! I think the cookies are my favorite. Oh, and the rosemary bread with the honey. So good. By the way, my name is Kathleen."

I tried really hard not to gag at the poor girl's name. It wasn't her fault I hated that name now. I internally rolled my eyes at myself. *Seriously, Brighton. How can you hate a name simply because the devil in disguise shares the same one?*

"It's nice to meet you...Kathleen," I choked out.

"Call me Lee, everyone does."

"Thank God," I whispered.

"Excuse me?" she asked with a tilt of her head that caused her ponytail to swish back and forth.

"Nothing," I said as held up the fruit plate. "Fruit?"

She smiled sweetly, took the large spoon, and put some on her plate.

My mother and Lee were soon lost in a conversation about all the hiking trails in the area. I listened halfheartedly as I tried not to look at Luke. Tried and failed. At least a dozen times. Lee's husband kept him engaged in conversation nearly the entire time.

When Lee finally decided they needed to get out and take advantage of the day, Luke leaned back in his chair, dabbed the corners of his mouth with his napkin, and looked at my mother. "Joanne, thank you so much for the lovely breakfast. I need to be heading off."

My mother beamed at Luke. "Of course. Leave your plate, we'll take care of it."

Luke nodded, smiled, and then stood. "Ron, thank you."

Daddy smiled politely. "Of course. Have a good day, son."

Son? Son? Did my father just call him...son?

When my father caught me staring at him, he shrugged. I turned and looked at Luke. My throat felt like it was clogged up with cotton.

When he looked at me and smiled, my insides warmed. "Brighton, enjoy your day."

All I could do was nod. I had woken up this morning honestly praying yesterday had been a dream. In case it hadn't, I took time to fix my hair, put on a bit of makeup, and dressed in something other than yoga pants and a Willow Tree B & B T-shirt.

168

I watched as Luke pushed his chair in and started out of the dining room. I wasn't sure how long I stared at the empty doorway before another guest excused themselves, and I pulled myself back into the moment.

Two other guests remained, and I somehow managed to engage in the conversation, when all I really wanted to do was run up the steps, throw open Luke's door, and ask him what in the hell he was doing here. Was he trying to torture me? Because if he was, he was doing a fine job of it.

I heard Lee, her husband—whose name I hadn't caught—and Luke all chatting as they walked through the lobby area and out the front door.

"Excuse me," I said as I quickly stood, nearly knocking over my chair in the process. My mother and father both stared at me with surprised expressions. I would have to deal with them later. Right now, I needed to talk to Luke.

I bolted out the front door and down the steps. The parking lot for the bed and breakfast was to my left, so I headed down the side path where I saw Lee and her husband get into a Ford Explorer. Lee waved, and I lifted my hand and waved back. Luke was opening the door to a black Toyota Camry. I called out his name, and he stopped right before he was about to slide in.

"Whose car is this?" I asked.

He looked at the car, then back at me. "It's mine."

"Where's your motorcycle?"

"Back in Boston. I didn't really want to draw attention to myself, so I bought this car."

"Draw attention to yourself?" I repeated.

He nodded. "Yes."

"Then why did you tell my parents who you were?"

"One of the guests recognized me, so I thought it would be best to fess up. When I said I was looking for a bit of privacy, they all understood."

I worked at swallowing the words that seemed to be stuck in the bottom of my throat. "And you didn't tell my parents about us?"

He tilted his head slightly. "No."

I nodded and realized I was wringing my hands together.

When he looked down, I dropped my hands to my side. "Are you heading to the set?"

"Yes."

"How long will you be here? I mean, how much longer is filming? If...you're planning on staying here the whole time."

"We've got a week left, then it'll wrap up. We only needed to be in this location for a few scenes."

My heart dropped, and I tried like hell not to show it. "A week?" Ugh. I hated that my voice sounded so pathetic. We stood there and stared at one another before I finally cleared my throat and asked, "Why are you here, Luke?"

His shoulders relaxed some as the corners of his mouth rose slightly. "I wanted to see you. And talk to you. I told you that yesterday."

My stomach flipped, and I had to fight the urge to throw myself at him. "Okay."

Luke's brows rose. "Okay?"

"Yes," I said with a firm nod. "We can talk."

When his mouth twitched, I knew he was holding back a smile. "Are you free for a late lunch? If Kyle doesn't mind, that is."

Oh man, you really dug a hole for yourself, Bree. "Kyle and I aren't dating."

"No?" Luke asked with obvious mock surprise.

I glared at him. "I think you already knew that, though."

He let out a soft laugh. "I had an idea, but your father confirmed it last night when he laughed his ass off and said you'd rather have your eyes ripped out than date Kyle Larson."

I let out an exasperated sigh and mumbled, "Good ol' Dad."

His smile faded, and he looked at his watch. "Listen, I wish I could stay and talk to you now, but I need to get going. Lunch around two?"

Ignoring the way my heart betrayed me with a little flutter of anticipation, I replied, "Sure. That works. I'll meet you at the front desk."

A brilliant smile appeared on his handsome face, and I couldn't help but notice those dark eyes of his sparkling with something that looked like hope. "See you then, Bree."

He slipped into the car, started it, then pulled away while I stayed rooted in the same spot until I could no longer see the car. All I could do now was pray that I wasn't opening myself up for more hurt.

I braced myself as I headed back toward the house and slowly made my way up the front steps. Quietly, I opened the door and stepped in. I could hear my mother and father in the kitchen cleaning up, and I tried to decide if I should turn and leave or help them. MaryLou wasn't here this morning, so I knew my mother needed the help.

"Chicken," I whispered as I walked into the dining room, grabbed some things off the table, and headed into the kitchen.

"Do you need me to make anything for dinner tonight before I head out for a run?" I asked, keeping my back to them both while I walked over to the sink. When neither of them said anything, I slowly turned around.

Two sets of narrowed eyes stared back at me. My father had his arms folded across his chest, and my mother looked like she wanted to be excited, but wasn't hatching her chickens quite yet.

"How about you tell us why you lied and told Luke you were dating Kyle?" my father said. "And while you're at it, fill us in on how, exactly, you know Mr. Luke Walters."

I swallowed hard and glanced at the doorway that led out of the kitchen.

Mom laughed. "Don't even think of running, Brighton."

With a defeated sigh, I said, "For starters, his name is Luke Morrison. And we dated for over a year."

My mother clutched at her chest. "Ron, get the whiskey."

He snapped his head around and looked at her. "It's eight in the morning, Joanne."

She sank down in a chair. "Trust me, I'm going to need it."

Chapter Sixteen

Luke

"**W**hy are you nervous?" I asked myself as I looked in the full-length mirror that hung on the wall in my room.

I ran my fingers through my hair, drew in a deep breath, and steeled myself for what Bree was going to say. The fact that she'd agreed to have lunch with me was huge. She could have told me to go fuck myself, which I had honestly expected her to do the moment she saw me.

Instead, I saw something in those beautiful light-brown eyes of hers. She might have acted upset to see me, but I was sure I saw a little spark of something there. And I saw it again this morning, when she came after me before I left. The Brighton Rogers I knew would never stand there and wring her hands nervously. I hated that I was the reason for that. That it was because of me she'd left her career and her life in Boston behind.

The alarm on my phone went off, alerting me that I had two minutes to get down to the desk to meet up with Bree. I grabbed my phone and gave myself another quick look, then shrugged. I had on jeans and a long-sleeve T-shirt. Bree had sent me a text informing me to dress casually. I wasn't sure how this would go, but I knew one thing: I wasn't going to walk away from her again. No matter how many times she told me to. I loved Brighton Rogers, and I would do whatever it took to prove that to her.

When I reached for the doorknob, I noticed my hand shaking slightly. I closed my eyes, counted to ten, then opened the door.

As I made my way down the steps, I could hear Bree's sweet voice floating up. She was speaking to a guest about popular hiking trails around the Boggy Creek Valley. I couldn't ignore the way my heartbeat picked up the closer I drew to the bottom of the stairs.

"It'll be a beautiful hike, I promise. Just make sure you stay on the trail and don't wander off. It's easy to get twisted around."

"Thank you so much, Brighton!" the young woman said as she waved and bounced down the front steps behind two other girls.

Brighton shut the door, then turned around and saw me. She still had a smile on her face, and I was pleasantly surprised that it didn't fade away when she noticed me. Admittedly, it wasn't as bright as when she'd first turned around, but at least she wasn't shooting daggers at me with her eyes.

"I'd love to check out some hiking trails," I said as she made her way back toward the desk that was set up at the end of the foyer. I glanced down and saw a plaque with the same quote I'd seen a few other times throughout the bed and breakfast. I read it out loud.

"'I love you a bushel and a peck.' I see that saying a lot throughout the house."

She glanced down and a soft smile played across her face. "My grandmother used to say it to my mother, then to me. Every time my mom sees something with that saying on it, she buys it."

"It's nice to have a reminder of your grandmother around."

Bree's eyes met mine, and she nodded. "Yeah, it is." She glanced away. "My father thinks Mom's gone a bit overboard, but it's fun to hear guests make comments about it to us or to read about it in the guest book."

Around that time, Joanne walked around the corner from the direction of the dining room and kitchen. "Luke!" she said, coming over to hug me.

My eyes widened, and I glanced over at Bree.

She shrugged. "Mom, let go of him."

Joanne did, but she looked up at me with a smile so wide, I couldn't help but return the gesture.

"I told them we dated," Bree said, leaning against the check-in desk. A smirk appeared on her face when Joanne cupped my cheeks with her hands.

"You are so handsome. No wonder Brighton was caught under your spell."

Frowning, I glanced over to Bree again. "Spell?"

She shrugged again.

"Brighton tells us the two of you are going out to lunch. How wonderful!"

"Mom," Bree warned as she pushed off the desk. She stepped in between me and Joanne. "There is nothing 'wonderful' about it. I asked you not to make a big deal out of this."

Joanne plastered on a fake expression of surprise. "Not make a big deal? I find out today my daughter dated someone for a year—a *year*—without my knowledge. Then that someone shows up and wants to rekindle the relationship, and I'm not supposed to make a big deal about it?"

I tried not to smile when Bree stomped her foot like a preteen girl furious with her mother for embarrassing her. "Rekindle?" she said. "I never said Luke was here to rekindle anything!"

Joanne dropped her chin and stared at Bree with a look only a mother could give. It screamed, "It's what you meant to say."

"Mom, I said Luke was here to talk. To. Talk. That's it."

Joanne folded her arms over her chest. "No man shows up to simply talk and ask how you've been the last four months." Her eyes darted up to me. "Isn't that right, Luke? Tell her the real reason you're here."

Oh shit.

Bree spun around and pointed her finger at me, then poked it in my chest. "Do not answer her."

"Brighton! No wonder he broke up with you."

Another spin, and Bree faced her mother. "I broke up with *him*. He didn't break up with me."

Joanne rolled her eyes. "Does it really matter?"

Before Bree could answer, Ron walked in. Thank God.

"Tonight's game night. Luke, I hope you'll join us."

I cleared my throat. "I'd love to come, sir. Thank you."

Joanne clapped her hands. "Wonderful! You kids can go on your date now."

Bree sighed. "Oh my God. It's not a date."

Joanna waved her hand in the air as she turned and followed Ron into the living room.

I watched Bree's shoulders slump. "Why did I think moving back home was a good idea?" she said.

"Should we, um, head on out?"

Turning to face me, Bree narrowed her eyes. "This is not a date. This is...us...talking. That's it."

"Okay."

"Okay?"

"Was that a question or a repeat? I'm sorta getting the sense you're not happy with my reply."

Her mouth opened, then shut. She finally shook her head, growled under her breath, and stalked toward the front door. Grabbing her purse off the long bench that sat against the wall, she flung the door open.

"I'm driving!" she called out as I pressed my mouth into a tight line to keep from laughing.

"Okay."

"Stop saying okay, dammit!"

It was strange to be in Bree's BMW driving around like two normal people. I hadn't once looked over my shoulder to see if anyone was following us. It was nice. Really nice.

It took less than five minutes to get to the restaurant, and neither one of us uttered a word during the short drive. I'd wanted to start up the conversation so many times but decided to wait.

Bree parked on Chestnut Street and slipped out of her car. "The Coffee Pot is on the corner."

"Ahh, the famous Coffee Pot you talked about."

She smiled, and it made my heart do a little jump in my chest. Christ, I had missed her something terrible. Simply feeling her next to me brought me such happiness. I only hoped I hadn't waited too long. Trying to get everything settled with my agent and contracts had already taken me longer than I'd hoped. And after I found out Bree had left Boston, it took me about a week to figure out that she'd moved back home to Boggy Creek, then another week to talk Katherine into filming the last scenes of the movie near her home in Boggy Creek Valley. Thankfully the director and studio were on board when I pitched the idea.

"A word of advice if you decide to come here alone: don't sit at table number four," Bree said. "It's the booth in the corner over there."

I looked at the booth, then back at Bree. "Why not?"

Lowering her voice as we headed toward a different booth, she replied, "Kyle had sex with the owner's daughter on that table."

I screwed up my face. "What? That's disgusting."

Bree chuckled. "Exactly. The owner, Tess, apparently didn't let Kyle in for like four or five years. Did I mention she caught them in the act?"

I laughed. "I'm surprised she even allowed him back at all."

"I'm pretty sure he laid on some heavy-duty charm to get back into her good graces."

"Must have."

We both slipped into the booth and a young waitress walked over and handed us our menus. I took a quick glance around and saw there was only two other people in the restaurant.

"Hey, Bree. How's it going?" the waitress said.

Bree smiled. "It's going well, thanks, Melissa. Where's Tess today? I don't think I've ever been here and not seen her."

Melissa smiled. "She took the day off! It's a big secret why, but I've got a fifty riding on her going on a date today. There's an older gentleman who's been coming in a lot lately. He lives up the valley some. They flirt. A lot."

Bree chuckled. "I hope she *is* seeing someone."

"So do I," Melissa said before she swung her gaze over to me. "What can I get you to drink, sir?"

I let out the breath I'd been holding in. "I'll have a Diet Pepsi."

"Diet Pepsi? When did you start drinking soda?" Bree asked.

With a shrug, I replied, "A couple of weeks ago. I think it's some weird phase."

"You know," Melissa added, "if it's the carbonation you like, you should try Waterloo sparkling water. The black cherry is to die for."

"No, it's not the same thing. That stuff tastes like shit," Bree stated as she shook her head and folded her arms over her chest.

Whipping her head to look back at Bree, Melissa gasped. "You're kidding me, right? Tell me you're lying right now."

"Nope," Bree said, popping the P. "That stuff is gross."

Melissa turned back to me and leaned in closer. "Don't listen to her. It's way healthier for you." Straightening, she grinned widely. "I'll get your drinks and be back for your order."

Bree handed me a menu. "She didn't ask what you wanted," I said.

With a chuckle, Bree replied, "You're in Boggy Creek now, Luke. It's a small town, and when you come to the same diner at least three to four times a week, they know what you drink."

I glanced at Melissa who was making our drinks and chatting with an older gentleman at the counter.

When I looked back at Bree, she was staring at me. Something was off with her expression. "What's wrong?" I asked.

She cleared her throat before she spoke. "This is the first time we've ever walked into a restaurant together and sat down in the open. We didn't slip in from the back kitchen area to a private room or meet in a dark corner after arriving separately."

My heart dropped, and all I could do was nod until I got my emotions in check. I hated that I assumed everything had been okay with us. That Bree would have been fine going on as we had been, while I lived the best of two fucking worlds. "I'm sorry, Bree. I'm sorry I made you do that."

She shook her head and let out a bitter laugh. "You didn't make me do anything. I went along with all of it because I wanted to, until..." Her voice trailed off, but then she smirked. "In case you've forgotten, I broke up with you."

With a slow shake of my head, I replied, "No, I haven't forgotten at all. There hasn't been a day that I haven't thought of you."

She raised a single brow, her face void of any real emotion. "Is that so?"

"Yes."

"You didn't seem to have a problem turning and walking out of my office that day." She sniffled and quickly wiped at a tear before she sat up straighter and whispered, "I'm no longer that woman you so easily walked away from."

I felt a pain so sharp in my chest, I could hardly breathe for a moment. It took me another few seconds to find my damn voice. "First, walking out of your office that day was the hardest thing I've ever had to do, Brighton. There wasn't anything fucking *easy* about it. You gave me no choice. I tried calling you, I texted you, but you wouldn't even let me explain. Then you demanded I leave."

Her expression remained the same, so I went on.

"The entire time we dated, I lived in fear." My words caused her brows to pull together. "Fear of letting the outside world into this perfect dream I was living. I wanted to believe everything was okay, that you were okay with how things were, that I was okay with it... when nothing could have been further from the truth."

She slowly shook her head. "I don't understand. What were you afraid of?"

I laughed bitterly and pushed my fingers through my hair before I sighed. "Everything. I was afraid if we let everyone else in, the walls would tumble down around us so fast, and I'd lose you. But in the end, me pretending everything was fine caused me to lose you anyway."

Bree looked down and then back up at me.

"I never cheated on you," I said. "And I haven't been with or even looked at another woman since that evening when you walked up to me at the Christmas party. As far as what you saw that night, Kathleen knew you were there. She was playing a game. I didn't kiss her; hell, I didn't even want to be there with her. If I'd known you were there, Bree, I would have gone straight to you."

"And how long would we have kept playing that game, Luke? I was tired of it."

"Why didn't you tell me how you felt?"

Her mouth opened, then shut before she looked away and let out a slow breath.

I sighed. "Neither one of us wanted to go public because we both knew the moment we did, things would change. I was scared to death everything would change."

She jerked her head back to look at me. "*You* were scared? I was terrified, and I didn't even realize it until that night. Seeing you with her on your arm. I kept telling myself it was fake. Surely it was all an act. Then when I saw the two of you inside the venue, I couldn't help but wonder why you kept the show going. Then she kissed you—"

"Tried to. I stopped it."

Bree rolled her eyes. "It doesn't matter, Luke. I knew in that moment I couldn't do it. I couldn't—no, I *wouldn't* stand by and watch you make movies with other women. Kiss them, have sex with them, all the while telling myself it was fake. You were pretending. Because that was exactly what *we* were doing. We were pretending."

"What?" I asked, confused. "First of all, I don't have sex with anyone, Brighton. I don't make porn."

180

"It's the same damn thing, practically. If I crawled into bed with Kyle and we were both covered by a patch of fabric and we started dry humping each other and kissing, how would you feel? I know you say it's acting and I shouldn't think otherwise, and maybe I am being a jealous twit about it all. But seeing you with Kathleen and how the two of you acted together—I'm not used to this world of yours, Luke, and I honestly don't think I could ever get used to it."

She sighed. "Did you feel anything at all when I kissed Kyle yesterday?"

I pulled my head back at her abrupt change. "I was...angry at first."

"I was acting," she stated, sarcasm dripping off the last word.

"Bree, it's not the same thing."

The waitress came back over and set down our drinks. "I'd have brought them sooner, but it looked like the conversation got pretty intense. I figured I'd give the two of you a chance to work it out, but it seemed to be heating up even more so I'm stepping in."

I stared up at her with a disbelieving look on my face.

She winked at me. "Do you know what you want to eat?"

Bree spoke. "I'll have the burger special with sweet potato fries."

To make things easier, I added, "I'll have the same."

"How do you want the burgers cooked?" Melissa asked.

"Well done," Bree and I said at the same time.

"Got it. Now you may go back to your heated discussion."

I watched Melissa walk back toward the counter while Bree let out a small chuckle, as if a waitress saying something like that was totally normal.

Chapter Seventeen

Bree

I tried not to laugh as Luke stared at a retreating Melissa. I failed.

"Were we being loud?" he asked. "I didn't think we were being loud."

Reaching for my drink, I shook my head. "We weren't. And besides, there's hardly anyone in here, and the few who *are* here don't care what we're talking about."

He frowned. "Why not?"

I shrugged after taking a sip. "They most likely think you're a tourist and a guest at my folks' bed and breakfast."

"And because of that, they won't pay any attention to us?"

"Yep. If they had any idea we used to date, they'd be straining to hear all the drama."

He shook his head. "Small towns."

After a few moments of Luke getting his thoughts back together, his gaze met mine. "I understand, Bree, why you couldn't do it. Be with me."

"Do you?"

He nodded. "Yes. But you never even gave me a chance."

My stomach dropped as I remembered the conversation with

everyone at dinner last night, and then the one I had later with Kyle. "A chance?"

"Yes. You assumed the worst of me, then decided that we weren't worth the fight."

I let a harsh laugh slip free. "*You're* the one who walked away and never looked back. You left."

"You told me to leave, Bree."

I felt my eyes rapidly blinking in disbelief at the idiot sitting across from me. Or maybe I was the idiot. "I thought...well, I thought you would...fight for us."

"Why couldn't you tell me your fears, Bree? Why talk to me in riddles and tell me you wanted me to leave?"

My heart hammered so hard in my chest, I was positive it was going to burst out at any moment. "Talk. In. Riddles?"

"You know what I mean. Wait. Let me take all that back and start over."

Dropping back in the booth, I crossed my arms over my chest and glared at him. I wasn't sure who to be angry with. Luke for listening to me and leaving, or me for being such a...girl. I had really expected him to read between the lines and then got upset when he didn't.

I stared at him—and it was then I got a really good look at him. He had dark circles under his eyes. When they opened again and he met my gaze, I noticed how bloodshot his eyes were and how tired he looked. His filming schedule must have been crazy up until this point. I was about to ask him if he'd gotten any sleep, but he went on.

"If I could go back in time and do things differently, I would. No, wait. I wouldn't. I got to be with you—alone with you, fall in love with you—without the outside world sticking their noses into our business and printing lies and negative shit about us. I wouldn't change any of that. But I wish I'd figured out a better way to do it, so that you never felt like I didn't cherish you."

His words repeated in my head. *Fall in love with you.* He had said he loved me plenty of times, and I had believed his words...until I told myself they couldn't have been true in a sad attempt to make the hurt go away. Deep down, though, I knew he loved me. Or had loved me.

The thought of him no longer loving me made me feel sick to my stomach.

"I never felt like you didn't cherish me, Luke."

"You obviously did at some point, Bree. You doubted us, my faithfulness, and that was my fault."

I gave a one-shoulder shrug. "I won't argue with you on that one."

The corner of his mouth rose into a small smile before he went on. "But you should have told me how you felt. I can't read your mind any more than you can read mine. You have fears, and so do I, but we can't expect each other to know what those fears are."

Nodding, I drew in a slow breath and let it out. "I agree. I should have told you how I was feeling. I'm sorry."

He reached across the table and took my hand in his. "And I'm sorry I wasn't completely open either. I never stopped loving you, Bree."

I could feel the tears pooling in my eyes. "It's been four months, Luke. Four. Did you think I'd wait for you?"

His jaw ticced, and he looked away for a moment before his dark gaze met mine. "Do you not love me anymore, Bree? Is that why you left Boston?"

"I left Boston because the idea of even *seeing* you hurt too much at the time. Of seeing your father and not asking about you or how you were. Or worse yet, him telling me you'd moved on and found someone new. I also left because someone told a reporter who I was, and they came to my office to ask about you. I lied and said I didn't know who you were, but if there was one reporter, there would be others. I freaked out and knew I needed to leave."

His face fell. "You left Boston, your job, because of me?"

I shook my head and looked down at where his hand covered mine. "No. That was only part of the reason."

"And the other part?" he asked.

"The other part doesn't matter."

A deep frown appeared on his handsome face. "If it caused you to leave your job and world behind in Boston, then it matters to you. And that means it matters to *me*."

My heart did a little tumble in my chest. *Lord, this man knows how to melt my insides.*

My cheeks got hot, and I looked down at my drink and started to run my finger along the glass with my free hand. "Over the last year, all the times I've returned to Boggy Creek, something inside me has changed."

"What do you mean?" he asked. I had to give him credit, he was desperately trying to understand the crazy that was me.

No matter how angry or hurt I still felt, I needed to be honest about my feelings. I knew deep in my heart that Luke was in Boggy Creek to rekindle our relationship, and for me, things hadn't changed. I loved him more than anything, but a life with him wasn't something I was sure I could do.

But like Kyle said, I needed to lay it all out and let Luke know where I stood. It was the only fair thing to do.

I closed my eyes, drew in a deep breath, and let all the words out. "All of my friends are falling in love, getting married, having babies. I'm so over-the-moon happy for them, but at the same time, it's only made me realize how much I want that."

I paused and waited to see if he'd react. He squeezed my hand and gave me a soft smile, silently urging me to go on.

"When I saw you with Kathleen, a whirlwind of emotions hit me...and the day you came to my office, I was afraid to tell you the truth."

"The truth about what?"

"That I wanted something more. Something you couldn't give me. The life I was living in Boston turned out not to be the life I thought I wanted. Deep down inside, I think I always knew it wasn't for me. From the time I was fourteen, all I ever wanted to do was leave Boggy Creek, explore what life would be like outside of the town where I grew up. In my head, it was the dream I wanted. My head was wrong, and my heart was so confused after you left. I was angry, hurt, sad. So I ran as fast as I could to the one place where I knew I would be okay. Home."

His eyes filled with something that looked like a mix of sadness and confusion. "What do you want, Bree? Tell me what you want that you don't think I can give you."

I forced myself to smile but couldn't let the words out, because the last thing I wanted to do was be the cause of this man giving up his entire career.

I want you. I want us to get married and have babies. I want to live a normal, simple life here in Boggy Creek like my parents and friends do. I want to walk down the street and hold your hand in plain sight and not have a photographer rush up and take our picture. I want simplicity.

I want what you can't give, and I would never in a million years ask you to give up everything for me.

Luke squeezed my hand, pulling me back from my internal monologue. "Bree?" he said, softly.

Pulling my hand out from under his, I turned and looked at the counter. "I want my burger. I'm starving."

When I looked back across the table, Luke was staring at me. I couldn't read the expression on his face...but for a moment, I thought I saw anger there.

Why was I so afraid to tell him the truth?

Fear. It was that simple. I was too much of a coward to even try to make it work because I was so worried about getting hurt.

"You're not going to tell me what you want," he stated. "Is it because you no longer want it with *me*?"

A sick feeling hit me right in the stomach. How could he even think I no longer loved him? A part of me thought it would be easier to agree with him. To tell him I no longer loved him. But I couldn't lie to him. I *wouldn't* lie to him.

My voice cracked when I went to speak, and I had to clear it before I could reply. "I honestly don't think I could ever want that life with anyone other than you. But I realized I couldn't have it."

"Why not?"

I let out a disbelieving laugh. "Because it would never work, Luke. I thought it would be okay in the beginning. But then I fell in love with you, and I fell so hard and I wanted things that..."

Luke leaned in toward the me. "That what? Goddammit, just tell me, Brighton. Come out and tell me," he said in a low voice so the few people in the café wouldn't hear us.

"I don't want to be married to an actor. I'm sorry, I know you were upfront and honest with me, but I can't do it." I felt a sob slip free, and I covered my mouth with my hand and looked away for a moment until I could get my emotions in check.

Drawing in a shaky breath, I focused back on him. "Damn you for making me cry. I swore I wouldn't."

His own eyes filled with tears as he whispered, "I don't want to be the reason you cry. Ever."

I sobbed again, and I wanted to pick up my glass and throw it at him.

I wiped my tears away and took a glance around the restaurant. We were the only two in here now. Thank freaking God. If anyone saw me crying, it would be all over town by the time we finished our burgers.

Clearing my throat, I went on. "I love you, Luke. But I don't think I can share you with the world, and I'm so sorry for that. I really am. And I would never in a million years ask you to give up what you love. It wouldn't be fair. I refuse to do it."

He nodded. "I know you wouldn't ask me to give up my career, but you also can't ask me to give up *you*—because that's something I cannot, I *will* not do, Bree."

My jaw ached as I fought to keep my emotions in place. "Luke," I said as I closed my eyes. When he started speaking, I looked back at him.

"I realized that day in your office that I needed to figure out a few things before I could make you any promises. I'm sorry it took me so long, and I'm sorry I didn't reach out to you in the meantime. Maybe deep down, I was also afraid that I was too late. But I never, not once, gave up on us, Bree. I prayed every night that God would make you feel my love for you, and when I found out you left Boston, I was scared to death I might have lost you forever."

From the corner of my eye, I saw the waitress making her way to us.

"Okay, it's burger time!" Melissa said as she set down two baskets on the table with our burgers and fries. She smiled at me, then turned and gave Luke a cold stare. She had clearly noticed me crying. Dammit all to hell.

"Thank you, Melissa," Luke said with a smile. She ignored him and turned back to me.

"Are we all good?" she asked.

I smiled. "Yes, I'm good. Luke?"

He nodded. "Yeah, I'm good."

Melissa grinned, turned, and walked away, leaving us alone again.

We proceeded to eat, neither one of us saying anything. It wasn't an uncomfortable silence. A few people entered the restaurant. Soon we had diners on both sides of our booth.

"Is there a place we can go and talk after we eat?" Luke asked.

I nodded. "I think that would be a good idea."

"I can't even tell you the last time I had an ice cream cone," Luke said with a wide smile on his face.

"This is not ice cream, it's custard."

He rolled his eyes and licked the cone, sending a flood of heat straight to my core as I watched. I nearly moaned. Christ, I needed to redirect my thoughts—and fast.

"Custard, ice cream. Either way, it's freaking good."

Smiling, I replied, "Yeah, Sandy's has the best *custard*."

He shot me a sideways glance and smiled before he went back to the cone.

I drew in a deep breath and decided we needed to get back to the discussion we'd stopped in the middle of earlier. "What did you need to figure out?"

Luke paused his licking and looked straight ahead at the benches in the small park along Maple Street. He motioned to them. "Want to sit down?"

"Sure," I replied and headed toward the park. There wasn't anyone around, so we'd have the privacy we didn't have at the restaurant. As we walked past a trash bin, I tossed my cone away. I didn't really feel like eating it. I had barely been able to force myself to eat half my burger and fries.

Once we sat, I felt my stomach drop, suddenly worried about what Luke was going to say.

"I knew that day in your office that I couldn't give you the things you wanted or deserved," he said. "I also knew that I couldn't let you go."

"Why did you wait so long to reach out to me? I know I told you to leave, Luke. And I know it's pure stupidity for me to think you could read my mind. I shouldn't have ignored your attempts to talk to me after I ran away from the benefit. And I know I told you to leave, but you had to know deep down I was so angry and hurt. Seeing that woman kiss you, and then to find out you slept with her in the past—it was all so much," I said in an almost defeated voice. "But I honestly thought deep down you'd simply give me some time. But you never even tried to reach out to me. Not once."

He sighed and rubbed the back of his neck as he looked at his cone. He stood and tossed it into a trashcan.

"Why did you throw it away?" I asked.

"Lost my appetite."

189

I wasn't going to apologize. My heart had been so broken, I had hardly been able to eat for weeks. I wasn't about to care that he threw away one damn cone.

"I fucked up, Bree, I know that. And for the last few months Hank has been reminding me of his own displeasure about how I handled things. I nearly fired him at least a dozen times." He shook his head. "This whole thing with us is new to me. I've never been in love with anyone before. Hell, I wasn't even sure I was *able* to love anyone. I've never experienced the things I felt until you showed up in my life. When you told me to get out of your office, that you couldn't stand by and watch me pretend to be with other women, I knew what I had to do."

My heart dropped to my stomach. "What did you do?"

"I knew that until I figured out where my own future was going, I couldn't keep you in the dark or expect you to wait and feel like you were being sidelined. Because that was never what I intended. I can't even begin to tell you how torn up I was when you said that. After I left your office, I went right to the airport and flew back to LA. I told my agent I was going to fulfill my last contract and then I was done. *Love Rebound* is my last movie."

"What do you mean...you're done?" I asked in a stunned voice.

Luke's eyes met mine. "I'm finished with acting, Bree. This is my last movie. I'm done."

Tears pooled in my eyes, though I wasn't sure how I should be feeling. A part of me wanted to scream out in pure happiness. The other part hated that I'd made him give up his career.

His face fell as he watched my tears fall. "Don't do that."

I wiped at my cheeks. "Do what?"

"Blame yourself. Because I know that's what you're thinking right now."

"I'm not sure *what* I'm thinking, to be honest with you. I never... oh God, Luke, I would never ask you to give up your career."

"You didn't."

"But...but..."

Luke took my hand in his. "Let me finish, okay?"

My head jerked a little as I tried to nod. "O-okay."

"Before you even came into my life, something felt off. Something was missing, and I couldn't figure out what it was. I told myself I was happy. I was doing what I'd always wanted to do and I was successful at it. I had a damn good career, money, a house on the beach, a house in Boston. I could fly anywhere in the world, anytime I damn well pleased. Then my mother begged me to come home for Christmas. Do you know how many times I've turned down an invite to go to that damn Christmas party?"

I shook my head. "No."

"Every single time, Bree. But for some reason...I knew I had to go. I told myself I was doing it for my mom. The moment you looked at me, I knew nothing would ever be the same. I won't lie and tell you I wasn't scared. Scared you would wake up one day and realize that you deserved someone better than me. Someone who would show you off to the world, not keep you hidden."

I squeezed his hand. "I did the same thing to you by not telling anyone about us. To be honest, even if you weren't an actor, I don't know how long it would have taken me to tell my parents about you. I think a part of me wanted to keep you a secret as well. I guess we both had our own reasons for that. You didn't want the press to tear our love apart, and I didn't want my mother to start planning a wedding and the names of our kids."

Luke laughed. "Your mom is not that bad, Bree."

"We're not dating right now, so you haven't seen the real Joanne Rogers."

A brilliant smile lit up his entire face. "I'd like to change that."

"You want to see the real Joanne?"

"No," he said as he placed his hand on the side of my face. I felt myself lean into his touch. "I would very much like to start dating you again, Bree. If you'll have me back."

I closed my eyes and drew in a deep breath before I exhaled and met his gaze. "I'm not sure how Kyle will handle this."

Luke laughed again and pulled me closer. Cupping my face in his hands, he said, "Are you still angry with me?"

"Yes."

He frowned. "Why?"

"Luke, I never wanted you to give up your life. Your career. Your passion. Your dream—"

Pressing his mouth to mine, he stopped my words with a powerful yet tender kiss. He deepened the kiss, and we both let out a soft moan. When we drew back, he leaned his forehead on mine. "You, Brighton Willow Rogers, *are* my life. My passion and all of my dreams. I've spent the last four months without you, and they were beyond miserable. I can't be without you for another minute. I don't *want* to be without you. I love you, and I want to marry you."

I gasped. "What?"

He smiled and drew back until we looked at one another. "I want to marry you."

Swallowing hard, I closed eyes and shook my head slightly. Had I heard him right? "You want to marry me?"

"Yes," he confirmed with a soft laugh.

"But...I want to live in Boggy Creek."

"So do I, Bree. I want to eat at The Coffee Pot two or three times a week, so they know what kind of drink I want. I want to walk our kids to school and stop at this park and push them on those swings."

I looked out over the playground, then back at Luke. Everything was starting to blur as more tears built up in my eyes.

"I want to be able to sit on a fucking park bench and kiss you out in public and not have it featured on *Entertainment Tonight*."

"But that would be such a simple life."

Luke laughed. "Life with you, Brighton, is never going to be simple. I already know that. But it's the only life I could ever imagine having. I can't promise there still won't be a stray photographer, or someone trying to take a picture of us. Or even our kids, if we're blessed with them someday. But if I'm no longer acting, no one is going to give two shits about me after a while. I don't want to do this life without you. So...will you do me the honor of marrying me?"

"We're not even dating!" I got to my feet and started to pace. "I was supposed to be mad at you for at least another few weeks. You know, make you work for it. Not let you walk right back into my life and then...and then..."

He lifted a single brow. "And then what?"

"And then realize that I can't live another moment without you either!"

Luke stood, and I threw myself into his arms. He held onto me so tightly, as if he was afraid I would slip away again.

"I love you, Bree. So fucking much, and I'm so sorry for everything."

I buried my face in his chest to muffle my cries as I held onto him with all my might. When I finally looked up, my breath caught in my throat. Luke was gazing down at me with so much love in his eyes, I felt my knees buckle.

"I love you too," I said. "And yes, I'll marry you."

A smile erupted across his face, and he pressed his mouth to mine in a searing kiss. When we drew apart, I started to laugh.

"What's so funny?" he asked with a chuckle.

"I don't know who's going to be happier about this news. My mother, your mother, or Hank."

He grinned. "Or Candace."

Chapter Eighteen

Luke

Bree flashed me that smile that melted my heart and stole my breath, and I kissed her once more. The crazy thing was, we were in public. At a park. And not a single person was around. Just like in the restaurant, where we'd openly argued.

If this was what life with Bree was going to be like, then sign me the fuck up.

"What do we do now?" Bree asked with a wicked gleam in her eyes.

"Well, if you're leaving it up to me, I vote for making up for lost time."

She waggled her brows. "We'll have to go to a hotel."

I frowned. "Why?"

She pulled back and gave me a look that said I had asked the stupidest question ever. "Luke, we cannot have sex in the bed and breakfast. Gross."

"Ooookay. What about your place?"

"Hard pass. With my luck, my mother would walk in on us. No, we're going to have to go somewhere else."

I blinked in confusion. "Where?"

She looked off into the distance as she thought about it. "We can't go to Boggy Creek Motel. I mean, it's super cute and all, but Joyce will be on the phone with my mother before we shut and lock the door. No, we need somewhere private. Somewhere no one will see us."

"I gotta tell ya, Bree, I'm experiencing a bit of déjà vu."

She laughed. "I'm sorry. We have two choices. We can go to the motel and risk my mother showing up with a basket of goodies, or we find somewhere more private to...catch up."

Bree's phone beeped, and she pulled it out of her pocket. Her mouth fell open. "Oh my God, it's like the woman has some sort of sixth sense!"

"Your mom?" I asked.

She nodded. "She wants me to call her. Probably for an update, or because someone overheard us in Tess's place." Bree tapped the phone and put it on speaker.

"Bree, darling."

"Mom, what's up?"

"How are things going with Walter?"

"Luke, Mom. His name is Luke."

"I thought he was incognito?"

"He is, but you don't have to call him that. You can call him Luke. And things are going...good."

"That's wonderful! Now, will you define good for me? Good as in you're working things out and you're no longer single? Or good as in you're talking but still in the friendzone?"

Bree looked at me and mouthed, "See!" All I could do was smile and shrug.

"Mom, I asked you to please not do this. Why do you think I never told you about Luke in the first place?"

"You said it was because you were afraid I'd tell Annie, and she'd tell Karen Larson, and then Karen would tell Millie. And if Millie found out, she'd say something in Schmick's Market, and then the whole town would find out. And someone would know someone in

Boston, and they'd tell someone else—and then the whole world would find out."

I had to press my mouth together into a tight line to keep from laughing as Bree drew in a long, deep breath.

"For the love of all things," she said. "I never tell you when I'm dating a guy because you do this!"

Joanne huffed. "And what is *this*?"

"Question me. First, it's are we back together? Then, it's when are we setting the wedding date? And am I really going to embarrass you by not getting married in the church?"

Joanne made another huffing sound. "I would do no such thing. But did you say marriage? Is that something the two of you have talked about?"

Bree's eyes shot back to me, and for a moment I thought she might throw her phone across the park. "I'm hanging up on you now."

"No, wait!" Joanne called out. "Your father and I have been invited to Boston with Lance and Karen."

"Lance and Karen Larson?" Bree asked.

Joanne sighed. "Well, what other Lance and Karen would there be, Brighton?"

Bree hit mute on the phone and said, "That's Kyle's parents. His dad's also the police chief."

I nodded.

"Brighton?"

"Sorry, Mom. Okay, when?"

"Well, they got tickets to a play tomorrow, and they'd like to spend a few days in Boston. Your father and I thought—"

"You should totally go!" Bree practically shouted.

"Oh, well, I was calling to see if you wouldn't mind if we left in the morning, and you manned the bed and breakfast for the day and night."

"I think you should leave with Lance and Karen. You and Dad deserve a little bit of downtime."

"Well, I mean, that would be nice. Are you okay handling things this evening and tomorrow?"

"Please, I've handled it before when you guys have gone on vacation. Besides, we only have a handful of guests."

She cleared her throat. "Eight now, if you count Walt...er...Luke."

"He doesn't count."

"He most certainly does, Brighton Rogers."

Bree sighed in frustration. "Fine, he counts. I'll take care of everything. And don't worry, MaryLou will be there to help—and Luke can help as well. Right, Luke?"

"Um, yes. Right."

"Oh, that's wonderful!" her mother said. "I'll go tell your father. When will you be back, so we can let Lance and Karen know what time we can leave?"

Bree looked at me and winked. "We're on our way back now."

Joanne let out a small excited sound. "Wonderful. See you soon, sweetheart."

Bree hung up, then looked at me. "Luck appears to be on our side, Mr. Morrison."

With a grin, I replied, "It appears so."

Bree and I walked back to her car and headed to Willow Tree. On the drive there, Jack texted me to see how things were going with Bree. I was more than happy to tell him we were back together. He sent a GIF of a guy jumping up and down in excitement, and then Lou texted me four words: *It's about damn time.*

Laughing, I said, "We can add Jack and Lou to the list of people who are happy we're back together."

"How are Lou and Jack?" she asked. "We should invite them to Boggy Creek when things settle down."

"They'd love that."

Bree pulled into the parking lot of the Willow Tree and stopped next to my car. We got out and started toward the front when I took her hand in mine and pulled her to a stop.

"Bree, I do need to mention that I'm obligated to promote the movie. I'll still need to go back to LA and appear at the premiere."

"Okay," she said with a smile.

"I wasn't sure if you wanted to keep us a secret until it's all over, or..."

She shook her head. "No, I'm tired of keeping us a secret. If we don't make a big show of us being together, maybe people won't make a big deal about it. And if you don't make a big announcement about retiring from acting and simply step away, people won't really pay attention."

I raised a brow. "Are you saying I'll be easy to forget?"

With a chuckle, she replied, "No. I'm saying if you make a big production about stepping away from acting, it will only cause people to be more curious."

"What about the premieres? My agent will want me to walk those red carpets with Kathleen."

A look passed over Bree's face, and I couldn't tell if it was anger or something else. "Well, that's too bad, because I'll be your escort from now on."

"You will?" I asked, surprised by her statement.

"Yes. Your *wife*."

"You're cheating on me?"

Luke and I both turned to see Kyle standing there with a wide smile on his face.

"Hey, Kyle," I said as we shook hands.

"Good to see you, Luke," Kyle said. He turned and looked at Bree. "I see we worked things out. What happened to making him work for it, Brighton?"

She rolled her eyes. "It's complicated, Larson. Why are you here? My God, do you ever do your job?"

Kyle faked a hurt expression. "Excuse me, but I *am* doing my job."

Bree folded her arms over her chest and glared at him, but I could see a hint of amusement on her face.

Kyle held up two tickets—and Bree let out a scream that would put her friend Candace's to shame.

"Are those the BLACKPINK tickets?" she asked, skipping over to Kyle.

He held them just out of her reach. "Yes, they are. But I do believe you owe me a favor for playing your fake boyfriend and making me kiss you." He pretended to gag.

Without warning, Bree punched Kyle in the stomach. He doubled over, giving her the opportunity to take the tickets from his hand and skip to the front door of the bed and breakfast.

"Shit, are you okay?" I asked as I leaned over to look at Kyle who was gasping for air.

"Yeah," he wheezed. "Fuck, I didn't see that coming."

I shook my head. "I can't tell if you two are friends or enemies."

He nodded. "Friends. I think. Christ, who taught her how to punch? She didn't hold back at all."

Lifting my hands, I took a step back. "Not me."

"I'm going to arrest you for assaulting an officer!" Kyle yelled out.

Looking back toward the front door, I said, "I think she's in the house."

"Yeah, I know she is—it's safer that way. Anyway, I'm going to go cough up blood now, maybe a kidney too. Tell Brighton I already gave Willa her ticket."

"For the BLACKPINK concert, I take it."

He nodded and spoke between gasps. "Yeah. Regretting...it... now."

Kyle turned and made his way back toward his vehicle. I could hear his K9 barking, most likely wanting to take a bite out of the woman who threw the punch.

Before he got in, Kyle cleared his throat. "Better think twice before marrying that one. She has a bit of...evil in her."

I couldn't help but laugh. "Thanks for the advice."

It didn't take Ron and Joanne long to get packed up and head out of town, leaving Bree and MaryLou in charge.

As her parents' car slipped from view, Bree turned to me. "Okay. You start on the bread and salad, and I'll get to work on the pasta sauce."

My brows shot up. "Um, excuse me?"

Bree tilted her head. "You do know how to make bread, right?"

I let out a laugh, only to stop when it was met with a glare. "This is a side of you I don't think I've ever seen before."

Smiling sweetly, Bree replied, "I have no idea what you're talking about. Now, back to the bread."

"Bree, why in the hell would you think I'd know how to make bread? I only know how to cut bread, dip it in olive oil, and eat the shit out of it."

She closed her eyes and sighed, then snapped them open. "I'm sorry. I lost my head for a moment. Can you make a salad?"

I scoffed. "Yes, I'm not *that* useless."

Reaching up onto her toes, she kissed me on the mouth. "I'll teach you how to make the bread. Then we need to make the gift bags for this evening, but it won't be that bad. We don't have a full house."

I'd only been at the bed and breakfast for one night, but yesterday evening there had been a little brown bag filled with lavender cookies hanging on my door when I went up to my room. When I'd checked in, Joanne had informed me that I could expect a little gift each night.

I pulled her to me and wrapped my arms around her waist. "I like this."

She beamed up at me. "What?"

"Helping you with the bed and breakfast. Is this something you want to do? Run the bed and breakfast with your folks?"

She chewed on her lip and thought about her answer. "Would it bother you if I said yes? I mean, I don't know how you feel about going from having people wait on you to turning around and waiting on others."

"As crazy as this may sound, I've never had people wait on me, Bree. Hank, yes, but I couldn't have done my job without his help. But I've always cleaned my own house, and when I wasn't getting takeout, I was making myself dinner."

Her eyes widened in surprise. "You cleaned your own house?"

"Yes. I find it relaxing, and besides, it's only ever been me. It wasn't that hard."

She ran the tip of her finger along my jawline. "And what types of meals did you make for yourself?"

I looked up as I thought about it. "Well, I make a mean hamburger. BLTs, tacos, spaghetti...oh, and I love grilling up salmon for fish tacos. A lot of nights I made myself cereal and cinnamon sugar toast."

She blinked a few times, then shook her head. "Cereal and toast?"

I nodded. "Yeah."

Taking in a deep breath, she patted me on the chest. "Well, when we do our weekly outdoor grill nights, you'll be in charge of the burgers."

A sense of happiness flooded my entire body. "Really?"

She winked. "Yep."

"Can I make the guests cinnamon sugar toast tomorrow?"

"Um—" Her eyes darted toward the now empty street where her folks had been parked moments ago. "We'll see."

I almost laughed with giddiness. What in the hell was wrong with me? Had I really been longing for a simple life so much that making toast was a thrill now?

Yes. And it was my duty to share this marvel with the world.

Bree laced her fingers in mine as we headed back toward the house.

"You won't be disappointed in the toast, Bree. Everyone will love it!"

She looked up at me through her lashes, clearly trying to keep from laughing. "I'm sure they will. And they won't even realize an award-winning actor made it for them."

Chapter Nineteen

Bree

It took everything I had not to laugh at the sight before me. Luke had flour in his hair, on his face, and covering his clothes. There was pasta sauce on his cheek, a blueberry inexplicably tangled up in his hair, and I was pretty sure that was a mint leaf stuck to his forehead.

"And you want to marry this man?" MaryLou whispered to me as she set the apple pie she'd made out on the counter to cool.

I sighed and took in the man I loved. He was trying to figure out how to zest a lemon for the vinaigrette dressing we were making for tonight's salad. "I do. I really do."

The only reason MaryLou knew about our plans to get married was because she'd walked in on Luke kissing me in the kitchen and asking how soon we could have a wedding. She'd gasped. Luke had jumped back and hit a bowl, causing fresh fruit to fly through the hair. I was going to guess that was where the blueberry in his hair came from.

"Brighton, he doesn't even know how to zest a lemon."

Turning to look at MaryLou, I replied in a hushed voice, "Everyone has to learn at some point."

When MaryLou could no longer stand it, she marched over and grabbed the lemon and the zester from Luke's hands. "Watch me."

He did as she commanded while MaryLou demonstrated. "Flip your wrist. Tap. Flip your wrist. Tap."

"Why are you tapping it?" Luke asked.

She glanced at him and then turned the zester over. "See all the zest there? You want to get it out, so you tap it."

"Ahh...that makes sense," Luke stated. "How do you know how much is a tablespoon?"

MaryLou stared at him with a disbelieving expression before she calmly opened a drawer and pulled out the measuring spoons. "You know what these are?"

Luke rolled his eyes, and I had to cover my mouth to keep from laughing. "Of course, I do. They're spoons for measuring."

"After a while, you'll get the visual of how much a tablespoon is and you won't need the spoons," MaryLou said as she tapped the zester once more, and they both looked in the bowl. "That's about a tablespoon. Now, you use the spoons and measure out the rest of the ingredients."

I watched Luke mix the mustard, olive oil, lemon juice, and seasonings all together with a whisk that MaryLou handed him. The buzzer on the oven went off.

"The bread's done. We have to take it out," MaryLou said, pushing at Luke to go get it.

He looked so confused that I giggled. "Wait, I'm whisking," he said. "I can't whisk this and get the bread out."

With a stern look on her face, MaryLou stated, "If I can make a whole Thanksgiving dinner while in labor with my second daughter, you can do this."

Luke gave me a pleading a look.

"I'll get the bread out," I said. "The sauce is simmering, and the pasta is cooking."

MaryLou clapped her hands together and then announced, "I've got to run now."

I nearly dropped the bread as Luke gasped, "You're leaving?"

"Wait, you're not staying through dinner?" I asked, setting the bread down on the rack.

MaryLou laughed. "Brighton, this is not the first time you've handled the bed and breakfast. And there are four guests joining you for dinner. You'll be fine."

"But it's only me," I exclaimed.

Luke huffed. "Hey, excuse me. I'm here, and I'm making dressing."

I rolled my eyes. "MaryLou, I'll pay you double if you stay. Tonight is game night. I can't do game night alone."

She jerked her thumb toward Luke. "You're not alone. Your boyfriend, I mean, fiancé is here."

"He's a guest too," I argued.

Dropping the apron on the hook by the back door, she exhaled and smiled. "Sorry, I've got a meeting I need to attend."

I frowned. "At night? With who?"

"Four other moms who need wine as much as I do. So now that I know the two of you are good, I'm off."

"Wait," Luke called out. "You can't leave us!"

Without another word, MaryLou was out the door.

"Oh my God, she left us," he said, sounding panicked. "How long do I whisk this for?"

I walked over and pulled the whisk from Luke's hand. "It's mixed." Taking a cucumber from the cutting board, I dipped it into the dressing, ate it, and then smiled. "And it's delicious. Good job, Mr. Morrison."

"How can you be so happy? She left us."

I waved my hand in the direction of the door. "We're fine. It's only a few guests, give or take. I think two of the couples aren't even planning on being here for dinner. We're golden either way. I made plenty of food, and game night really isn't that big of a deal."

"What about the evening bags?"

"Shit," I muttered. "I forgot about them. Maybe my mom made them up already."

Pulling out my phone, I hit her number.

"Brighton, is everything okay?"

"MaryLou needs to be fired for leaving me."

Her laugh came through the phone. "What are you talking about? You have four guests for dinner—the others told me they'd be eating out—so why are you acting like it's a full house?"

I gave another eye roll. "Did you make the evening gift bags?"

"Yes. They're in the hall closet."

"Oh, good, one less thing I need to do since the traitor left me all alone."

My mother chuckled. "Make sure you pour the garlic butter sauce over the bread."

"Right." Turning to Luke, I asked, "Will you pour the garlic dressing over the bread?"

He nodded.

"How's Luke doing?" she asked. "I love that he offered to help you this evening. What a sweet boy."

Turning my body away from him, I grinned. "Mom, he's covered in food. Flour, sauce—he even has a blueberry in his hair, and I don't have the heart to tell him it's there."

She giggled. "You should have seen your father the first few times we prepared dinner for the guests. He would be covered head to toe in food."

"I was not!" my father protested.

"I'm sure he's doing a fine job," she said. "Such a handsome boy he is."

Sighing, I replied, "He's not a boy and yes, he's very..." My voice trailed off as I looked back at Luke. "Oh. My. God. I'm going to kill him."

"Why?" my mother asked, her voice laced with concern.

"He's pouring the lemon vinaigrette over the bread...*why*? Dear God, why? LUKE!"

He jumped and the glass bowl in his hands fell to the floor and broke. "Jesus, Bree! Look what you made me do!"

"Was that glass? Brighton, what broke? Oh my goodness, it didn't get in any food, did it?" my mother asked.

"Why were you pouring the dressing over the bread?" I asked as I made my way over to him.

He looked at the bread, then down at the floor where the rest of the dressing had splattered. "You told me to."

My mouth fell open. "I did no such thing. I said pour the garlic dressing over the bread."

"You should have said garlic butter, sweetheart," my mother added.

I pulled the phone back and glared at it before I brought it to my ear again. "I need to go, Mom."

After hitting End, I looked down at the fresh loaf of Italian bread, then back at Luke.

"You said dressing," he said. "Was that not dressing I made?"

I placed my thumb and pointer finger on the bridge of my nose and took in a few calming breaths. "Why would I ask you to pour salad dressing over the bread?"

"Don't know. I thought it was kind of strange."

I dropped my hand to my side. "We'll need to run to the bakery and buy some more bread. Do you know where it's at?"

He shook his head.

"I'll call Candace."

He nodded. "Good plan. Should I, um, make more salad dressing?"

We both looked down at the floor. "Yeah, probably."

Candace answered her phone, thank goodness, and was soon on her way with the bread and the bottle of wine I'd asked her to pick up. For me.

"Table is all set," I said as I walked back into the kitchen—and stopped dead in my tracks. Luke stood there with a worried look on his face. "What's wrong?"

He smiled a boyish, almost embarrassed smile, and I couldn't help but return it. "I did something."

My smile instantly faded. "What did you do?"

"Well, I always heard you can tell when pasta's done by throwing it against a wall."

I scanned the kitchen for the pasta. When I didn't see any, I focused back on Luke and lifted one single brow.

"I couldn't really find an open wall...so I sorta threw it higher."

Slowly dropping my head back, I saw the long noodle hanging onto the ceiling.

"It's done!" Luke announced with a nervous laugh.

"Okay, we'll have to worry about that later."

A knock at the back door had us both turning to see Candace walking in, followed by Kyle and Hunter. All three of them took one look at Luke and their eyes went wide.

"Jesus Christ, what in the hell happened to you?" Kyle asked.

Candace walked up to Luke, wiped her finger over the sauce on his cheek, and then proceeded to lick it. "Needs more salt."

"What?" Luke asked as his hand went to his cheek.

"Dude, you have food in your hair." Hunter reached up and took the blueberry out, showing it to Luke.

Candace folded her arms and shot me a dirty look. "What have you done to this poor man?"

"What? Me? I haven't done anything. He's helping me since my parents decided to go to Boston."

Luke ran his fingers through his hair. "If I remember right, you *wanted* them to leave tonight."

"Yes! So we could have sex! I haven't had sex in four months, and I can't have sex if my parents are here!"

A throat cleared from behind me—and we all quickly turned to see a woman standing in the doorframe. My face instantly heated.

"Mrs. Cole, what can I help you with?" I asked.

With an embarrassed smile, she cleared her throat again. "I was going to see if you might have a banana?"

"A...banana? Well, dinner will be ready in about ten minutes."

She stepped into the kitchen and looked around at everyone, her eyes widening when she took in Luke. "It's for the, um...the...ahh...

As she tried to find her words, the stray piece of spaghetti that had been on the ceiling decided to fall. And land in her hair.

I gasped, and so did Candace. Mrs. Cole, however, didn't seem to notice. She was too busy staring at Luke.

Hunter grabbed a banana and handed it to Mrs. Cole. "Here you go, a banana for you or whoever's in need of it. Don't forget that dinner will be served shortly, so don't get too full."

As Hunter ushered Mrs. Cole out of the kitchen, Candace and Kyle fell into a fit of laughter.

Pointing my finger at them, I whispered, "Hush!" Then I spun and faced Luke. "You need to go get cleaned up. You can't go to dinner looking like this."

"No, what Luke needs is to get the hell out of here," Kyle stated.

"I agree," Hunter added. "Dude, you look like you've been through the ringer. What has she been making you do?"

Luke sighed. "I had to zest a lemon. Twice."

I blinked several times as I watched Hunter and Kyle take pity on Luke.

Kyle walked over and put a hand on his shoulder. "It's poker night. You're coming with us. I'm afraid if we leave you here any longer, you'll be high-tailing it back to Boston."

"Wait, what?" I said, stomping my foot. "I need him here! To help me!"

Hunter looked at me and winked. "Don't worry, we'll have him back in time for you to be able to...you know."

"Have sex," Kyle deadpanned.

Candace slipped on the apron that MaryLou, the traitor, had hung up. "Let them go. You and I can handle this."

I faced Candace, wanting to hug her. "Are you serious? For some reason I feel so flustered and unorganized."

She gave me a knowing look. "It's the lack of sex. And the fact that the man you want to have it with is standing right here, and you can't do anything about it."

I pointed at her. "Yes! That is exactly it."

"Right," Kyle said, giving Luke a little push. "Go take a shower and meet us in the living room."

"Candace is right, this does need more salt," Hunter said after he tasted the sauce in the pan.

I glared at him. "If you don't want me to take this pan and hit it upside your head, you'll get the hell out of my kitchen. Now."

Hunter lifted his hands in surrender and headed out of the kitchen. "Some thanks I get for rescuing Spaghetti Head from the kitchen."

I closed my eyes and fell back against the counter. "I'm exhausted. You'd think I made a seven-course meal. I spent more time trying to keep Luke from messing everything up that I would have been better off doing this alone."

Candace chuckled. "I think it's kind of cute he was trying to help. He looked adorable with all that flour on his face."

Smiling, I nodded. "He did look rather adorable, didn't he?"

"Yes. Now, come on, let's get your guests served. I can hear them all talking in the living room with Kyle and Hunter. Lord knows what those two will say or do."

After announcing that the food was ready, Candace and I successfully served dinner and dessert without an issue. It was hard to sit through dinner, though, and not focus on the spaghetti that was still in Mrs. Cole's hair. Her husband had clearly not noticed, and if the other two guests did, they pretended not to.

At some point after we sat down, Kyle, Hunter, and Luke slipped away from the house and headed to Kyle's house for poker night.

As Candace and I cleared the dishes from the table, I informed everyone that game night would be in the living room, and I'd have pie and ice cream available.

"Game night?" Candace asked while bouncing on her toes. "We're having game night?"

I nodded. "Yes. Do you want to stay? You can be my partner; that way we'll have an even number of teams."

"Hell yes, I want to stay!" Candace said as she placed some plates on the counter. "What are we playing?"

"Um, I think we have charades and Pictionary on the calendar."

Candace fist pumped. "Yes! We're going to kick some ass tonight, Bree!"

I stared at her. "Well, my folks tend to let the guests win."

With a laugh that sounded like pure evil, Candace shook her head. "Yeah, no. That's not how it's going to work tonight." She rubbed her hands together and smiled. "We're taking Mrs. Cole down!"

I couldn't hold my laugh in even if I had tried.

Chapter Twenty
Luke

Kyle slapped me on the back. "Make yourself at home, Luke."
I glanced around his place, taking it all in. It was for sure a bachelor pad, with white walls and brown leather furniture and very few other things in the living room. There was, of course, a large TV mounted, but the rest of the walls were empty. To the side of the leather sofa was a large brown leather recliner, and next to that was a crate for Cat, his K9 partner.

"Want a beer?" Hunter asked, holding up a bottle.

With a smile, I replied, "That'd be great, thanks."

He grinned and handed it to me.

"Okay," Kyle said as he walked back into the living room. "Aiden, Bishop, and Hudson will be here in a few."

I took a drink from the beer and then said, "Thanks for inviting me."

Hunter and Kyle both laughed before Kyle said, "Dude, I took one look at you and knew we needed to step in and get you the hell out of there."

"I have to ask," Hunter said with a slight smile. "Was she punishing you, or did you willingly walk into that mess?"

I gave a one-shoulder shrug. "Willingly walked into it."

Hunter smiled at me while Kyle shook his head. "Kyle said the two of you made up?" Hunter asked. "I wasn't even aware she'd been dating anyone. I mean, I figured something happened when she asked me and Kyle to come to Boston and help her move back to Boggy Creek."

Rubbing at the back of my neck, I let out a sigh. "Yeah, I didn't really handle things all that well. Of course, I also didn't know when she told me to get out of her office that she wasn't actually telling me to leave her alone."

"Women," Kyle scoffed. "This is why I'm the only single one left. I'm the only one with any brains."

"Adam," Hunter stated.

Kyle rolled his eyes. "He doesn't count."

"Who's Adam?" I asked.

"Friend of ours who was engaged, but she broke his heart. He moved to Boston to drown his sorrows away by working endless hours in the emergency room."

Hunter added, "He's a doctor."

"Oh, I see."

"I've got to know," Kyle said as he sat down on the sofa and motioned for me to sit as well. "How did it go from Brighton asking me to pretend to be her boyfriend to the two of you talking about getting married?"

"Married?" Hunter asked in a surprised voice. "You didn't tell me that part."

Kyle shrugged. "Probably because I was still trying to get my liver back in place after Brighton punched me."

I couldn't help but laugh before I answered him. "We ate lunch at The Coffee Pot, talked, argued a little, then went and sat on a park bench and laid it all out on the line. I told her I gave up acting."

Both men's mouths dropped open.

"Dude, you did *what*?" Hunter asked.

With a nod, I said, "I'm giving it up. I love her too much to lose her, and if I stay in the business, that's exactly what will happen."

The corner of Kyle's mouth twitched with a hidden smile. "Mad respect for you, Luke. That had to be hard."

I studied the beer in my hand and let out a soft laugh before I looked back up at them. "Honestly, it was the easiest thing I've ever done. I haven't been happy for the last few years. Yes, I've been incredibly blessed with my career, but something was missing. I found it one night at my father's Christmas party when a set of light-brown eyes looked up at me and said, 'You look like Gene Kelly.' I was lost to her."

Hunter and Kyle both laughed.

"Yeah, Brighton is as obsessed with Gene Kelly as Kyle is with Jane Austen."

That caused me to raise my brows. I glanced over to see Kyle nodding. "I'm man enough to admit I like Jane Austen."

"Are you man enough to admit you're also in my sister's book club?" Hunter asked.

"Willa told you that?" Kyle sat up straight on the sofa. "I can't believe she told you."

Hunter grinned at his friend. "Of course, she told me. Willa tells me everything."

Kyle shook his head. "Damn women."

"What kind of book club is it?" I asked.

"Romance," Hunter answered, trying not to laugh.

"You're an asshole," Kyle said. "Luke is new to the group. Can we not have him thinking I'm a pansy ass right off the bat?"

I held up my hands. "No judgment from me. I was in a romance book club in college. The only guy with about thirty single women. That was a good semester," I said, looking up in thought.

Pointing his beer at me, Kyle said, "I knew I liked you. We're going to be good friends."

There was a quick knock at the door before it opened and three men walked in. Kyle stood, and I did the same.

"About damn time you guys got here. The pizza will be here any minute." He turned to me and said, "Luke Morrison, this is Aiden O'Hara. He's married to Hunter's sister, Willa."

I reached for Aiden's hand and shook it. "It's nice to meet you, Aiden. Thank you for your service."

He looked taken aback for a moment. "Um, thank you. It's nice to meet you, Luke."

"Brighton talked a lot about all of you. I feel as if I've known you for a while."

They all exchanged a look before all eyes were back on me.

"She didn't say shit about you, dude," the taller one with blond hair and blue eyes said. "The name is Bishop Harris. I'm married to Abby."

"The Christmas tree farmer," I said. "Pleasure to meet you, Bishop."

He nodded and gave me a warm smile.

"And last but not least is the man who's going to marry my sister, Greer. This is Hudson Higgins."

"The writer," I said as we shook hands. "I've read your work and really enjoyed it."

He gave me a grin. "Thank you. I've enjoyed your work as well. Especially *The Time Before Us*. Very powerful performance."

"I thought we weren't mentioning the fact that he's an actor?" Bishop said.

I laughed. "Was. I'm officially retiring after I finish up this last movie I'm filming. We've only got a few days left, and then it'll be done."

"Wow," Aiden said as he took the beer Kyle handed him. Bishop and Hudson also took one from their host. "You're walking away from it all?"

"I am," I said with a nod. "If it means being able to have Brighton in my life, then it's a no-brainer."

"What took you so long to come back for her?" Kyle asked.

I exhaled. "It took longer than I thought to finalize things, and honestly, I was an idiot for staying away as long as I did."

Kyle looked at me with a serious expression. "Brighton is probably one of the strongest women I've ever known. It was hard to see her with so much sadness in her eyes." Before I could say anything, he added, "And if you ever tell her I said that, I'll deny it and call you a lying bastard."

I drew my brows in. "I really don't understand the relationship you two share."

Bishop hit me on the back as he made his way over to the card table that was set up on the other side of the large living room. "Welcome to the club."

Two hours later, I reached for the middle of the table and pulled my latest winnings toward me.

"I don't think I've ever lost this many hands of poker. What the fuck, dude?" Kyle said as he threw his cards down on the table.

Bishop tipped back a beer and shook his head. "I haven't won a damn round yet."

All I could do was smile and look around the table. "Should we deal again?"

Aiden laughed. "I'm broke, so count me out."

"I'm expecting a baby in October, so I think I better save my coins. Good playing, Luke," Bishop said, tapping his beer bottle to mine.

Hunter chuckled. "Same."

"Congratulations to you both," I said. "When's your baby due, Hunter?"

His face morphed into a look of pure happiness, and a strange pang hit me right in the middle of my chest. Was that jealousy?

"November ninth."

"Are you finding out if it's a boy or girl?" I asked them both.

They both said no at the same time, then grinned at each other.

"What about you, Luke? Do you want kids?" Aiden asked.

Nodding, I answered, "Yes. More than anything. That's another reason I want a simpler life. I don't want my kids growing up with cameras shoved in their faces. Again, not that I'm not grateful. I knew what I was getting into when I moved to LA. Once Brighton walked into my life, though, my eyes were opened to a whole other world I never even knew I wanted."

"Has she mentioned if she wants to practice law here in Boggy Creek?" Hunter asked. "I know Earl Watkins, the one and only lawyer in Boggy Creek, is well past his retiring years."

I shook my head. "No, she hasn't mentioned it."

"What about you?" Bishop asked. "Brighton mentioned you were once a lawyer."

"I was. I think if my father hadn't pushed me into becoming one, I could have really enjoyed it. Might not have ever gone to LA to pursue acting. Don't get me wrong, I was in drama in high school and college and fucking loved it. But I think my dad pushing me away from it actually drove me to it. If that makes sense."

They all nodded. "That's like me and my dad," Kyle said. "He was a cop, and from the time I was little, I remember him telling me what a great cop I'd make."

Everyone focused on him.

"Dude, do you not like being a cop?" Hunter asked.

He shook his head. "I love it. It's just...sometimes I wonder if my father hadn't been a cop, would I have done something different with my life?"

There was a long silence as we all glanced around the table. Bishop finally broke it. "Okay, so I'll ask. If you're not going to be a lawyer or act, what are you going to do? I'm assuming you don't need to work."

With a grin, I replied, "No, I'm financially good, and I have a lot of side projects and investments as well. I *have* thought about offering my services as a lawyer for a nonprofit, maybe."

Aiden sat up straighter. "Really?"

I nodded, then finished off my beer.

"Another one?" Kyle asked as he stood up.

Waving my hand, I replied, "No, I'm good."

He nodded and looked around the table. "Anyone?"

"I'm designated driver, so have at it," Hudson said to Aiden and Bishop, but they both declined.

Kyle rolled his eyes. "My God, you all got tied down with women and stopped being adventurous."

"I have two kids who'll both be up at the crack of dawn tomorrow. The last thing I need is a hangover," Aiden commented.

"Whatever," Kyle mumbled, heading into the kitchen.

Hunter slowly shook his head. "Someday, a woman is going to come along and knock him on his ass."

"I think one already has," Bishop stated.

All eyes were now on him. "What do you know?" Hunter asked.

Bishop glanced around, then his gaze landed on Hudson. "Ever since your sister came to visit, haven't you guys noticed how Kyle hasn't gone out or dated anyone? It's almost like he's pining over someone..."

Hudson leaned back in his chair and gave Bishop a thoughtful expression. "You think he likes my sister?"

Bishop nodded.

"I'm going to agree," Hunter added. "I saw the way Kyle looked at Everly. He couldn't keep his eyes off her. Sorry, Hudson."

He shrugged, then looked back at the kitchen to see if Kyle was coming. "Everly seemed to be taken with Kyle as well. It was hard not to notice the way the two of them looked at each other. But do you honestly believe that short encounter with Everly would keep him from seeing anyone else?"

Bishop shook his head. "I don't know. All I know is, he hasn't dated anyone since your sister came to town."

"Where's your sister now?" I asked.

A proud smile moved across Hudson's face. "She's in Alaska. She's a climatologist. She was supposed to take a job in Boston, but she suddenly hopped on a plane and left for Alaska. Her job keeps her traveling a lot, otherwise she lives in Washington, DC."

"Wow, that's kind of cool," I said.

Hudson nodded. "Yeah, she was in Greenland for a few years. She got engaged to another climatologist but broke things off with him. I never got a good vibe from the guy. Met him twice and each time he gave me...a bad feeling."

"I can't imagine what it would be like to have my sister Jenn date a douchebag, let alone get engaged to one."

"You just have the one sister?" Aiden asked as Kyle walked back into the room.

"I do, and I highly doubt she'll get married anytime soon."

"Why's that?" Kyle asked. He took a seat back down at the table, clueless to the previous conversation about him and Everly.

"My sister is too much in love with herself and her shoes and clothes."

"Does she get along with Brighton?" Kyle asked with a laugh.

I chuckled. "They get along famously. Clothing is their connection."

"Yeah, Brighton has a way with clothes. Last fall, she threw a little welcome home party for Abby," Bishop said. "That's a long story we'll fill you in on later...but Brighton brought outfits for each girl to wear."

Lifting a brow, I asked, "What kind of outfits?"

"I'm surprised she never told you," Hunter said with a laugh. "They were...very suggestive outfits."

"Willa was nearly eight months pregnant at the time, and Brighton had her in short boy shorts and a half T-shirt with the number sixty-nine on it. Needless to say, I smuggled it out of the party."

The entire table erupted in laughter.

"Were you guys there for the party?" I asked.

"Oh no," Kyle said with a shake of his head. "Brighton had the whole thing planned out. She got them all wasted—well, everyone except Willa, of course. Had them dress up in these skimpy outfits, then called in a noise complaint and bribed the responding officer to page me and Hunter so we'd show up."

I frowned. "Why would she do that?"

Bishop and Hunter both looked at each other and smiled.

"Let's just say Bishop and I weren't with Abby and Arabella at the time," Hunter said, "and Brighton was trying to give us a little push."

"Fucking worked," Bishop added.

I couldn't help but smile. "That sounds like something she'd do. She adores all of you. Talked about you a lot."

They all grinned.

Kyle held up his beer. "I, for one, am glad you showed up in Boggy Creek. I think you're a great actor, but you're an even cooler guy."

The rest of the guys held up their bottles, and I picked up mine. "Thanks for including me tonight. You have no idea how nice this was."

"You're stuck with us now, dude," Hudson said. "Poker twice a month."

For the first time in a long time, I truly felt like I was somewhere I belonged, with people who wanted to hang out with me...and not because I was an actor.

We played another hand of poker and then decided to call it a night. As we were leaving, Aiden walked up to me. "Luke, I wouldn't mind setting up a business meeting with you."

I raised a brow, curious about why Aiden would want to talk business. He must have seen that curiosity on my face.

"Me and another ex-Navy SEAL—his name is Mitch Hathaway and he's also a Boggy Creek police officer—have a counseling clinic in Boggy Creek. It's mostly to help veterans and people who suffer from PTSD, but we also offer counseling for other things, such as domestic violence, sexual assault, or other traumatic experiences. I've got a law firm in Boston that handles a lot of our stuff, but I'd really like to work with someone here in Boggy Creek. If that's something you'd be interested in, I'd love to talk to you about it."

I couldn't help but notice the hopeful look on his face as he waited for my answer, and a part of me really wanted to explore the opportunity. "I'd love to sit and chat with you about it."

A wide smile spread across his face. "Great. Um, here's my card, and it's got my cell phone on there. Give me a text and let me know some days and times you're open, and we'll set up a time to talk."

I took the card and pulled out my wallet, slipping it inside one of the pockets. "Will do."

Aiden reached his hand out to shake mine. "I really am glad you and Brighton were able to work things out."

"Thank you, so am I."

"Welcome to Boggy Creek, Luke."

"Yeah, welcome to BC," Bishop said as he tapped the side of my arm.

"Thanks."

Hunter and Hudson repeated the welcome, and I was soon left standing on the front porch with Kyle. Before I headed to my car, I turned to face him. "Thank you for tonight, Kyle. I had a really good time."

He winked. "I have a feeling your evening will get even better."

Chapter Twenty-One

Bree

Exhaustion.

I had never been so tired in my life. Four guests. We only had four guests, and I'd been running around like a crazy woman. After Candace and I had cleared off the dinner table, I got to work cleaning up while she got everyone set up in the living room for game night.

Once I'd gotten all the dishes cleaned and put in the dishwasher, wiped down the table and the kitchen, I joined them. What started off as fun, quickly turned into a Pictionary showdown between Mrs. Cole and Candace.

The younger couple, Lee and Will, decided to duck out of game night when things became too heated. They decided to go and check out our local bar, Brew's Place. I was almost positive they'd seen the look on my face pleading them to take me too.

When Candace almost called Mrs. Cole a cheating whore, I put an end to game night and suggested the Coles sit by the outdoor firepit to enjoy the nice evening.

Candace decided to head home while I put the three gift bags on the doors for our guests. I smiled as I placed Luke's bag on his door. Even though I wanted to text him, I knew he was with the guys and they would make him feel welcome. Well, almost all of them would. Lord only knew what in the hell Kyle would say or do.

I walked through the house and turned on the small lights that we kept on all the time for guests who might arrive during the night. The Coles had already come back inside and made their way up to the room. I sat on the sofa in the main living room and yawned. I had already let both couples know I lived in the cabin down the path past the firepit and told them to call the desk if they needed anything.

My eyes felt heavy, and I decided to close them for a second while I let the evening's activities slowly fade away.

Warm breath tickled the side of my neck, and I let out a soft moan.

"Sweetheart, wake up."

"Go away," I mumbled, turning away from the person who'd woken me up from a dream. A very lovely dream. Luke had been making love to me, and the last thing I wanted to do was wake up.

"Bree, wake up, love."

It was Luke, whispering into my ear.

"Luke?" I turned and opened my eyes to see him staring down at me, a brilliant smile on his face. "How was poker night?"

"I'll be surprised if they ask me back."

Frowning, I slowly pushed myself up into a sitting position. "Why do you say that?" I asked with a yawn.

He chuckled. "I pretty much won every hand."

My brows shot up. "Really? I didn't know you liked poker." A blush moved over his cheeks and I narrowed my eyes. "Did you cheat?"

"No! Of course not. But...I neglected to tell them I was taught how to play by William Lawrence Parker."

"I don't know who that is."

He laughed softly. "He's one of the best, if not *the* best, poker player in the world. I played him in a movie a few years ago that was filmed in Vegas where he lives. He used to live at Caesars Palace and played the high stakes poker games. He won millions back when he was in his thirties."

I brought my hand to my mouth and giggled. "Oh my God, please don't tell them for at least another few poker nights! That's hilarious. Was Kyle pissed he kept losing?"

Luke gave me a one-shoulder shrug. "He wasn't happy." Standing up, he said, "Let's get you to bed."

He headed for his room before I stopped him. "I already told the guests I'll be in the cabin in the back, and if they need anything they should call the number for the front desk. I forwarded it to my cell already."

"So what you're saying is, we'll have privacy to make up for the last four months?"

I nodded and gave him a wicked smile. "Yes. And we don't have to be quiet either."

Before I knew what was happening, Luke swept me up into his arms and headed to the back door. "Do the doors lock automatically?" he asked as he slipped outside and paused.

"Yes," I replied. "They're programed to lock at nine. Didn't you have to use your code to get in?"

He nodded. "I did. But I wanted to make sure they're all locked."

As he started down the path, I snuggled into his chest and breathed in his scent. It sent a thrill straight to my core, and I instantly felt a pulse of need between my legs.

"You know, I'm going to need to find a place to live," he said, "And sooner rather than later, Bree."

"Why's that?" I asked, pretending to be confused.

"I'm not fucking you steps away from your parents, where your mother could interrupt us at any moment. Especially after we get married."

My heart warmed, and my stomach did a little flip. "Married," I whispered. A part of me screamed that we needed to slow the hell down. We had been broken up for four months. But now that Luke was back and I was in his arms and had tasted his sweet kisses again, there was no way in hell I was letting him go. Ever.

"I've been looking at places to buy. I saved up some money and have enough for a down payment, but I haven't been in a huge rush," I replied. "I'd like to find a historical home."

He looked down at me and smiled while he picked up his pace. Once we got to the cottage, Luke set me down and I punched in the code. The moment the door opened, he pushed me inside and we got to work on undressing each other. It was rushed and sloppy, with my hands getting in the way of his and vice versa. But soon we were both standing naked in the middle of my little living room and I couldn't keep my hands off of him. I trailed my fingers up his chest, over his shoulders, down his arms.

When I brushed a fingertip lightly over his cock, Luke hissed and grabbed my hand. "I want you too badly to play games. Sit down in the chair, Bree."

My entire body hummed with anticipation. I glanced over my shoulder at the antique chair that sat in the corner of the living room. "That chair?" I asked innocently.

Luke growled and began gently pushing me back until my legs bumped into it, and I sank down. He dropped to his knees, pushed my legs apart, and stared for the longest time before he let out a low moan. "Fuck, I've missed you."

The feel of his hot gaze on me was nearly enough to make me come on the spot. I squirmed in my seat, needing him to do something.

"I want to taste you, Bree."

All I could do was nod, grip the chair arms, and hold on.

Then his head was between my legs, and I jumped when I felt him lick through my folds and then softly blow on my skin, causing my entire body to shudder.

"Luke," I pleaded, lifting my head and staring down at him. He never took his eyes off of me as he placed his mouth on me and started to lick and nibble my clit.

He moaned, and I cried out in pleasure. "Yes. Oh God, Luke, yes!"

He worked magic with his mouth, tongue, and fingers. When I wouldn't stay still anymore, he pressed his hands on my hips, forcing me to let him take what he wanted.

"Oh God," I panted. "I'm...so...close."

It didn't take long before the familiar sensation started in my toes and rushed up, unleashing an orgasm that nearly stole the breath from me.

"Luke!" I screamed out as I pushed my fingers into his hair. I couldn't decide if I needed to pull him closer or push him away.

Ripples of pleasure coursed through my entire body until I was almost positive I'd pass out from utter bliss. Before I could fully come back down to reality, I felt Luke lift me from the chair.

"Bedroom?" he whispered.

My arm felt like it weighed a hundred pounds when I lifted it and pointed to the door on the left. Luke quickly headed in that direction and, once inside my room, gently placed me on the bed.

He leaned down and kissed me. A mixture of myself and the faint hints of alcohol on his tongue created a heady response in me. I wrapped my hand around his neck and drew him closer, deepening the kiss.

When we broke apart, I whispered, "Please tell me I'm not dreaming."

His beautiful face stared down at me and when he smiled, it felt like the sun had burst through the small window to light up the room. "You're not dreaming, love."

I moved my hand to the side of his face and let out a long, slow sigh. "I've missed you so much, Luke."

He closed his eyes for a moment, and then his gaze met mine. "I swear to you, I'll never leave you again."

"Promise?"

He dropped to his knees, and I turned on my side to look at him.

"I swear on my life, I will never walk away from you. I will never be the reason you cry again."

My heart started to beat faster in my chest while my breath caught in my throat. I grinned. "What if they're happy tears?"

He lifted his hand and ran his finger along my jawline and then down my throat, watching the path it took before he looked into my eyes. "Happy tears don't count."

"Good, because I'm so very happy right now I think I might cry."

I felt a tear slip free and glide down my face. Luke leaned up and kissed it.

"Make love to me, Luke. Please."

His lips found mine once again, and he kissed me so passionately there was no doubt in my mind that this man was in love with me. The fact that he'd given up his entire life for me hit so intensely, I fought to keep from crying harder.

He gave up everything. *For me.*

I drew back and looked into his eyes. "I love you, and I will never be able to repay you for what you've done for me. What you've given up for me. All I can do is hope and pray that I love you enough each day that you never regret your decision."

He frowned slightly. "I will *never* regret it, Bree. Never. Because the only thing I need in this life to make me happy is you. I love you more than I'll ever be able to express. You're the reason I breathe. The first time we made love, I knew you were the missing piece of my life. The one thing that would make me feel complete. Your love..."

His voice cracked, and he closed his eyes as he drew in a deep breath before looking at me again. He picked up my hand and placed it over his heart. "If these last few months without you have shown me anything, it's that I cannot live this life without you in it. I will love you until I take my last breath and then some. You are my heart, Brighton."

Tears streamed down my face, and I sat up and wrapped my arms around his neck. I buried my face against him as he wrapped his arms around me.

"I love you." We said it in unison and laughed as we drew back and looked at each other.

"Can I make love to you now?" he asked.

Nodding, I whispered, "Yes."

Luke laid me back down on the bed and covered me with his body. The feel of his bare skin against mine was heavenly. My dreams would never even come close to the real thing. I moved my fingers softly over his back while he placed kisses on my neck, across my breasts, and back up to my mouth.

"When can we get married?" he asked against my lips.

"As soon as you want."

"Tomorrow."

I placed my hand on his chest and pushed him back slightly. "Tomorrow?"

He smiled. "Yes. There has to be a justice of the peace in Boggy Creek."

A soft chuckle slipped free. "There is. He's, um...he's my dad's best friend."

Luke laughed. "Then I say we go to the courthouse, get our license, and get married. I need to be on set by two, though."

I opened my mouth, then closed it. "But...I need to make breakfast for the guests. I need to..."

When my voice faded away, Luke looked at me with a serious expression. "Am I pushing things?"

"No. I can call Candace. I'm positive she'll help me."

He smiled, and it took my breath away. "Good, because I don't want to wait another minute."

A sudden fit of giggles came over me, and Luke pushed up and peered down at my face. "What is it?"

I shook my head and wiped at my tears—these ones from laughing. "My mother is going to be *pissed* if we elope."

He gave me another brilliant smile. "We'll make it up to her. If you want to plan the biggest wedding Boggy Creek has ever seen, then do it. As long as you become Mrs. Brighton Morrison within the next twenty-four hours, I'm fine with anything."

Raising a brow, I replied, "Biggest wedding ever seen, huh?"

He nodded and started to kiss along my breasts again, pulling one of my nipples into his mouth and sucking. I gasped and lifted my hips, feeling the weight of his hard length press against my core.

"Luke, I need you. Now."

He reached between us and positioned himself at my entrance. Taking my mouth with his, he slowly pushed in, one delicious inch at a time. We both moaned once he was fully seated inside me.

"Bree," he whispered against my mouth as he stilled.

"God, the way you feel inside me... It's the most amazing feeling in the world."

He smiled and moved his hips, teasing me. "I agree. Being inside you is one of my very favorite places to be."

Our eyes met, and a rush of warmth hit me in the chest at the love in his gaze. "Make love to me, Luke."

He pulled out a bit before pushing back in. "My pleasure, sweetheart."

It didn't take long for the two of us to become completely lost in one another. Our lovemaking started off sweet and slow and quickly turned passionate when it was clear we both needed more.

Luke rolled over onto his back, and I repositioned myself on top of him.

"Take what you want, sweetheart."

Smiling, I did exactly that. With my hands on his chest, I rotated my hips until I found the rhythm I needed to ease the throb between my legs.

"Christ, you're so fucking beautiful. That's it, baby. Ride me. Make yourself come."

His words caused a flood of lust and desire to rush through me, and I felt my orgasm building. I pushed off his chest and threw my head back, my hands going to my breasts while I moved on top of him.

"Luke. Oh God, I'm so close."

When I felt his thumb touch my clit, I screamed. The orgasm hit me so hard, I was positive I might black out. Waves and waves of pleasure rippled through my entire body, and I felt myself clench around his cock.

"Fuuuuuck! Oh God, Bree. I'm going to come."

"Yes!" I cried out. "Come, Luke! Come!"

Like the sweetest music my ears had ever heard, he cried out my name, grabbed onto my hips, and came inside me. Lord, it was heavenly. I could feel his warmth, feel his dick grow harder right before his own release.

When I could no longer stay upright, I collapsed onto his chest, my panting breaths coming one right after the other. I could hear Luke's heart beating a mile a minute with my ear pressed to his body. He wrapped his arms around me, and we worked together at calming our heart rates.

"How soon will you be ready to do that again?" I asked. My body shook with his laughter. I loved the sound of that laugh.

"Give me a few minutes. Then I'll try my best."

I pushed up and looked down at him, my heart filled with so much happiness and love. I ran my fingertip over his lips and sighed. "I'm so utterly happy right now."

His eyes sparkled as he cupped my face and looked so deeply into my gaze that it felt like he was staring right into my soul. "That makes two of us."

Rolling us, he hovered above me and peppered kisses all over my face and down my neck. "We have a lot of time to make up for."

I moaned and wrapped my legs around him. "I agree. But maybe we should go shower and talk about all the ways we're going to make up for lost time."

He laughed, then kissed the tip of my nose. "Lead the way, baby."

Chapter Twenty-Two
Luke

I woke to the feel of Bree pressed against my body, her warm breath a slight tickle on my chest. Drawing in a slow, deep breath, I exhaled and closed my eyes. Last night hadn't been a dream. The feeling of being inside Bree twice and then making her come with my mouth two more times hadn't been a fantasy.

It was then I noticed my arm was asleep. I tried to move it, but when Bree groaned in protest, I stilled. If it meant keeping her near me, I'd let my whole damn body go numb.

Closing my eyes, I drifted back to sleep. That was, until an obnoxious alarm went off, causing Bree to sit up so fast she nearly flew over my body and off the bed.

"Breakfast!" she screamed out. "We need to make breakfast!"

I watched as she stumbled over to the dresser, where she wrenched open drawers and pulled out clothes.

"Bree."

"I can't, Luke. I mean, I want to, but I can't. I need to get breakfast going for the guests."

Sitting up, I let the sheet fall below my waist and watched her run around like a chicken with its head cut off. "Bree..."

"Shit. I need to make the gravy. I hate making gravy!" she said, rushing into the bathroom. I heard her electric toothbrush turn on, and I threw off the sheet and made my way to the bathroom.

Stopping in the open door, I leaned against the jamb and watched her brush her teeth with one hand while combing her long dark hair with the other.

"You sent Candace a text last night," I said. "Don't you remember?"

She stopped and met my gaze. I couldn't help but smile.

"Candace called you back," I reminded her, "and you told her our plan for this morning. She screamed that rather loud scream of hers, then said she and Arabella would take care of the guests today."

The hand that was holding the brush fell to her side and she smiled around her toothbrush.

I nodded. "That's right, love. We're getting married this morning. The quicker I get you in front of a justice of the peace, the less likely it is you'll come to your senses and decide not marry me."

Pulling the toothbrush from her mouth, she dropped it in the sink and then threw herself into my arms. I caught her in time, nearly stumbling back in the process. She went to kiss me, but I turned my head.

"I love you, but not enough to kiss you with a mouth full of toothpaste." I fake gagged.

"Fit, forry!" she said, turning and spitting into the sink and then rinsing her mouth. She opened the drawer and pulled out a disposable toothbrush, smiling as she held it out for me. I knew she'd have one. She always had one available.

"Thank you," I said, taking it from her and proceeding to brush my own teeth.

"Let me call Candace—they should be on their way here by now."

She slipped out of the bathroom, and I soon heard her talking on the phone. She popped her head back in. "They're already here. I have the best friends ever!"

Laughing, I rinsed my mouth, used the restroom, and then headed back into the bedroom to get dressed.

Bree was standing at her closet, still talking on the phone.

"Do you think white? I was thinking something more like pink. What do you mean, you can't see me in pink? I've worn pink before."

I slipped on my jeans and tried not to laugh again. I had never once seen Bree in pink.

"Fuck you, Candace. I can pull off pink if I want to. Fine, whatever. What do you mean green? I'm not wearing *green* to my wedding."

There was a long pause. "I don't care if I'm getting married at the justice of the peace; I'm not wearing green."

After slipping my shirt back on, I put on socks and shoes while Bree pulled dress after dress out of her closet and tossed them onto the floor.

I turned and headed into the kitchen area and found her coffeepot and coffee.

"I'm not wearing red to my wedding!"

Laughing, I opened the fridge and took in what little food she had. "Okay, looks like we're grabbing breakfast on the way."

"I found it!" Bree called out. "Do you remember that white sundress in Boston that Arabella and you talked me into buying? Yes, the one with the lace and tulle that fell to my thighs. It's perfect!"

I walked over to the bedroom door and peered in to see Bree holding up a white lace dress. She spun around and glared at me. "What are you doing?"

"Seeing what you found to wear."

Her eyes went wide. "You can't see the dress!"

My mouth dropped open, and I was positive I had something to say—I just couldn't figure out what.

"Yes, I know that, Candace. Shut up."

I didn't hear what Candace said. Clearing my throat, I replied, "Um, how are you going to keep me from seeing it? We have to drive together."

"No, we don't. I'll meet you there."

"But we have to get the marriage license."

She let out a frustrated sigh. "Okay, you leave, go get dressed. I'll meet you at the front desk in...thirty minutes."

I glanced down at my watch. It was six forty-five. "We've got plenty of time. Nothing will open until eight."

Bree laughed. "Please, you forget this is Boggy Creek. I texted Kyle last night, who texted his dad, who texted Gina, who said she'd start the marriage license first thing. She'll be there by seven. All she needs is your info."

I shook my head in disbelief. "And when did you text all of this? If memory serves me, we were pretty tied up having sex most of the night."

She shot me a dirty look. "Luke!" She hit something on her phone and put it back up to her ear. "Shut up, Candace! I'll be over there in a bit. No, I don't need help with my makeup. Take care of the guests, and if my mother calls...don't tell her I'm not there. Tell her I'm...busy."

Hitting a button on her phone again, she dropped it onto the bed and then looked at me. "Why are you still here, Luke? Go get changed!"

"Right," I said, turning on my heels and heading to the coffee. "Thank God we're not having a real wedding."

"I heard that!"

Thirty minutes later, I was standing in front of the check-in desk, listening to the hustle and bustle of breakfast going on in the dining room. Candace and Arabella sounded like they were having a great time as they chatted with the guests.

The front door to the bed and breakfast opened and Bree poked her head in.

"Hey," I said softly, making my way over to her. Once I got close enough, she pulled me through the door.

"We need to hurry!"

It was then I noticed she was in a long trench coat. "Why are you wearing a coat?"

She grabbed my hand and pulled me down the steps of the front porch and around the path to the parking lot. "So you don't see my dress. We need to hurry, Luke!"

"Why?" I asked with a laugh.

She stopped, nearly causing me to run into her. "My mother found out."

"What?"

Rolling her eyes, she said, "My mother found out about the marriage license because apparently Gina stopped at The Coffee Pot first thing this morning to get her coffee, and she told Tess about the marriage license. And Maddie Brooks was in there."

Confused, I asked, "Who's Maddie Brooks?"

"She owns the quilt shop."

"Um, okay," I said, even more confused. "And did she tell your mom?"

Bree laughed. "God, no. But she was talking to Cindy Hamilton, who owns Schmick's, and *she* told Millie Parks."

"Millie Parks?" I asked.

"Yes, she owns the candy store on Main. Anyway, she immediately called my mother to congratulate her, and you can imagine my mother's shock. She called me and I answered, thinking she was going to ask about the morning and breakfast and all of that."

I nodded. "And did she?"

"Hell no, she didn't." Bree grabbed my hand again and pulled me toward her car. "She asked me about the rumor she'd heard about me getting married."

Bree unlocked her BMW and then handed me the keys. "I can't drive. I think Kyle is on duty, and if I get pulled over for speeding, he'll for sure give me a ticket, especially after I punched him."

I stood there, my mouth hanging open as I stared at Bree, who was now opening the door to the passenger side of her car. Before she got in, she looked at me with a confused expression. "Why are you standing there?"

"Who are you?" I asked.

"Ha!" she said, shooting me a look. "This is what happens when you tell your mother you're dating someone!"

I tried not to laugh as I got in the car and started it. "Wow, news travels pretty fast in town."

She nodded. "Just wait until someone realizes who you are. But don't worry, they won't call *People* or anything. The most that'll happen is they'll ask you to pull the switch for the Christmas tree lighting in the square."

I jerked my head to the right and stared at her. "What?"

She waved off my question. "Let's go! If my father drives fast enough, they'll get here sooner rather than later. You're going to go down Althorpe Street, and then take a left. The municipal building where we can get our license is a couple blocks down. Justice of the peace will be there as well—he called and said he'd meet us there. It'll be a one and done."

"A one and done?" I repeated. "This really is small-town living."

"Yep." She turned and looked at me, a wide smile on her face. "Are you excited? I'm excited. And nervous! Oh my God, we're getting married! Are you nervous?"

I gripped the steering wheel and tried not to laugh. I had no idea who the crazy woman was beside me, but one thing I did know for sure—I had fallen even more in love with her. "I'm excited and a bit nervous."

She chuckled. "Me too! Oh, here! Park here."

I pulled into a parking spot, and we made our way across the street and up the steps of the courthouse.

"I just realized the last time I was here, Willa was getting a divorce," she said. "Now I'm here, and I'm getting married."

I intertwined my fingers with hers, as I opened the door and we stepped inside.

"Brighton!"

We both turned to see an older woman walking toward us.

Bree smiled. "Gina! Thank you so much for getting here early. And for arranging this."

She took Bree into her arms and hugged her. "You mother called my cell, but I sent her to voicemail. She's going to be ticked off at me!"

Bree smiled. "Thank you. It's not that I don't want her here...I just don't want her here."

The older woman nodded in understanding. "Let's get that marriage license. Now, how far along are you, sweetheart?"

"What do you mean?" Bree asked as we followed Gina down the hallway and into a large room. When we went through another door, down a second hall, and into a small office, where she gestured for us to sit down.

Gina sat behind the desk and then looked at us both and winked. "How far along are you?"

Bree looked at me with a crease between her eyes, then back at Gina. "Do you mean how long have we dated?"

Gina's smile faded. "Wait, you're not...pregnant?" She whispered the last word.

"Pregnant!" Bree nearly shouted. "No! We simply want to get married as quickly as possible."

"Oh!" Gina said, turning and looking at me. "I'm so sorry I assumed."

I held up my hands. "If she was pregnant, I'd be just as happy."

Both women now looked at me, dreamy smiles on their faces.

"Mister...?" Gina started.

"Morrison."

She nodded. "First, I need to get some information from you."

After sharing our information, we followed her out of her office and down another hall.

We walked into a small courtroom where three people stood at the far end. They all turned and faced us.

Bree gasped. "Willa! Aiden!"

Willa practically ran down the aisle. "Arabella called me. She said you might need witnesses."

Aiden reached his hand out for me to shake. "You went from winning poker to getting married. Fast player."

"How did you find out we were here?" Bree asked Willa.

"It wasn't hard. I called Hunter, who called Kyle, who called Gina."

"Christ, I'm going to need a list of people in this town," I mumbled.

"You ready to get married?" Willa asked Bree as both girls hugged once more.

"Yes, I'm sweating my ass off in this coat." Bree turned to the justice of the peace. "Sorry, Sam."

He waved it off.

Bree looked at me and said, "Turn around."

"Why?"

"Dude," Aiden whispered. "You've got a lot to learn. Turn around."

I looked from Bree to Aiden. When he gave me a look that said I'd better do as she requested, I turned.

"Oh, here. I picked these from the garden while we were rushing out," Willa said.

"Who's watching the kids?" Bree asked.

"My mom," Willa stated.

I heard Willa suck in a deep breath and watched Aiden smile a big, goofy smile. He looked at me and nodded, then mouthed *she looks beautiful.*

Bree cleared her throat. "Okay, you can turn around!"

When I turned, I saw Bree standing there in the same white lace dress she'd been holding up earlier. My heart nearly pounded right out of my damn chest. I swallowed and tried to remember how to make my mouth move. All I could do was stare at the gorgeous woman who stood in front of me in a simple white dress and white heels—that she'd clearly switched out in the last thirty seconds which explains why the pockets in her trench coat looked so full—holding a small bouquet of flowers in her hands.

"You look beautiful," I whispered, stepping closer to her.

"Thank you," she replied softly, her cheeks turning a slight shade of pink.

"You're sure this is what you want? You don't want to wait for a big fancy wedding?"

She shook her head. "Nope. This is what I want."

I took her hand in mine, and we turned to face the justice of the peace. Who was apparently named Sam.

Once he started to speak, I didn't hear a damn word. All I could do was stare down at Bree. When he asked us for the rings, we both looked at him.

"Oh, I didn't even think about rings," Bree said with a laugh.

We all looked around at each other before Gina cried out. "Hold on!"

She ran out of the courtroom and was back in less than a minute. She walked up and handed me a straw.

I stared down at it. "What am I supposed to do with this?"

She rolled her eyes, opened the straw, and handed me the wrapper. "Make the rings."

When I still stared at it, Aiden took it from my hands, tore it in two, and handed the pieces to Sam. It was *his* turn to stare down at it.

Clearing hit throat, Sam went on. "Right. Okay, well, let's continue on."

When it came time to put the rings on, it finally dawned on me what to do. I tied one piece around Bree's finger, and she tied the other on mine.

"By the power vested in me by the state of New Hampshire, I now pronounce you Mr. and Mrs. Morrison," Sam said. "You may kiss your bride."

Bree looked up at me, her eyes glistening with unshed tears. I cupped her face in my hands, leaned down, and brushed my lips across hers as I whispered, "I love you, Mrs. Morrison."

She half laughed, half sobbed. "I love you, too, Mr. Morrison."

Then I kissed my wife.

Hank stared at me as I sat in the chair on the movie set while getting ready for my next scene. "What do you mean, you got married this morning?"

Smiling, I said, "I got married this morning."

"To who?"

I shot him a dirty look. "Who do you think? Brighton."

He stared at me with a blank expression for a good two minutes. I sighed and looked up at Kimberley, the makeup artist.

"Congratulations, Luke!" Kimberley said.

"Thank you," I replied.

Hank shook his head. "But I thought you were trying to make up with her."

"Oh, we made up."

Kimberley chuckled.

"And she married you?" Hank asked with a smile.

"I know, I'm still feeling a little surprised by it too."

Hank lifted his hands up in a 'hold on' gesture and looked at me in the mirror. "Brighton forgave you and then married you? Did you drug her?"

"Ha ha, very funny. I have to say, it was the strangest wedding I've ever been to." I held up my left hand and showed Kimberley and Hank my ring. "See the ring?"

Kimberley laughed. "Is that a piece of paper?"

I nodded.

She sighed. "That is so romantic."

Hank pulled his head back as if someone struck him. "Excuse me? You think a paper ring is romantic?"

Looking at him, she replied, "What? It is!"

Rolling his eyes, Hank said, "I'll never understand women."

I couldn't help but chuckle.

Hank slapped me on the side of the arm. "I'm happy for you, Luke. Glad it finally happened. Now, I think I'll go...get something to drink. Do you need anything?"

"No," I said. "Hank—wait." He turned and looked at me. "Bree should be getting here around three. She had to stay behind in Boggy Creek and calm down her very upset mother. I already gave her name to security, so they should let her in with no problem, but I'd like for you to be there too. Will you show her around, then bring her to our filming location by the lake?"

Hank grinned. "So you're going public, huh?"

I couldn't help but think of our meal at The Coffee Pot and the ice cream we had in the park. Smiling, I replied, "We already have."

He nodded and then slipped out of the trailer.

Kimberley leaned down and looked at me in the mirror. "Are the rumors true, then? This is your last film?"

"They're true."

She smiled. "I'm really happy for you, Luke. What's your wife like?"

A warm rush of happiness washed over me. "She's the most amazing woman I've ever met. She's kind, funny, compassionate. Loves clothes and makeup."

"I like her already."

I laughed. "She's the love of my life."

"Are you giving this up for her?"

Our eyes met in the mirror. "I'm giving this up for both of us."

With a wink, she went back to work. I had one more damn scene to shoot, and then I was done. My life as an actor would officially be over, with the exception of promoting this movie. I was counting down the minutes until I could drive back to Boggy Creek in my wife's BMW with the top down while she sang her heart out to BLACKPINK.

Life had never been better.

Chapter Twenty-Three
Bree

I got to the filming location earlier than expected. After talking my mother down off her ledge of despair and promising to have a real wedding in the near future, I set off to meet up with Luke.

There was no denying how excited I was to see the movie set. I wanted to at least see Luke in action one time before he walked away from it all. He had assured me it wouldn't be a love scene. No kissing, no pretend sexy time. It was a scene where he and Kathleen were walking around a lake. It was odd to me because it was one of the first scenes that would be in the movie—the moment they first meet—yet they were filming it last.

I pulled up to the temporary security gate and smiled at the young gentleman who walked up to the car. "Hi, my name is Brighton Rogers...er, I mean, Brighton Morrison. I'm a guest of—"

"Mr. Walters. Yes, he told us he was expecting you. His assistant isn't here yet to escort you in—looks like you're a bit early."

I looked for Hank on the other side of the gate. "Should I wait?"

The young man shook his head. "No, I'll call him and let him know you're here. Follow this road, and you'll see a parking area on the left. Once you park, head on over to the tent that's set up. There are drinks and food if you're hungry. I'll have him meet you there."

Smiling, I replied, "Thank you so much."

He waved at me as I pulled in and followed the road to the parking lot. I got out of my car and took a look around. People were everywhere. Directly in front of me were at least ten trailers. I wondered if one of them was Luke's. I looked to the left and spotted the tent. I started to make my way there when a young woman with blonde hair holding a little dog came up to me.

"Ms. Rogers?"

I stopped. "Yes?"

"Hi, my name's Lanny. Hank asked me to let you know that Luke is in his trailer, and I should bring you there."

"Oh," I said with a smile. "Okay."

I had to admit, I was excited to see Luke's trailer.

"Follow me, please."

I did as she asked. We walked in silence for a bit until I said, "Is that your dog?"

She looked at the little dog and laughed. "No. This is Sweet Pea. She belongs to Kathleen Daughtry."

I tried not to gag at the mention of her name. "And are you pet sitting for her?"

The woman looked at me, and for a moment, I had the feeling she wanted to say something she wasn't supposed to. Instead, she plastered on a fake smile and nodded. "Yes. I'm her assistant. Pet sitting is one of the many things I do for Kathleen."

"Lucky you," I said under my breath.

We came to a stop at a trailer, and a rush of pride hit me when I saw Luke's name on the door. "Here it is," she said. "I'll let you show yourself in."

"Thank you, Lanny. It was nice meeting you."

She paused for a moment, looked at the door, then back to me. "Wait..."

I had walked up the two steps to the door, but stopped when she spoke. "Yes?"

Her eyes darted from me to the door. She let out a defeated sigh and whispered, "I'm sorry."

I frowned. "For what?"

Without answering, she turned and walked away.

Staring at her as she retreated, I shook my head and whispered, "No wonder he wants to leave."

I opened the trailer door and stepped inside. It looked like a typical RV trailer with a small kitchen area, a sofa, a table, and in the front were two chairs and a large TV screen.

"I'm back here, darling."

The voice from the other end of the RV caused me to freeze. I slowly turned to see a door cracked open slightly.

"Luke? Darling? Is that you? I'm waiting."

I balled my fists, anger pulsing through my body like someone had injected it straight into my blood.

That. Bitch.

I started for the back of the RV. When I got to the door, I pushed it open—and gasped at what I saw.

A very naked Kathleen Daughtry was lying across the bed, a glass of wine in her hand. For an award-winning actress, she sure sucked at acting surprised.

"Oh my God! Who are you and what are you doing in here?"

I pulled out my phone and took a picture before I folded my arms across my chest and gave her body a clinical study of the eye. "I'm Luke's wife, and thanks for the blackmail photo."

Her mouth dropped open, and this time the bitch really *was* surprised. "I'm sorry, what did you say?"

With a tilt of my head, I asked, "Do you honestly think I'm stupid enough to fall for this little stunt?"

This time her eyes went wide with horror. "I beg your pardon?"

"This little show. Honestly, this is some terrible acting on your part."

Okay, it was a bitch thing to say, but honestly. The whole scene was ridiculous.

She scrambled off the bed and reached for a robe. "How dare you! I'll have you know I've been nominated for an Oscar."

I shrugged. "Really? I hadn't known that."

Gasping, she set the glass of wine down on the small table next to the head of the bed. She pulled on the robe with angry, jerky movements. "You're not the least bit concerned I'm in Luke's trailer? *Naked*?"

I looked her over one more time. "No. Do you know why?"

The woman shook her head.

Holding up my left ring finger, I showed off the tied piece of paper. "Because he's *mine*—and I trust him."

"As you should," came a voice from behind me.

Turning, I smiled when I saw Hank.

"Hank!" I threw myself into his arms. "I've missed you."

He laughed. "I've missed you, too, Brighton."

After I drew away, I glanced back at Kathleen, who was standing there looking utterly confused.

"You might want to let Luke know he needs to have them clean out his trailer better," I said. "It appears someone left the trash in here."

"How dare you!" Kathleen exclaimed as she attempted to stomp out of the small bedroom and doing a piss-poor job of it. "You have no idea about the man you married! He was with *me* all morning."

I raised a brow. "How have you've been nominated for an Oscar? You're terrible at lying. Or are lying and acting that different?"

She glared at me. "Fuck you, you little twit! He'll get tired of you, you wait and see."

Pushing past me, she made her way out of the trailer. She let out a little scream, and I imagined it was because she nearly fell going down the two steps.

"You shouldn't have pissed her off, Brighton," Hank said. "She could tell the press your name and where you live."

I looked at Hank. "She could, but I seriously doubt she wants Luke to be pissed at her. And I don't think she wants a picture of her naked ass displayed for the world."

Hank looked back toward the door where Kathleen had disappeared. "You're probably right."

"How did you know I was in here?"

He motioned for me to head out of the RV. "Lanny told me you were here, and she also confessed to Kathleen being in here as well. It appears Kathleen saw your name on the list for security and quickly hatched this little plan. Luke is going to be furious when he finds out."

I chuckled. "Maybe we shouldn't tell him."

"Why wouldn't you tell him?"

Shrugging, I said, "I kind of feel sorry for her."

Hank stopped walking and looked at me. "You feel sorry for Kathleen Daughtry?"

With a nod, I replied, "Yes. From what I understand, she seems to throw herself at men. To me, that screams that she's a woman who's unhappy and insecure with herself. Hopefully she realizes that sooner rather than later, or she's going to be one very lonely woman."

Slowly shaking his head, Hank said, "No wonder Luke is so in love with you."

I gave a half shrug before we started walking again. Stopping at a golf cart, Hank motioned for me to climb in.

"I'll take you over to where they're filming the next scene. Kathleen should have been in makeup, not playing in Luke's trailer. You'll have a few minutes to talk to Luke, and I'm sure he'll want to introduce you to some folks."

I smiled and tried not to let my excitement show, but I was so curious to see Luke in action. I still hadn't watched one of his movies, so I'd never seen him act.

When we finally pulled up and I saw all the cameras and what looked like small train tracks set up around a stretch of the lake, my heart was pounding in my chest. I wasn't sure if I was nervous, excited, or worried.

It still bothered me that Luke was walking away from his career. But a part of me was also so happy, and that part filled me with guilt.

Luke was standing with three other men in a circle. They were holding something that I assumed was the script. As I approached, his eyes lifted up from the paper and he looked directly at me as if he sensed I was there. A brilliant smile spread across his face, and he hurried over to me. "Hey, you're here."

When he leaned down to kiss me, I froze for a moment. Then I relaxed and kissed him back.

He drew away and leaned his forehead on mine. "Hi, wife."

With a giggle, I replied, "Hi, husband." It was then I realized he still had the paper ring on. "You kept it on?"

He reached down for my hand and brushed a kiss across my knuckles. "So did you."

"I'm not taking it off until we get real rings."

Luke smiled. "Neither am I."

My eyes darted over to the lake, and Luke must have been able to read my mind.

"They can digitally edit it out, because I am *not* taking this paper ring off my finger."

"Well, we do need to take it off to shower," I stated with a wicked smile. I was hit with memories of last night, and I almost moaned thinking about Luke's mouth making me come while the water rained down around us.

"Someone's having dirty thoughts," Luke whispered against my ear.

Laughing, I replied, "Just thinking about last night."

He drew back and looked down at me, his eyes dark with promises of more. "Wait until our honeymoon this evening. Since your folks are back in town—and I cleared it with your father—I booked us a room at the country club here."

I felt my eyes go wide. "What? Are you a member?"

He tilted his head and gave me a look that said he couldn't believe I'd even asked. "I believe that country club is the whole reason you and I are married, Mrs. Morrison."

My stomach did a little flip. "Then there's no better place for us to spend our honeymoon."

Luke kissed my forehead. "I agree."

I looked around at everyone and everything. A few people watched us curiously, but for the most part they all seemed to be carrying on as usual. "So this is a movie set, huh?"

Luke followed my gaze. "It's one of them, yes." Turning back to me, he winked. "Come on, I want to introduce my wife to everyone."

I pulled back against his hand. "Um, before we do, there's something I need to tell you."

His brows drew down in concern. "You just got very serious."

Smiling, I replied, "No, it's nothing big. It's just...I got here a bit early, and they sent me ahead to meet Hank at the catering tent. A young woman approached me and said I was supposed to meet you in your trailer."

Luke immediately grew angry.

"Kathleen Daughtry was in your trailer," I said. "In your bed. Naked."

"What!" Luke shouted, causing a few people to turn in our direction.

"It's okay. I'm not upset or angry. I do think she might be a little butt hurt and might try and take it out on you, though."

"Butt hurt?" he asked with a wicked gleam in his eyes.

"I might have called her trash."

His eyes went wide. "You did?"

With a little shrug, I smirked. "More or less. The reason I'm telling you is if you even think I'm going back to that trailer, you've got another thing coming."

He chuckled. "I was thinking we could go straight to our room after this. We still have a lot of time to make up for."

I couldn't help the wide grin that spread over my face. "Yes, we do."

"Come on, let's go shock everyone even more by telling them I'm married."

Luke led me over to the men he'd been talking to. Two women had joined them. One was the producer, the other the assistant director. Everyone was nice and polite and said how much they'd miss working with such a class act like Luke, but completely understood why he wanted to leave the industry. The guilt I had weighing around my heart eased up a little, but I knew it would take a while for me to work through it entirely. After all, Luke was giving up so much for me and our future. I planned on doing everything in my power to make sure he never doubted his decision.

It was an hour later when Kathleen was finally on set and ready to film. The scene was supposed to be their first encounter, where Luke was jogging and Kathleen's dog—who was being played by a beautiful golden retriever named Lucy—ran up and knocked him over. Then the long-lost lovers caught up.

My heart swelled with pride as I watched Luke work. They had to start over a few times when the dog's attention was focused on a squirrel in a tree or on one of the extras walking by. When they finally got the take with Luke falling, I couldn't help but swoon.

"He's an amazing actor," someone next to me said. Turning, I looked up to see an older gentleman standing there.

Smiling, I focused back on Luke. "He is."

"I've got to say, when I heard this would be his last film, I wondered what in the world would make a man who was on top of his game walk away from such an incredible career."

My heart dropped, and I glanced down at the grass before taking in a breath. Then I caught Luke's gaze as he looked over at me. He lifted his hand and waved, and I waved back.

"Then I heard him talking about you."

I snapped my head to the side. "Me?"

The older gentleman looked down at me. "Yes. It was so evident in the way he smiled when he mentioned you. That look in his eyes. It reminded me of myself. When I was a bit younger than Luke— the ripe ol' age of eighteen back in 1978—I met the love of my life at the grocery store, if you can believe that. I'd recently filmed my third movie and there was Oscar buzz. I was flying high. Then I met Joyce...and my God, I fell head over heels in love with her. But life crept in and things started to turn."

"What do you mean?" I asked, turning my body to face him—and suddenly realizing who in the hell I was talking to. I nearly gasped but managed to stay calm. The man next to me was Jake Lenard. One of Hollywood's most acclaimed actors. He'd actually starred in a film with my beloved Gene Kelly, playing Gene's son. I drew in a few deep breaths and fought the urge to ask him what it was like to work with Gene.

"The press found out and started following us around everywhere. We couldn't even go to a club and get a drink and dance. Joyce was a teacher. She taught fourth grade."

The way he smiled at the memory made my heart jump.

"I went to her house one night—had to sneak in through the backyard so no one would see me going in. She'd made us dinner." He chuckled. "Spaghetti and meatballs. She was Italian, you see, and made the best sauce I'd ever had."

I grinned.

He smiled back at me, then looked back out over the scene. They were getting ready to start filming again and were attempting to get Lucy to stand next to Kathleen. Apparently, the dog smelled a rat.

Jack's smile faded. "That was the night she told me she could no longer see me."

I took in a sharp breath.

"She said she loved me, but she also liked her quiet, simple life, and that she couldn't take the chaos that would come from being with me."

I covered my mouth with my fingers as I felt this man's pain down to my core. Had this been how Luke felt that day I'd told him to leave my office? I'd said nearly the same words to him.

"I'm so sorry," I whispered.

Jake drew in a deep breath and smiled sheepishly. "Nothing like having the woman you love tell you that you bring chaos to her life.

Luke told me about you right after you met. I told him the story of me and Joyce. He asked if I'd change anything if I could go back."

"Would you?" I asked.

He looked out over the lake, seemingly lost in another world. The sadness on his face was so evident it nearly brought me to tears. He finally spoke.

"I would have walked away from all of this. Instead, I threw myself into it even harder in hopes of forgetting her. I found out two years later she'd gotten married. He was a teacher as well. They had two kids. I got married four times, had six kids with four different women. I love my kids and wouldn't take that back for the life of me. But I never truly loved their mothers."

I blinked to keep my tears back. "Have you...have you ever reached out to Joyce?"

He laughed. "No. She moved on with her life, and I'm happy she's happy."

It was my turn to look out over the lake. If I had moved on from Luke, gotten married and had kids, would I have been truly happy? I searched the group of people until I found him. He threw his head back, laughing at something someone said, and I quickly wiped away the single tear that was sliding down my cheek.

"Most of my friends think I'm this strong, independent woman," I said. "I talk a lot of shit. But when I told Luke to leave and he turned and walked out of my life, I've never felt so devastated. I was positive my heart would never be the same."

I could feel Jake's gaze on me.

"If he hadn't come back to me, I probably would have settled down and gotten married eventually. But that's the key word, Jake. I would have settled. And even though it wouldn't have been fair to the man I married, my heart—I can say with every ounce of my being— would have belonged to Luke. Always."

His dark blue eyes misted with tears before he nodded and cleared his throat.

"Will you tell me one thing?" I asked.

Jake looked back at me. "Of course."

"What was it like to work with Gene Kelly?"

He let out a roar of laughter. "Your young Luke reminds me of him. Looks like a younger version of Gene too."

"I know," I said with a smile. "Did you know he can sing too? He sings in the shower."

Jake laughed and shook his head. "I did not know that, dear."

The somber mood quickly changed as Jake told me what it was like to work with Gene Kelly. I got lost in the conversation, and when they called him over to do his part, I was a bit sad. The immediate connection we had formed was amazing.

"Jake?"

He turned and looked at me.

"Will you do me one more favor?"

"Yes, I will."

I chewed on my lip for a moment. "Will you look her up? Joyce, I mean. Will you do that for me?"

He stared at me for a long moment and then gave one nod of his head before he headed over toward where Luke was standing. He'd told me he was playing Luke's father in the movie. My heart ached as I thought about Jake's story and how easily that could have been me and Luke.

Glancing down at my paper ring, I clutched my hand and pressed it to my heart.

I spent the rest of the afternoon sitting in Luke's chair and watching them film the final scenes of the movie. I watched as Luke and Jake had a private moment set apart from everyone else. They embraced, and I saw Luke quickly wipe a tear from the corner of his eye. He made his way around to the crew, thanking them and shaking hands.

There was one person who was noticeably missing. Kathleen Daughtry. She had apparently stormed off to a golf cart and was whisked away to her trailer. She had another few hours of filming to do today, but Luke was finished.

The producer of the movie was the last one to speak to Luke, and I was standing next to him by that point. His arm was around my waist, almost as if he was afraid I'd bolt.

"You don't even want to think about it, Luke?" the producer asked.

With a soft laugh, Luke replied, "Mike, I appreciate you asking me to direct a film, but I honestly *am* walking away. I have another life I'm anxious to start."

Mike looked at me and sighed, but then smiled. "I get it. But you could have both worlds, you know."

"I could, but that's not what I want."

Looking up at Luke, I felt my knees go weak. I loved this man so much, and I couldn't wait to show him exactly that the moment we got to our hotel room.

"Then I won't keep you any longer. I'll see you around, Luke Walters."

Luke reached his hand out and shook Mike's. "Later, Mike."

Steering me toward a golf cart where Hank was sitting at the wheel, Luke and I walked toward our new life together. Arm in arm.

Chapter Twenty-Four

Luke

My phone buzzed on the side table, and I rolled to pick it up. It was the text I'd been waiting for.

Hank: They're here and waiting in the lobby.

With a smile, I typed back my reply.

Me: Give me ten minutes to wake up my bride and get dressed.

Hank: This is Bree we're talking about, Luke. I'll give you thirty.

Laughing, I set my phone down and rolled back over. Bree was sleeping on her stomach, her back rising and falling with each breath she took. I kissed her soft skin, then chased it with my tongue.

"Mmm, have I mentioned how much I love your kisses on my body?" she said.

"You may have screamed it out a time or two."

She chuckled and rolled over. "What time is it?"

"It's two."

Shooting up, she replied, "In the afternoon?"

I laughed. "Yes. We've officially been in this hotel room for nearly three days."

"We probably need to get back to reality. I feel bad leaving my folks alone at the bed and breakfast."

Running my finger down the side of her arm, I watched as goosebumps appeared on her flawless body. "Don't worry, I plan on making it up to them."

"Making what up?" she asked as she stretched. My eyes landed on her perfect breasts.

"Stealing their daughter away from them."

She smiled. "What do you plan on doing?"

"I thought they might like a trip."

"A trip?" she asked.

"Yeah. I overheard your mom telling another guest that she's always wanted to go to Ireland."

Bree raised a single brow. "You're going to send my parents to Ireland?"

I nodded. "Ireland in September, I hear, is the perfect time of year...and isn't that when their anniversary is?"

She laughed and nodded. "Yes, it is."

Her eyes turned smoldering as her gaze drifted over my bare chest.

"As much as I want to make love to you," I said, "we have company coming up to the room."

With wide eyes, she asked, "Company? Can Hank not leave you alone for a single day?"

Laughing, I leaned over and took one of her nipples into my mouth and sucked on it before moving to the other one. She let out a little sigh of pleasure.

Glancing up, I said, "It's a jeweler from Boston. Hank arranged for them to come and bring some rings for us."

She blinked a few times. "Excuse me?"

Rolling over and slipping out of bed, I reached for my new pair of jeans that were sitting on the chair next to the large, king-size bed, along with a new shirt. Bree and I had managed to slip away yesterday evening to do some shopping, since neither one of us had any clothes here except what we had on our backs. We'd also needed toiletries.

The country club boasted a few designer clothing stores, and Bree had quickly gotten lost in one of the boutiques. She'd even FaceTimed Candace, and they'd made arrangements to come back for a shopping trip soon.

"I asked Hank to have some rings brought up from a jeweler in Boston," I repeated. "They're here."

Her eyes went wide, and she flew out of bed. "They're *here* here? As in the hotel here?"

I nodded and pulled the shirt over my head. "Yep."

She darted one way and then another. "Oh my God, I need to get dressed. Fix my hair. Put makeup on!"

Laughing, I sat down on the bed to put on socks. "Bree, you only need to get dressed. They don't care if you have makeup on."

She paused while looking at the two dresses she was holding up, one in each hand. "Do you not know me at all, Luke Morrison?"

"Touché," I replied.

I had never seen Bree get ready so fast. She'd slipped on a light blue sundress with white sandals. Her hair was pulled up into what she called a sloppy bun, but I thought it looked stunning with all those locks of soft brown hair piled up on her head, a few stray strands hanging down and curling up around her neck. She'd put on a little bit of makeup, but I knew the glow on her cheeks wasn't from anything artificial. It was from the last few days of endless lovemaking. A few rounds of fucking, and some amazing shower and tub sex.

Since I had pretty much kidnapped her and brought her here, she hadn't brought anything from home with her—and that included her birth control pills, which we'd both agreed she would stop taking. We were going to let things happen as they happened.

Clearing my throat, I looked away from my stunning wife before I embarrassed myself with a hard-on.

The jeweler came into the room. "Mr. and Mrs. Morrison, it's a pleasure to help you this afternoon with your purchase of wedding bands."

"We need an engagement ring as well. You did bring some with you?" I asked.

The older man with gray hair and kind green eyes nodded. "I did, indeed."

We were staying in one of the larger suites in the resort. It had a full-size kitchen as well as a living area with a large dining room table that sat eight.

Lacing my fingers with Bree's, we made our way over to the table and sat while the jeweler began to take out the boxes from a locked container. A security guard stood close by, but not enough to be in the way.

"I wasn't sure if you wanted precious jewels as an option, so I brought some with me as well as the traditional diamonds."

Bree practically bounced in her seat, her eyes widening with delight at the sight before her.

"Do you have a favorite cut, miss?" the jeweler asked.

Looking back at him with a wide grin, she replied, "I've always liked a cushion cut."

He nodded. "And do we prefer color or a traditional diamond?"

She chewed on her fingernail for a few moments. "Traditional."

He quickly took out a large box and slid it open to reveal some rings. Bree gasped and looked at me, then back at the rings.

I noticed her gaze immediately went to one.

"Do you like that one?" I asked as I pointed to it.

She drew in a breath and whispered, "It's beautiful."

"Which one?" the jeweler asked.

Bree pointed to it.

"Ahh, yes. That is a two-and-a-half-carat cushion-cut diamond. It's framed by brilliant sparkling round diamonds that sweep across the entire band. The milgrain beading adds a vintage touch to the ring, don't you think?"

Bree nodded. "Yes, that's why I love it."

He went on. "The color is F, the clarity one. The metal is fourteen-karat gold with a white rhodium finish on it. It's a very beautiful ring. Shall we try it on?"

When Bree looked at me, I nodded. She turned back to the jeweler. "How much is it?"

I held up my hand. "The price doesn't matter. What matters is if you love it."

Her cheeks turned the most beautiful shade of pink.

I held my hand out to the jeweler. "May I?"

He smiled and handed me the ring. I took Bree's left hand and smiled down at the tied piece of paper. It was almost falling apart from how many times we'd taken them off and on. I untied it and then slipped the diamond ring on her finger. It was a perfect fit.

"It's a sign when the ring fits like a glove," the jeweler stated with a wide smile.

Bree stared down at the ring, and I could see the tears forming in her eyes. "It's beautiful."

"Is this the one?" I asked softly.

She nodded. "Yes."

"The wedding band?" I asked the gentleman.

"Yes, of course."

It didn't take long for Bree to pick a band. It was fourteen-karat white gold trimmed in the same classic milgrain detailing with a row of brilliant round-cut diamonds.

Sliding the engagement ring off her finger, I slid the band on and then put the engagement ring over it.

"It's a bit bigger," she said, twisting the band around.

"We can easily size it for you," the jeweler said.

"I don't want to take it back off," Bree said as she looked up to me.

With a slight laugh, I replied, "How big is it?"

"Not that big."

"Then we'll get it sized at a later date."

She held her hand up against her heart and beamed at me. "Your turn!"

I laughed. "You pick out your favorites."

"What metal do you want, sir?" the jeweler asked.

Looking at Bree, I shrugged. "How about platinum." The only reason I suggested it was because I'd overheard Aiden talking about *his* ring, and it was platinum.

Bree picked out three different bands.

"Do you have a favorite of the three?" I asked.

"It's your band, Luke. I want you to like it."

I nodded. "I have a favorite."

She smiled. "Okay, let's label them. One, two, and three."

The third one was the one I liked the most. It had a stain finish in the middle with polished edges. I couldn't wait to see which one she'd picked.

"Let's say the number on three," Bree said with a gleeful look on her face.

Holding up her hand, she counted down. On three, we both said, "Three."

"There you go," the jeweler stated. He handed Bree the ring, and she slipped it onto my left ring finger. After we untied the paper ring, of course.

One month later

I watched as my fishing line bobbed in the water while Kyle, Hunter, and Bishop talked about the proper way to cook trout.

"Why would you put garlic on it, Kyle?" Hunter asked.

Kyle replied, "Because I like garlic, Hunter."

"I'm telling you, you put a bit of seasoning on it, some lemons, and wrap it up in foil and bake it. Best damn trout you'll ever eat."

That came from Bishop.

"You shouldn't cook with aluminum foil."

We all turned to look at Kyle as he cast out.

"Why not?" I asked.

He looked at me as if I should know the answer. "It's not good for you."

"What?" Hunter and Bishop said at the same time.

"Yeah," Kyle stated. "I can't remember who told me that."

"The salesman who sold you that expensive set of pans," Hunter stated.

Kyle shot Hunter a dirty look.

Bishop sighed. "Well, hell. That's the only way I make my fish."

"You're fine, Bishop," Hunter said with a laugh. "Kyle here got duped into buying expensive-ass pans."

"I did not! And besides, I only bought them from her because she was pretty."

Hunter laughed. "I rest my case. There's this paper you can buy that's for baking. I put some lemon pepper on my fish, asparagus, and slices of lemon, fold it up in the paper and bake it. Best damn meal you've ever had."

"Christ," I said as I reeled in my empty line. "If you three keeping talking about food, I'm packing up and leaving you here to go get something to eat."

Now all three of them looked at me.

"I'm down for that," Kyle said with a half smile. "I haven't caught one damn fish that was a keeper."

Hunter groaned. "At least you caught something."

We packed up our stuff and started for Hunter's truck.

"How's the house hunting going?" Bishop asked while Kyle and Hunter walked ahead of us.

"We've found a few places, but nothing that's jumped out at us yet."

"You ever think about buying land and building?"

I nodded, rubbing at the back of my neck. "We talked about it, but I think Bree wants something more historical."

Kyle was putting his fishing rod in the holder that Hunter had set up in the back of his truck when he stopped and looked at me. "When I was patrolling yesterday, I saw a house for sale down from my folks'. They live on one of the oldest streets in Boggy Creek. The house was right around the corner from them on Clay Street. It's about three blocks from Main."

"Really? What does it look like?"

"Typical colonial-style. Most likely built in the 1800s."

A spark of excitement hit me. "No kidding?"

He nodded. "You guys should go check it out."

"I'll let Bree know."

After we got all of our stuff packed up and slipped into the truck, Kyle turned around from the front passenger seat and said, "I expect a finder's fee if you buy the house."

I raised a brow. "And what exactly is your price?"

He smiled. "Ah, still so new to the fold."

Bishop and Hunter both laughed.

"I'll call in a favor when least expected."

"Is that so?" I deadpanned. "I'm going to guess since you're a cop, it wouldn't be anything illegal."

Kyle simply smiled, then faced forward. I looked at Bishop, who shrugged.

I drew in a deep breath and exhaled. "Why do I feel like the three of you have had some adventures?"

They all laughed.

"Wait until ice fishing," Hunter stated.

I couldn't help but smile. The three guys in the truck, along with Hudson and Aiden, had welcomed me into their group with open arms. They held nothing back and treated me like one of the guys. And I would forever be thankful for that. They'd made settling into this new life easier than I'd honestly thought it would be.

I pulled out my phone and sent Bree a text, letting her know about the house Kyle had mentioned. I also told her that we needed to go in knowing that if we bought it, Kyle wanted a "finder's fee" in return.

The next morning, Bree and I stood in the kitchen of the house Kyle had told us about.

"It was built in 1830 and sits on one acre of land," the realtor said. "Three bedrooms, two bathrooms, and it's three-thousand square feet."

Bree smiled. "Look at these wide plank floors, Luke."

I glanced down at the very old, much-in-need-of-restoration, wide plank floors. "This house needs a lot of work, Bree."

She nodded. "I know!"

I couldn't help but laugh as we followed the real estate agent through the house. The previous owners had added on to the back of it, and there was a large screened-in porch and, behind it, a barn that looked like it was ready to fall down.

I stared at the barn for the longest time.

"What's wrong?" Bree asked.

"That barn could be turned into an office."

Bree studied it. "I guess it could."

Turning to face her, I asked, "Do you like the house?"

She looked around and smiled. "It *would* be a lot of work."

I nodded in agreement.

"But I do love it. That old fireplace in the kitchen is amazing. And did you see the wood beams on the ceilings?"

Laughing, I pulled her to me. "Are you up for an adventure, Mrs. Morrison?"

"A remodeling adventure?"

"That...and I've been thinking."

She raised a brow. "About?"

"Mr. Watkins approached me yesterday morning in The Coffee Pot when I was eating breakfast with Aiden. He found out I was doing law work for Aiden's nonprofit. He wants to retire...and asked if I'd be interested in taking over his practice."

Bree's eyes went wide.

"I told him I'd talk to my wife about it. I know you've been helping your folks at the bed and breakfast, but I was thinking...this might be something I'd like to do."

"You want to practice law full time again?"

"I think so. Would you be willing to work with me?"

A wide smile spread over her face. "You want me to work for you?"

Laughing, I said, "Not work for me. Partners."

Her smile faded slightly before it was replaced with a smirk. "Morrison and Morrison law firm. I like the sound of it."

I drew her body closer to mine and pressed my lips to hers before pulling back slightly and whispering, "So do I."

She lightly ran her finger down my cheek. "A new house. A new law practice. And a new puppy. That's a lot to take on all at once."

I jerked my head back. "New puppy?"

She played innocent. "I mean, you can't expect to buy a house and not get a dog, Luke. Besides, we're going to need her for practice."

Laughing, I asked, "Practice for what?"

The real estate agent stepped back out onto the screened-in porch. "So what do we think?"

"What do we think, husband?" Bree asked.

My heart about burst from pure happiness as I gazed down at my wife. "I think we should buy it, wife."

She stepped out of my embrace and flashed a wide smile at the agent. "We love it and want to put an offer in."

The young woman practically jumped ten feet in the air. "Oh my gosh! My first sale! This is so exciting. Let's head back to the office, and we can draw up the offer and get it sent over!"

As Bree followed the agent back into the house, I asked, "Bree, what were you talking about? Practice for what?"

She glanced over her shoulder and gave me a smile that took my breath away. "Our Valentine's Day gift."

I frowned. "Our Valentine's Day gift?"

She spun back toward me. The way her eyes sparkled and her cheeks glowed made me stop and take a good look at my beautiful wife. She raised one single brow, and I instantly knew. Somehow, I knew.

"Holy shit," I whispered.

With a laugh, she replied, "Holy shit is right. We only have eight months to get this house ready."

And with that, she headed into the house and left me on the porch while her announcement settled into my soul.

We were pregnant. *Pregnant.*

"Wait!" I called out as I ran back into the house, my heart flooding with joy. "I think we need to negotiate that puppy!"

Look for *Looking for Love* – book six in the
Boggy Creek Valley series. Coming on May 17, 2022

The last person I ever expect to find waiting on the front porch for me in the middle of the night is Everly Higgins. To say I'm both surprised and thrilled to see her would be an understatement. I haven't been able to stop thinking about her since we met last fall when my sister, Greer, fell in love with Everly's brother, Hudson.

When I see her bruised-up face, I instantly want to hurt someone. The problem is, Everly won't tell me who hurt her or who she's running from. The only thing she'll say is that she needs a safe place to stay where no one can find her.

Being a cop, I have an urge to unravel this mystery, but another side of me simply wants to protect Everly from whatever she's running from.

But as the people she's hiding from catch up with her, I quickly discover there's nothing I wouldn't do for Everly Higgins.

I'd even die for her.

Other Books by Kelly Elliott

What's next from Kelly?
Returning Home (The Seaside Chronicles #1) July 12, 2022
Part of Me (The Seaside Chronicles #2) September 6, 2022
Lost to You (The Seaside Chronicles #3) November 1, 2022
Someone to Love (The Seaside Chronicles #4) January 3, 2023

Stand Alones
The Journey Home
Who We Were*
The Playbook*
Made for You*
*Available on audiobook

Boggy Creek Valley Series
The Butterfly Effect*
Playing with Words*
She's the One*
Surrender to Me*
Hearts in Motion (releases on March 22, 2022)

Looking for You (releases on May 3, 2022)
Surprise Novella TBD
*Available on audiobook

Meet Me in Montana Series
Never Enough*
Always Enough*
Good Enough*
Strong Enough*
*Available on audiobook

Southern Bride Series
Love at First Sight*
Delicate Promises*
Divided Interests*
Lucky in Love*
Feels Like Home *
Take Me Away*
Fool for You*
Fated Hearts*
*Available on audiobook

Cowboys and Angels Series
Lost Love
Love Profound
Tempting Love
Love Again
Blind Love
This Love
Reckless Love
*Series available on audiobook

Boston Love Series
Searching for Harmony
Fighting for Love
*Series available on audiobook

Austin Singles Series
Seduce Me
Entice Me
Adore Me
*Series available on audiobook

Wanted Series
Wanted*
Saved*
Faithful*
Believe
Cherished*
A Forever Love*

The Wanted Short Stories
All They Wanted
*Available on audiobook

Love Wanted in Texas Series
Spin-off series to the WANTED Series
Without You
Saving You
Holding You
Finding You
Chasing You
Loving You
Entire series available on audiobook
*Please note Loving You combines the last book of the Broken and
Love Wanted in Texas series.

Broken Series
Broken*
Broken Dreams*
Broken Promises*
Broken Love
*Available on audiobook

The Journey of Love Series
Unconditional Love
Undeniable Love
Unforgettable Love
*Entire series available on audiobook

With Me Series
Stay With Me
Only With Me
*Series available on audiobook

Speed Series
Ignite
Adrenaline
*Series available on audiobook or coming to audiobook soon

COLLABORATIONS
Predestined Hearts (co-written with Kristin Mayer)*
Play Me (co-written with Kristin Mayer)*
Dangerous Temptations (co-written with Kristin Mayer*
*Available on audiobook